The Contributors

M. Christian . . . Contributor to numerous magazines, editor of a number of anthologies, and author of an upcoming short story collection

Storm Constantine . . . author of fourteen novels, including the *Wraeththu* trilogy

Esther Friesner . . . Two-time Nebula Award–winning author of twenty-nine novels and over a hundred short stories

Nina Kiriki Hoffman . . . Bram Stoker Award–winning short story writer and novelist

Jack Ketchum . . . Author of ten novels and three story collections, including the highly controversial *Off Season*

Kathe Koja . . . Bram Stoker Award winner and author of one of the original Dell *Abyss* novels, *The Cipher*

Edward Lee . . . Novelist, short story writer, and comic book author, and a contributing editor for *Barnes & Noble Online*

Tanith Lee . . . Two-time World Fantasy Award–winning author of sixty-six books and two hundred short stories

Brian McNaughton . . . Prolific author and winner of the World Fantasy and International Horror Guild Awards for his collection *The Throne of Bones*

Yvonne Navarro . . . Acclaimed author of eleven novels and over sixty short stories

Kathryn Ptacek . . . Prolific author and editor of *The Gila Queen's Guide to Markets*, a newsletter for writers and artists

Robert Silverberg . . . Five-time Nebula winner and four-time Hugo winner

Lois Tilton . . . Vampire novelist and acclaimed short story writer

Lawrence Watt-Evans . . . Hugo Award–winning author and former president of the Horror Writers Association

Gene Wolfe . . . Author of the classic and cr[...] Sun

Chelsea Quinn Yarbro . . . Author of the [...] novels, cartographer, musician, and tarot reade[...]

Graven IMAGES

Edited by

NANCY KILPATRICK
and THOMAS S. ROCHE

ACE BOOKS, NEW YORK

GRAVEN IMAGES

An Ace Book / published by arrangement with
the editors

PRINTING HISTORY:
Ace edition / October 2000

The Penguin Putnam Inc. World Wide Web site address is
http://www.penguinputnam.com

Check out the ACE Science Fiction & Fantasy
newsletter and much more at Club PPI!

ISBN: 0-441-00766-X

ACE®
Ace Books are published by
The Berkley Publishing Group, a division of Penguin Putnam Inc.,
375 Hudson Street, New York, New York 10014.
ACE and the "A" design are trademarks belonging to
Penguin Putnam Inc.

PRINTED IN THE UNITED STATES OF AMERICA

10 9 8 7 6 5 4 3 2 1

Contents

Acknowledgments   ix

Editors' Introductions   xi
NANCY KILPATRICK AND THOMAS S. ROCHE

Diana of the Hundred Breasts   1
ROBERT SILVERBERG

The Face of Sekt   28
STORM CONSTANTINE

The Goddess Danced   50
LOIS TILTON

The Grotto   71
KATHRYN PTACEK

The Eleventh City   90
GENE WOLFE

Heart of Stone   97
LAWRENCE WATT-EVANS

Cora   118
ESTHER FRIESNER

Contents

Ascension   133
YVONNE NAVARRO

Mud   142
BRIAN McNAUGHTON

Shaped Stones   159
NINA KIRIKI HOFFMAN

Wanderlust   183
M. CHRISTIAN

Giotto's Window   190
CHELSEA QUINN YARBRO

Masks   206
JACK KETCHUM AND EDWARD LEE

At Eventide   221
KATHE KOJA

That Glisters Is   231
TANITH LEE

Graven Images (Contributors' Notes)   247

Acknowledgments

Thanks to my delightful collaborator, a sincere, intelligent, and funny guy who values dancing on the edge of the paradox as much as I do. Also thanks to our editor, Ginjer Buchanan, to whom I am extremely grateful for backing this project. Ginjer not only recognizes the value in spirituality as it manifests in creativity, but she also has a sharp eye and a keen sense of timing!

Then there are the people who love me, and without whom I cannot manage: Christine Christolakis, Eric Kauppinen, Mike Kilpatrick, Alison Graham, Sephera Giron, Stephen Jones, Mitchell D. Krol, Eric Paradise, Michael Rowe, Mandy Slater, Caro Soles, Mari Anne Werier, and *mon compagnon*, Hugues Leblanc, guardian of my soul.

— Nancy Kilpatrick

Thanks once again to my family, both immediate and extended, whose support is invaluable to me. And sincere thanks to Nancy for being a pleasure to work with — as always!

Acknowledgments

Other people who deserve much thanks for their support on this project are Ginjer Buchanan, M. Christian, Paula Guran, Zach, and Mr. Fuzzy.

Since humility is an important trait for an editor, thanks also to my friends at Zeitgeist, the local biker bar, who kept me humble throughout this project by repeatedly skunking me at pool.

—Thomas S. Roche

Both Thomas and Nancy would like to thank the contributors to this volume for writing amazing stories, which we found an utter joy to edit.

Introductions

What is it about a Graven Image that won't allow us to look away?
Many societies have worshiped images of the sacred carved in
stone or formed of other materials. In its infancy, Christianity absorbed such
pagan or pre-Christian traditions. Statues of Celtic deities in grottoes were
transformed into images of Jesus; statues of the Virgin Mary, found in grotto-
like altars in churches, supplanted earlier images of pagan goddesses.

Concretized sacred figures reflect the essence of the mysterious source of
life and death. Many of these representations from the land of metaphor are
neither pleasant to look at nor especially comforting. They can be hauntingly
beautiful or terrifyingly grotesque. Either way, we seem drawn to them. From
the artifacts of prerecorded history to the sophisticated modern tomes analyz-
ing our current spiritual dilemmas, one thing is obvious—all religions have
allowed for the dark side. Graven Images incorporate both the dark and the
light in one figure. They portray primitive gods that can be swayed either
way—to help or hinder us. We mere mortals seem to find this paradox compelling.

Introductions

History abounds with such enigmatic figures. Every society has managed to create images that blend the nurturing with the destructive. The mix of the dark with the light is what Carl Jung deemed our task, both individually and collectively: integrating the shadow side. It is, some believe, the only hope we have of saving us from ourselves!

The marvelous stories in *Graven Images* are like a path cutting through humanity's spiritual history. In chronological order, they permit us to tour the ages, beginning with an entity as old as time and leading us on an exciting journey through ancient Egypt to India, and then to pre-Christian Tuscany. These superb authors allow us via their imagination to witness a South American possession by a 2,000-year-old biblical devil, to marvel at a wizard's creation in medieval Europe, to experience a 500-year-old manticore, and to shudder as we face a Mexican stonework from the eighteenth century that one cannot forget. We move through the horrors of World War I in France, to the stark Depression of the 1930s in New York City, to a kitsch figure from the '50s seen on dashboards all over North America. We end with modern images that accompany us into the new millennium.

It was Sartre who twigged us to the notion that the battle between being and nothingness—our existential struggle—is won or lost on ground rooted in and limited only by our imagination and our willingness to think and be and change. Graven Images can go either way, but so can we. In the end, it is always a moral struggle, and those who can face the dark without being swallowed by it are far better able to look into the light and see what is really there. These stories strike a chord because they reflect the paradox of primal forces, the paradox of consciousness.

—Nancy Kilpatrick

In the Bible, the term "Graven Image" is used frequently to refer to the forbidden idols of non-Judaic worship. The sense in which we use the term here indicates the artwork of one belief system when it appears within the sacred place of another—also known as a "grotesque" in historical terms. In the case where one of the faiths has died out, or is dormant, the Graven Image often takes on a sinister, demonized aspect, as it did with the Jews and, later, the Christians (as well as with many other faiths). However, because Christianity, especially, absorbs aspects of the indigenous faiths of the realms it conquers, Christian places of worship often still bear the symbols of a pagan past. For example, the gods and goddesses of the *Niebelungenlied* appear on the wall of the Cathedral at Worms.

In broader terms, a Graven Image can be an image or representation of a god or goddess who no longer rules but who still holds power. The myriad of supernatural beings in *Graven Images* are all powerful creatures who have, to some degree, lost their significance in a subsequent age. But their essence persists. They wait, slumbering or half-asleep, waiting to flex their muscles, waiting for their place in the world to return. In a very real sense, then, Graven Images represent the displaced archetypes of spirituality which echo complex needs we mortals don't even know we still have, or ever had. They haunt our modern faiths as the shadows of the ancient ones. They are the ghosts of humanity's makers, the specters of our cultural dreams.

There's a tendency in modern life to pooh-pooh the beliefs of ancient, supposedly more "primitive" cultures, while maintaining our own kinds of superstitions — those of science or of whatever other belief system currently holds sway. For example, the vast majority of North Americans believe in God and an afterlife — but do not attend church. And how many of us in my hometown of San Francisco walk around with crystal necklaces or sleep with pyramids under our beds?

"Science," the new-age aliens-are-coming millennialists tell us; "spirituality is all about science. Man has a soul — we can prove it on a gas spectrometer. Oh, and there's a monkey face on Mars." Maybe that's what those strange lights in the sky have been trying to tell us since shortly after the hungry ghost of the atom bomb claimed its first victim at Hiroshima: "Slay your old gods, and others will take their place. And these gods might not be so friendly."

We have built a society where our only living deities are ghosts of previous belief systems. There is a widespread tendency to return to "spirituality" and to justify it through science—even as trust in science and technology fades with every CNN story about the hole in the ozone layer or every government-subsidized report that Jell-O causes cancer and terrorists may have seized anthrax weapons from former Soviet states.

And yet technology still holds sway, still rules the world, still gains power with every new Internet address—even as the cracks appear in the face of technology, as it starts to crumble for lack of resources and lack of faith. We all know that technology must ultimately fail in its most immediate task: to preserve, prolong, and improve human life. It must fail, because it cannot preserve our lives indefinitely—nothing can. That fact haunts us as we drive our sedans and fly in our airliners, as we eat low-fat foods and gulp vitamin C and walk on our infinite treadmills. And so the Graven Image of today's world is the face of any god or God who predates technology: It is a fierce one, because there, but for the grace of God, go we—into the shadows.

Our gods, current and past, are but Graven Images, because every belief system is out of date somewhere, somewhen. But those images still wield power—immense, terrifying power, power human beings cannot hope to fully grasp. Because the old gods are the embodiment of human attempts to understand the universe; maybe they were purer than the gods who now reign, because the old gods did not have the pesky necessity of proof, documentation, and market share to dilute their perception. They are the forces which shaped our world and our culture. We are their children—and in a very real sense, whether you believe in them or not, they are ours.

Our gods and saints, old and new, are our conscience, our aspiration, our desperation, our need. Their faces, like ours, are graven in stone—they pass out of the world, but those etchings remain to haunt the next generation and the next world.

Enjoy your journeys, alongside the brilliant storytellers in *Graven Images*, to the lands of the old gods. And remember that reality, like the grotesque, is the mirror to Bertolt Brecht's hammer.

—Thomas S. Roche

To Hugues Leblanc
—Nancy Kilpatrick

To Cathie, for everything
—Thomas S. Roche

Diana of the Hundred Breasts

ROBERT SILVERBERG

The two famous marble statues stand facing each other in a front room of the little museum in the scruffy Turkish town of Seljuk, which lies just north of the ruins of the once-great Greek and Roman city of Ephesus. There was a photograph of the bigger one in my guidebook, of course. But it hadn't prepared me—photos never really do—for the full bizarre impact of the actuality.

The larger of the statues is about nine feet tall, the other one about six. Archaeologists found both of them in the courtyard of a building of this ancient city where the goddess Diana was revered. They show—you must have seen a picture of one, sometime or other—a serene, slender woman wearing an ornamental headdress that is all that remains of a huge, intricate crown. Her arms are outstretched and the lower half of her body is swathed in a tight cylindrical gown. From waist to ankles, that gown is decorated with rows of vividly carved images of bees and of cattle. But that's not where your eyes travel first, because the entire midsection of Diana of Ephesus is festooned with a grotesque triple ring of bulging pendulous breasts. Dozens of them, or several dozens. A great many.

"Perhaps they're actually eggs," said my brother Charlie the professor, standing just behind me. For the past eighteen months Charlie had been one of the leaders of the team of University of Pennsylvania archaeologists that has been digging lately at Ephesus. "Or fruits of some kind—apples, pears. Nobody's really sure. Globular fertility symbols, that's all we can say. But I think they're tits, myself. The tits of the Great Mother, with an abundance of milk for all. Enough tits to satisfy anybody's oral cravings, and then some."

"An abomination before the Lord," murmured our new companion Mr. Gladstone, the diligent Christian tourist, just about when I was expecting him to say something like that.

"Tits?" Charlie asked.

"These statues. They should be smashed in a thousand pieces and buried in the earth whence they came." He said it mildly, but he meant it.

"What a great loss to art that would be," said Charlie in his most pious way. "Anyway, the original statue from which these were copied fell from heaven. That's what the Bible says, right? Book of Acts. The image that Jupiter tossed down from the sky. It could be argued that Jupiter is simply one manifestation of Jehovah. Therefore this is a holy image. Wouldn't you say so, Mr. Gladstone?"

There was a cruel edge on Charlie's voice; but, then, Charlie is cruel. Charming, of course, and ferociously bright, but above all else a smart-ass. He's three years older than I am, and three times as intelligent. You can imagine what my childhood was like. If I had ever taken his cruelties seriously, I suspect I would hate him; but the best defense against Charlie is never to take him seriously. I never have, nor anything much else, either. In that way Charlie and I are similar, I suppose. But only in that way.

Mr. Gladstone refused to be drawn into Charlie's bantering defense of idolatry. Maybe he too had figured out how to handle Charlie, a lot quicker than I ever did.

"You are a cynic and a sophist, Dr. Walker," is all that he said. "There is no profit in disputing these matters with cynics. Or with sophists. Especially with sophists." And to me, five minutes later, as we rambled through a room full of mosaics and frescoes and little bronze statuettes: "Your brother is a sly and very clever man. But there's a hollowness about him that saddens me. I wish I could help him. I feel a great deal of pity for him, you know."

THAT anyone would want to feel pity for Charlie was a new concept to me. Envy, yes. Resentment, disapproval, animosity, even fear, perhaps. But pity? For the six-foot-three genius with the blond hair and blue eyes, the movie-star face, the seven-figure trust fund, the four-digit I.Q.? I am tall too, and when I reached twenty-one I came into money also, and I am neither stupid nor ugly; but it was always Charlie who got the archery trophy, the prom queen, the honor-roll scroll, the Phi Beta Kappa key. It was Charlie who always got anything and everything he wanted, effortlessly, sometimes bestowing his leftovers on me, but always in a patronizing way that thoroughly tainted them. I have sensed people pitying me, sometimes, because they look upon me as Charlie-minus, an inadequate simulacrum of the genuine article, a pallid secondary version of the extraordinary Charlie. In truth I think their compassion for me, if that's what it is, is misplaced: I don't see myself as all that goddamned pitiful. But Charlie? Pitying Charlie?

I was touring Greece and Turkey that spring, mostly the usual Aegean resorts, Mykonos and Corfu and Crete, Rhodes and Bodrum and Marmaris. I wander up and down the Mediterranean about half the year, generally, and, though I'm scarcely a scholar, I do of course look in on the various famous classical sites along my way. By now, I suppose, I've seen every ruined Roman and Greek temple and triumphal arch and ancient theater there is, from Volubilis and Thuburbo Majus in North Africa up through Sicily and Pompeii, and out to Spain and France on one side and Syria and Lebanon on the other. They all blur and run together in my mind, becoming a single generic site — fallen marble columns, weather-beaten foundations, sand, little skittering lizards, blazing sun, swarthy men selling picture postcards — but I keep on prowling them anyway. I don't quite know why.

There are no hotels remotely worthy of the name in or around the Ephesus ruins. But Charlie had tipped me off that I would find, about six miles down the road, a lavish new deluxe place high up on a lonely point overlooking the serene Aegean that catered mostly to groups of sun-worshipping Germans. It had an immense lobby with marble floors and panoramic windows, an enormous swimming pool, and an assortment of dining rooms that resounded day and night with the whoops and hollers of the beefy Deutschers, who never seemed to leave the hotel. Charlie drove out there to have dinner with me the night I arrived, and that was when we met Mr. Gladstone.

"Excuse me," he said, hovering beside our table, "but I couldn't help hearing you speaking in English. I don't speak German at all and, well, frankly, among all these foreigners I've been getting a little lonely for the mother tongue. Do you mind if I join you?"

"Well . . ." I said, not really eager for his company, because tonight was the first time I had seen my brother in a couple of years. But Charlie grandly waved him to a seat.

He was a grayish, cheerful man of about sixty, a small-town pastor from Ohio or Indiana or maybe Iowa, and he had been saving for something like twenty years to take an extensive tour of the Christian holy places of the Middle East. For the past three months he had been traveling with a little group of . . . pilgrims, I guess one could call them, six weeks busing through Israel from Jerusalem to Beersheba, down to Mount Sinai, back up through the Galilee to Lebanon to see Sidon and Tyre, then out to Damascus, and so on and so on, the full Two-Testament Special. His traveling companions all had flown home by now, but Mr. Gladstone had bravely arranged a special side trip just for himself to Turkey—to poky little Seljuk in particular— because his late wife had had a special interest in an important Christian site here. He had never traveled anywhere by himself before, not even in the States, and going it alone in Turkey was a bit of a stretch for him. But he felt he owed it to his wife's memory to make the trip, and so he was resolutely plugging along on his own here, having flown from Beirut to Izmir and then hired a car and driver to bring him down to Seljuk. He had arrived earlier this day.

"I didn't realize there was anything of special Christian interest around here," I said.

"The Cave of the Seven Sleepers of Ephesus," Mr. Gladstone explained. "My wife once wrote a little book for children about the Seven Sleepers. It was always her great hope to see their actual cave."

"The Seven Sleepers?"

He sketched the story for me quickly: the seven devout Christian boys who took refuge in a cave rather than offer sacrifices in the temple of the Roman gods, and who fell into a deep sleep and came forth two hundred years later to discover that Christianity had miraculously become the official religion of Rome while they were doing their Rip van Winkle act. What was supposedly their cave may still be seen just beyond the Roman stadium of Ephesus.

"There's also the Meryemana," Charlie said.

Mr. Gladstone gave him a polite blank smile. "Beg your pardon?"

"The house where the Virgin Mary lived in the last years of her life. Jesus told St. John the Apostle to look after her, and he brought her to Ephesus, so it's said. About a hundred years ago some Eastern Orthodox priests went looking for her house and found it, sure enough, about three miles outside town."

"Indeed."

"More likely it's sixth-century Byzantine," said Charlie. "But the foundations are much older. The Orthodox Christians go there on pilgrimage every summer. You really ought to see it." He smiled his warmest, most savage smile. "Ephesus has always been a center of mother-goddess worship, you know, and apparently it has continued to be one even in postpagan times."

Mr. Gladstone's lips quirked ever so slightly. Though I assumed—correctly—that he was Protestant, even a Presbyterian was bound to be annoyed at hearing someone call the Virgin Mary a mother-goddess. But all he said was "It would be interesting to see, yes."

Charlie wouldn't let up. "You will, of course, look in at the Seljuk Museum to see the predecessor goddess's statue, won't you? Diana, I mean. Diana of the Hundred Breasts. It's best to visit the museum before you begin your tour of the ruins, anyway. And the statues—there are two, actually—sum up the whole concept of the sacred female principle in a really spectacular way. The primordial mother, the great archetype. The celestial cow that nourishes the world. You need to see it, if you want truly to understand the bipolar sexual nature of the divine, eh, Mr. G?" He glanced toward me. "You too, Tim. The two of you, meet me in front of the museum at nine tomorrow, okay? Basic orientation lecture by Dr. Walker. Followed by a visit to ancient Ephesus, including the Cave of the Seven Sleepers. Perhaps the Meryemana afterward." Charlie flashed a dazzling grin. "Will you have some wine, Mr. Gladstone?"

"No, thank you," Mr. Gladstone said, quickly putting his hand over the empty glass in front of him.

AFTER the museum, the next morning, we doubled back to the ruins of Ephesus proper. Mobs of tour groups were already there, milling around befuddledly as tour groups will do, but Charlie zipped right around them to the best stuff. The ruins are in a marvelous state of preservation—a nearly intact Roman city of the first century A.D., the usual forum and temples and stadium and gymnasium and such, and of course the famous two-story library that the Turks feature on all those tourist posters.

We had the best of all possible guides. Charlie has a genuine passion for archaeology—it's the only thing, I suspect, that he really cares for, other than himself—and he pointed out a million details that we would otherwise have missed. With special relish he dwelled on the grotesqueries of the cult of Diana, telling us not only about the metaphorical significance of the goddess's multiplicity of breasts, but about the high priest who was always a eunuch— "His title," said Charlie, "meant 'He who has been set free by God' "—and the staff of virgins who assisted him, and the special priests known as the Acrobatae, or "walkers on tiptoe," et cetera, et cetera. Mr. Gladstone showed signs of definite distaste as Charlie went on to speculate on some of the more flamboyant erotic aspects of pagan worship hereabouts, but he wouldn't stop. He never does, when he has a chance to display his erudition and simultaneously offend and unsettle someone.

6

Eventually it was midafternoon and the day had become really hot and we were only halfway through our tour of the ancient city, with the Cave of the Seven Sleepers still a mile or two in the distance. And clearly Mr. Gladstone was wilting. We decided to call it a day, and had a late lunch of kebabs and stewed eggplant at one of the innumerable and interchangeable little bistros in town. "We can go to the cave first thing tomorrow morning, when it's still cool," Charlie offered.

"Thank you. But I think I would prefer to visit it alone, if you don't mind. A private pilgrimage—for my late wife's sake, do you see? Something of a ceremonial observance."

"Certainly," Charlie intoned reverently. "I quite understand."

I asked him if he would be coming out to the hotel again that evening for dinner with me. No, he said, he would be busy at the dig—the cool of the evening was a good time to work, without the distraction of gawking tourists—but we arranged to meet in the morning for breakfast and a little brotherly catching up on family news. I left him in town and drove back to the hotel with Mr. Gladstone.

"Your brother isn't a religious man, is he?" he said.

"I'm afraid that neither of us is, especially. It's the way we were raised."

"But he really isn't. You're merely indifferent; he is hostile."

"How can you tell?"

"Because," he said, "he was trying so hard to provoke me with those things he was saying about Diana of Ephesus. He makes no distinction between Christianity and paganism. All religions must be the same to him, mere silly cults. And so he thinks he can get at my beliefs somehow by portraying pagan worship as absurd and bizarre."

"He looks upon them all as cults, yes. But silly, no. In fact Charlie takes religion very seriously, though not exactly in the same way you do. He regards it as a conspiracy by the power elite to remain on top at the expense of the masses. And holy scriptures are just works of fiction dreamed up to perpetuate the authority of the priests and their bosses."

"He sees all religions that way, does he, without making distinctions?"

"Every one of them, yes. Always the same thing, throughout the whole of human history."

"The poor man," said Mr. Gladstone. "The poor empty-souled man. If only I could set him straight, somehow!"

There it was again: the compassion, the pity. For Charlie, of all people! Fascinating. Fascinating.

"I doubt that you'd succeed," I told him. "He's inherently a skeptical person. He's never been anything else. And he's a scientist, remember, a man who lives or dies by rational explanations. If it can't be explained, then it probably isn't real. He doesn't have a smidgen of belief in anything he can't see and touch and measure."

"He is incapable of giving credence to the evidence of things not seen?"

"Excuse me?"

" 'The substance of things hoped for, the evidence of things not seen.' Book of Hebrews, 11:1. It's St. Paul's definition of faith."

"Ah."

"St. Paul was here, you know. In this town, in Ephesus, on a missionary journey. Gods that are fashioned by human hands are no gods at all, he told the populace. Whereupon a certain Demetrius, a silversmith who earned his living making statuettes of the many-breasted goddess whose images we saw today in the museum, called his colleagues together and said, If this man has his way, the temple of the great goddess Diana will be destroyed and we will lose our livelihoods. 'And when they heard these sayings, they were full of wrath, and cried out, saying, "Great is Diana of the Ephesians." And the whole city was filled with confusion.' That's the Book of Acts, 19:28. And there was such a huge uproar in town over the things that Paul was preaching that he found it prudent to depart very quickly for Macedonia."

"I see."

"But the temple of the goddess was destroyed anyway, eventually. And her statues were cast down and buried in the earth, and now are seen only in museums."

"And the people of Ephesus became Christians," I said. "And Moslems after that, it would seem."

He looked startled. My gratuitous little dig had clearly stung him. But then he smiled.

"I see that you are your brother's brother," he said.

I was up late reading, and thinking about Charlie, and staring at the moonlight shimmering on the bay. About half past eleven I hit the sack. Almost immediately my phone rang.

Charlie. "Are you alone, bro?"

"No," I said. "As a matter of fact, Mr. Gladstone and I are hunkering down, getting ready to commit abominations before the Lord."

"I thought maybe one of those horny Kraut ladies—"

"Cut it out. I'm alone, Charlie. And pretty sleepy. What is it?"

"Can you come down to the ruins? There's something I want to show you."

"Right now?"

"Now is a good time for this."

"I told you I was sleepy."

"It's something big, Tim. I need to show it to somebody, and you're the only person on this planet I even halfway trust."

"Something you discovered tonight?"

"Get in your car and come on down. I'll meet you by the Magnesian Gate. That's the back entrance. Go past the museum and turn right at the crossroads in town."

"Charlie—"

"Move your ass, bro. Please."

That "please," from Charlie, was something very unusual. In twenty minutes I was at the gate. He was waiting there, swinging a huge flashlight. A tool sack was slung over one shoulder. He looked wound up tight, as tense as I had ever seen him.

Selecting a key from a chain that held at least thirty of them, he unlocked the gate and led me down a long straight avenue paved with worn blocks of stone. The moon was practically full and the ancient city was bathed in cool silvery light. He pointed out the buildings as we went by them: "The baths of Varius. The basilica. The necropolis. The temple of Isis." He droned the names in a singsong tone as though this were just one more guided tour. We turned to the right, onto another street that I recognized as the main one, where earlier that day I had seen the gate of Hercules, the temple of Hadrian, the library. "Here we are. Back of the brothel and the latrine."

We scrambled uphill perhaps fifty yards through gnarled scrubby under-brush until we came to a padlocked metal grate set in the ground in an otherwise empty area. Charlie produced the proper key and pulled back the grate. His flashlight beam revealed a rough earthen-walled tunnel, maybe five feet high, leading into the hillside. The air inside was hot and stale, with a sweet heavy odor of dry soil. After about twenty feet the tunnel forked. Crouching, we followed the right-hand fork, pushing our way through some bundles of dried leaves that seemed to have been put there to block entrance.

"Look there," he said.

He shot the beam off to the left and I found myself staring at a place where the tunnel wall had been very carefully smoothed. An upright circular slab of rough-hewn marble perhaps a yard across was set into it there.

"What is it?" I asked him. "A gravestone? A commemorative plaque?"

"Some sort of door, more likely. Covering a funeral chamber, I would suspect. You see these?" He indicated three smaller circles of what looked like baked clay, mounted in a symmetrical way over the marble slab, arranged to form the angles of an equilateral triangle. They overlapped the edges of the slab as though sealing it into the wall. I went closer and saw inscriptions carved into the clay circles, an array of mysterious symbols and letters.

"What language is this? Not Greek. Hebrew, maybe?"

"No. I don't actually know what it is. Some unknown Anatolian script, or some peculiar form of Aramaic or Phoenician—I just can't say, Timmo. Maybe it's a nonsense script, even. Purely decorative sacred scribbles convey-ing spells to keep intruders away, maybe. You know, some kind of magical mumbo jumbo. It might be anything."

"You found this tonight?"

"Three weeks ago. We've known this tunnel was here for a long time, but it was thought to be empty. I happened to be doing some sonar scanning overhead and I got an echo back from a previously uncharted branch, so I came down and took a look around. Nobody knows about it but me. And you."

Gingerly I ran my hand over the face of the marble slab. It was extraordinarily smooth, cool to the touch. I had the peculiar illusion that my fingertips were tingling, as though from a mild electrical charge.

"What are you going to do?" I asked.

"Open it."

"Now?"

"Now, bro. You and me."

"You can't do that!"

"I can't?"

"You're part of an expedition, Charlie. You can't just bust into a tomb, or whatever this is, on your own. It isn't proper procedure, is it? You need to have the other scientists here. And the Turkish antiquities officials—they'll string you up by the balls if they find out you've done a bit of secret freelance excavating without notifying any local authorities."

"We break the seals. We look inside. If there's anything important in there, we check it out just to gratify our own curiosity and then we go away, and in the morning I discover it all over again and raise a big hullabaloo and we go through all the proper procedure then. Listen, bro, there could be something big in there, don't you see? The grave of a high priest. The grave of some prehistoric king. The lost treasure of the temple of Diana. The Ark of the Covenant. Anything. Anything. Whatever it is, I want to know. And I want to see it before anybody else does."

He was lit up with a passion so great that I could scarcely recognize him as my cool brother Charlie.

"How are you going to explain the broken seals?"

"Broken by some tomb-robber in antiquity," he said. "Who got frightened away before he could finish the job."

He had always been a law unto himself, my brother Charlie. I argued with him a little more, but I knew it would do no good. He had never been

11

much of a team player. He wasn't going to have five or six wimpy colleagues and a bunch of Turkish antiquities officials staring over his shoulder while that sealed chamber was opened for the first time in two thousand years.

He drew a small battery-powered lamp from his sack and set it on the ground. Then he began to pull the implements of his trade out of the sack — the little chisels, the camel's-hair brushes, the diamond-bladed hacksaw.

"Why did you wait until I got here before you opened it?" I asked.

"Because I thought I might need help pulling that slab out of the wall, and who could I trust except you? Besides, I wanted an audience for the grand event."

"Of course."

"You know me, Timmo."

"So I do, bro. So I do."

He began very carefully to chisel off one of the clay seals. It came away in two chunks. Setting it to one side, he went to work on the second one, and then the third. Then he dug his fingertips into the earthen wall at the edge of the slab and gave it an experimental tug.

"I do need you," he said. "Put your shoulder against the slab and steady it as I pry it with this crowbar. I don't want it just toppling out."

Bit by bit he wiggled it free. As it started to pivot and fall forward I leaned all my weight into it, and Charlie reached across me and caught it too, and together we were able to brace it as it left its aperture and guide it down carefully to the ground.

We stared into the blackest of black holes. Ancient musty air came roaring forth in a long dry whoosh. Charlie leaned forward and started to poke the flashlight into the opening.

But then he pulled back sharply and turned away, gasping as though he had inhaled a wisp of something noxious.

"Charlie?"

"Just a second." He waved his hand near his head a couple of times, the way you might do when brushing away a cobweb. "Just — a — goddamn — second, Tim!" A convulsive shiver ran through him. Automatically I moved toward him to see what the matter was and as I came up beside him in front

12

of that dark opening I felt a sudden weird sensation, a jolt, a jab, and my head began to spin. And for a moment—just a moment—I seemed to hear a strange music, an eerie high-pitched wailing sound like the keening of elevator cables far, far away. In that crazy incomprehensible moment I imagined that I was standing at the rim of a deep, ancient well, the oldest well of all, the well from which all creation flows, with strange shadowy things churning and throbbing down below, and from its depths rose a wild rush of perfumed air that dizzied and intoxicated me.

Then the moment passed and I was in my right mind again and I looked at Charlie and he looked at me.

"You felt it too, didn't you?" I said.

"Felt what?" he demanded fiercely. He seemed almost angry.

I searched for the words. But it was all fading, fading fast, and there was only Charlie with his face jammed into mine, angry Charlie, terrifying Charlie, practically daring me to claim that anything peculiar had happened.

"It was very odd, bro," I said finally. "Like a drug thing, almost."

"Oxygen deprivation, is all. A blast of old stale air."

"You think?"

"I know."

But he seemed uncharacteristically hesitant, even a little befuddled. He stood at an angle to the opening, head turned away, shoulders slumping, the flashlight dangling from his hand.

"Aren't you going to look inside?" I asked, after a bit.

"Give me a moment, Timmo."

"Charlie, are you all right?"

"Christ, yes! I breathed in a little dust, that's all." He knelt, rummaged in the tool sack, pulled out a canteen, took a deep drink. "Better," he said hoarsely. "Want some?" I took the canteen from him and he leaned into the opening again, flashing the beam around.

"What do you see?"

"Nothing. Not a fucking thing."

"They put up a marble slab and plaster it with inscribed seals and there's nothing at all behind it?"

"A hole," he said. "Maybe five feet deep, five feet high. A storage chamber of some kind, I would guess. Nothing in it. Absolutely fucking nothing, bro."

"Let me see."

"Don't you trust me?"

In fact I didn't, not very much. But I just shrugged; and he handed me the flashlight, and I peered into the hole. Charlie was right. The interior of the chamber was smooth and regular, but it was empty, not the slightest trace of anything.

"Shit," Charlie said. He shook his head somberly. "My very own Tutankhamen tomb, only nothing's in it. Let's get the hell out of here."

"Are you going to report this?"

"What for? I come in after hours, conduct illicit explorations, and all I have to show for my sins is an empty hole? What's the good of telling anybody that? Just for the sake of making myself look like an unethical son of a bitch? No, bro. None of this ever happened."

"But the seals—the inscriptions in an unknown script—"

"Not important. Let's go, Tim."

He still sounded angry, and not, I think, just because the little chamber behind the marble slab had been empty. Something had gotten to him just now, and gotten to him deeply. Had he heard the weird music too? Had he looked into that fathomless well? He hated all mystery, everything inexplicable. I think that was why he had become an archaeologist. Mysteries had a way of unhinging him. When I was maybe ten and he was thirteen, we had spent a rainy evening telling each other ghost stories, and finally we made one up together, something about spooks from another world who were haunting our attic, and our own story scared me so much that I began to cry. I imagined I heard strange creaks overhead. Charlie mocked me mercilessly, but it seemed to me that for a time he had looked a little nervous too, and when I said so he got very annoyed indeed; and then, bluffing all the way, I invited him to come up to the attic with me right then and there to see that it was safe, and he punched me in the chest and knocked me down. Later he denied the whole episode.

"I'm sorry I wasted your time tonight, keed," he said, as we hiked back up to our cars.

"That's okay. It just might have been something special."

"Just might have been, yeah." He grinned and winked. He was himself again, old devil-may-care Charlie. "Sleep tight, bro. See you in the morning."

But I didn't sleep tight at all. I kept waking and hearing the wailing sound of far-off elevator cables, and my dreams were full of blurry strangenesses.

THE next day I hung out at the hotel all day, breakfasting with Charlie—he didn't refer to the events of the night before at all—and lounging by the pool the rest of the time. I had some vague thought of hooking up with one of the German tourist ladies, I suppose, but no openings presented themselves, and I contented myself with watching the show. Even in puritanical Turkey, where the conservative politicians are trying to put women back into veils and ankle-length skirts, European women of all ages go casually topless at coastal resorts like this, and it was remarkable to see how much savoir faire the Turkish poolside waiters displayed while taking bar orders from zaftig bare-breasted grandmothers from Hamburg or Munich and their stunning topless granddaughters.

Mr. Gladstone, who hadn't been around in the morning, turned up late in the afternoon. I was in the lobby bar by then, working on my third or fourth postlunch raki. He looked sweaty and tired and sunburned. I ordered a Coke for him.

"Busy day?"

"Very. The Cave of the Seven Sleepers was my first stop. A highly emotional experience, I have to say, not because of the cave itself, you understand, although the ancient ruined church there is quite interesting, but because—the associations—the memories of my dear wife that it summoned—"

"Of course."

"After that my driver took me out to the so-called House of the Virgin. Perhaps it's genuine, perhaps not, but either way it's a moving thing to see. The invisible presence of thousands of pilgrims hovers over it, the aura of centuries of faith." He smiled gently. "Do you know what I mean, Mr. Walker?"

"I think I do, yes."

"And in the afternoon I saw the Basilica of St. John, on Ayasuluk Hill."

I didn't know anything about that. He explained that it was the acropolis of the old Byzantine city—the steep hill just across the main highway from the center of the town of Seljuk. Legend had it that St. John the Apostle had been buried up there, and centuries later the Emperor Justinian built an enormous church on the site, which was, of course, a ruin now, but an impressive one.

"And you?" he said. "You visited with your brother?"

"In the morning, yes."

"A brilliant man, your brother. If only he could be happier, eh?"

"Oh, I think Charlie's happy, all right. He's had his own way every step of his life."

"Is that your definition of happiness? Having your own way?"

"It can be very helpful."

"And you haven't had your own way, is that it, Mr. Walker?"

"My life has been reasonably easy by most people's standards, I have to admit. I was smart enough to pick a wealthy great-grandfather. But compared with Charlie—he has an extraordinary mind, he's had a splendid scientific career, he's admired by all the members of his profession. I don't even have a profession, Mr. Gladstone. I just float around."

"You're young, Mr. Walker. You'll find something to do and someone to share your life with, and you'll settle down. But your brother—I wonder, Mr. Walker. Something vital is missing from his life. But he will never find it, because he is not willing to admit that it's missing."

"Religion, do you mean?"

"Not specifically, no. Belief, perhaps. Not religion, but belief. Do you follow me, Mr. Walker? One must believe in something, do you see? And your brother will not permit himself to do that." He gave me the gentle smile again. "Would you excuse me, now? I've had a rather strenuous day. I think a little nap, before supper . . ."

Since we were the only two Americans in the place, I invited him to join me again for dinner that night. He did most of the talking, reminiscing about his wife, telling me about his children—he had three, in their thirties—and describing some of the things he had seen in his tour of the biblical places. I had never spent much time with anyone of his sort. A kindly man, an earnest man; and, I suspect, not quite as simple a man as a casual observer might think.

He went upstairs about half past eight. I returned to the bar and had a couple of raw Turkish brandies and thought hopeful thoughts about the stunning German granddaughters. Somewhere about ten, as I was considering going to bed, a waiter appeared and said, "You are Mr. Timothy Walker?"

"Yes."

"Your brother Charles is at the security gate and asks that you come out to meet him."

Mystified, I went rushing out into the courtyard. The hotel grounds are locked down every night and nobody is admitted except guests and the guests of guests. I saw the glare of headlights just beyond the gate. Charlie's car.

"What's up, bro?"

His eyes were wild. He gestured at me with furious impatience. "In. In!" Almost before I closed the door he spun the car around and was zooming down the narrow, winding road back to Seljuk. He was hunched over the wheel in the most peculiar rigid way.

"Charlie?"

"Exactly what did you experience," he said tightly, "when we pulled that marble slab out of the wall?"

My reply was carefully vague.

"Tell me," he said. "Be very precise."

"I don't want you to laugh at me, Charlie."

"Just tell me."

I took a deep breath. "Well, then. I imagined that I heard far-off music. I had a kind of vision of—well, someplace weird and mysterious. I thought I smelled perfume. The whole thing lasted maybe half a second and then it was over."

17

He was silent a moment.

Then he said, in a strange little quiet way, "It was the same for me, bro."

"You denied it. I asked you, and you said no, Charlie."

"Well, I lied. It was the same for me." His voice had become very odd— thin, tight, quavering. Everything about him right now was tight. Something had to pop. The car was traveling at maybe eighty miles an hour on that little road and I feared for my life. After a very long time he said, "Do you think there's any possibility, Tim, that we might have let something out of that hole in the ground when we broke those seals and pulled that slab out?"

I stared at him. "That's crazy, Charlie."

"I know it is. Just answer me: do you think we felt something moving past us as we opened that chamber?"

"Hey, we're too old to be telling each other spook stories, bro."

"I'm being serious."

"Bullshit you are," I said. "I hate it when you play with me like this."

"I'm not playing," Charlie said, and he turned around so that he was practically facing me for a moment. His face was twisted with strain. "Timmo, some goddamned thing that looks awfully much like Diana of Ephesus has been walking around in the ruins since sundown. Three people I know of have seen her. Three very reliable people."

I couldn't believe that he was saying stuff like this. Not Charlie.

"Keep your eyes on the road, will you?" I told him. "You'll get us killed driving like that."

"Do you know how much it costs me to say these things? Do you know how lunatic it sounds to me? But she's real. She's there. She was sealed up in that hole, and we let her out. The foreman of the excavations has seen her, and Judy, the staff artist, and Mike Dornan, the ceramics guy."

"They're fucking with your head, Charlie. Or you're fucking with mine."

"No. No. No. No."

"Where are we going?" I asked.

"To look for her. To find out what the hell it is that those people think they saw. I've got to know, Tim. This time, I've absolutely got to know."

The desperation in Charlie's voice was something new in my experience of him. I've absolutely got to know. Why? Why? It was all too crazy. And dragging me out like this: why? To bear witness? To help him prove to himself that he actually was seeing the thing that he was seeing, if indeed he saw it? Or, maybe, to help him convince himself that there was nothing there to see?

But he wasn't going to see anything. I was sure of that.

"Charlie," I said. "Oh, Charlie, Charlie, Charlie, this isn't happening, is it? Not really."

WE pulled up outside the main gate of the ruins. A watchman was posted there, a Turk. He stepped quickly aside as Charlie went storming through into the site. I saw flashlights glowing in the distance, and then four or five American-looking people. Charlie's colleagues, the archaeologists.

"Well?" Charlie yelled. He sounded out of control.

A frizzy-haired woman of about forty came up from somewhere to our left. She looked as wild-eyed and agitated as Charlie. For the first time I began to think this might not be just some goofy practical joke.

"Heading east," the woman blurted. "Toward the stadium or maybe all the way out to the goddess sanctuary. Dick saw it too. And Edward thinks he did."

"Anybody get a photo?"

"Not that I know of," the woman said.

"Come on," Charlie said to me, and went running off at an angle to the direction we had just come. Frantically I chased after him. He was chugging uphill, into the thorny scrub covering the unexcavated areas of the city. By moonlight I saw isolated shattered pillars rising from the ground like broken teeth, and tumbledown columns that had been tossed around like so many toothpicks. As I came alongside him he said, "There's a little sanctuary of the Mother-Goddess back there. Wouldn't that be the logical place that she'd want to go to?"

"For shit's sake, Charlie! What are you saying?"

He kept on running, giving me no answer. I fought my way up the hill

19

through a tangle of brambles and canes that slashed at me like daggers, all the while wondering what the hell we were going to find on top. We were halfway up when shouts came to us from down the hill, people behind us waving and pointing. Charlie halted and listened, frowning. Then he swung around and started sprinting back down the hill. "She's gone outside the ruins," he called to me over his shoulder. "Through the fence, heading into town! Come on, Tim!"

I went running after him, scrambling downhill, then onward along the main entrance road and onto the main highway. I'm in good running shape, but Charlie was moving with a maniacal zeal that left me hard pressed to keep up with him. Twenty feet apart, we came pounding down the road past the museum and into town. All the dinky restaurants were open, even this late, and little knots of Turks had emerged from them to gather in the crossroads. Some were kneeling in prayer, hammering their heads against the pavement, and others were wildly gesticulating at one another in obvious shock and bewilderment. Charlie, without breaking stride, called out to them in guttural Turkish and got a whole babble of replies.

"Ayasuluk Hill," he said to me. "That's the direction she's going in."

We crossed the broad boulevard that divides the town in half. As we passed the bus station half a dozen men came running out of a side street in front of us, screaming as though they had just been disemboweled. You don't expect to hear adult male Turks screaming. They are a nation of tough people, by and large. These fellows went flying past us without halting, big men with thick black mustachios. Their eyes were wide and gleaming like beacons, their faces rigid and distended with shock and horror, as though twenty devils were coming after them.

"Charlie—"

"Look there," he said, in an utterly flat voice, and pointed into the darkness.

Something—something—was moving away from us down that side street, something very tall and very strange. I saw a tapering conical body, a hint of weird appendages, a crackling blue-white aura. It seemed to be floating rather than walking, carried along by a serene but inexorable drifting motion almost as if its feet were several inches off the ground. Maybe they were.

As we watched, the thing halted and peered into the open window of a house. There was a flash of blinding light, intense but short-lived. Then the front door popped open and a bunch of frantic Turks came boiling out like a pack of Keystone Cops, running in sixty directions at once, yelling and flinging their arms about as though trying to surrender.

One of them tripped and went sprawling down right at the creature's feet. He seemed unable to get up; he knelt there all bunched up, moaning and babbling, shielding his face with outspread hands. The thing paused and looked down, and seemed to reach its arms out in fluid gestures, and the blue-white glow spread for a moment like a mantle over the man. Then the light withdrew from him and the creature, gliding smoothly past the trembling fallen man, continued on its serene silent way toward the dark hill that loomed above the town.

"Come," Charlie said to me.

We went forward. The creature had disappeared up ahead, though we caught occasional glimpses of the blue-white light as it passed between the low little buildings of the town. We reached the man who had tripped; he had not arisen, but lay facedown, shivering, covering his head with his hands. A low rumbling moan of fear came steadily from him. Hoarse cries of terror drifted to us from here and there as this villager or that encountered the thing that was passing through their town, and now and again we could see that cool bright light, rising steadily above us until finally it was shining down from the upper levels of Ayasuluk Hill.

"You really want to go up there?" I asked him.

He didn't offer me an answer, nor did he stop moving forward. I wasn't about to turn back either, I realized. Willy-nilly I followed him to the end of the street, around a half-ruined mosque at the base of the hill, and up to a lofty metal gate tipped with spikes. Stoned on our own adrenaline, we swarmed up that gate like Crusaders attacking a Saracen fortress, went over the top, dropped down in the bushes on the far side. I was able to see, by the brilliant gleam of the full moon, the low walls of the destroyed Basilica of St. John just beyond, and, behind it, the massive Byzantine fortification that crowned the hill. Together we scrambled toward the summit.

"You go this way, Tim. I'll go the other and we'll meet on the far side."

"Right."

I didn't know what I was looking for. I just ran, leftward around the hill. Along the ramparts, into the church, down the empty aisles, out the gaping window frames.

Suddenly I caught a glimpse of something up ahead. Light, cool white light, an unearthly light very much like moonlight, only concentrated into a fiercely gleaming point hovering a couple of yards above the ground, thirty or forty feet in front of me.

"Charlie?" I called. My voice was no more than a hoarse gasp.

I edged forward. The light was so intense now that I was afraid it might damage my eyes. But I continued to stare, as if the thing would disappear if I were to blink for even a millionth of a second.

I heard the wailing music again.

Soft, distant, eerie. Cables rubbing together in a dark shaft. This time it seemed to be turned outward, rising far beyond me, reaching into distant space or perhaps some even more distant dimension. Something calling, announcing its regained freedom, summoning—whom? What?

"Charlie?" I said. It was a barely audible croak. "Charlie?"

I noticed him now, edging up from the other side. I pointed at the source of the light. He nodded.

I moved closer. The light seemed to change, to grow momentarily less fierce. And then I was able to see her.

She wasn't exactly identical to the statues in the museum. Her face wasn't really a face, at least not a human one. She had beady eyes, faceted the way an insect's are. She had an extra set of arms, little dangling ones, coming out at her hips. And, though the famous breasts were there, at least fifty of them and maybe the hundred of legend, I don't think they were actual breasts because I don't think this creature was a mammal. More of a reptile, I would guess: leathery skin, more or less scaly the way a snake's is, and tiny dots of nostrils, and a black slithery tongue, jagged like a lightning bolt, that came

22

shooting quickly out between her slitted lips again and again and again, as though checking on the humidity or the ambient temperature or some such thing.

I saw, and Charlie saw. For a fraction of a second I wanted to drop down on my knees and rub my forehead in the ground and give worship. And then I just wanted to run.

I said, "Charlie, I definitely think we ought to get the hell out of—"

"Cool it, bro," he said. He stepped forward. Walked right up to her, stared her in the face. I was terrified for him, seeing him get that close. She dwarfed him. He was like a doll in front of her. How had a thing this big managed to fit in that opening in the tunnel wall? How had those ancient Greeks ever managed to get her in there in the first place?

That dazzling light crackled and hissed around her like some sort of electrical discharge. And yet Charlie stood his ground, unflinching, rock-solid. The expression on my brother's face was a nearly incomprehensible mixture of anger and fear.

He jabbed his forefinger through the air at her.

"You," he said to her. It was almost a snarl. "Tell me what the hell you are."

They were maybe ten feet apart, the man and the—what? The goddess? The monster?

Charlie had to know.

"You speak English?" he demanded. "Turkish? Tell me. I'm the one who let you out of that hole. Tell me what you are. I want to know." Eye to eye, face to face. "Something from another planet, are you, maybe? Another dimension? An ancient race that used to live on the Earth before humans did?"

"Charlie," I whispered.

But he wouldn't let up. "Or maybe you're an actual and literal goddess," he said. His tone had turned softer, a mocking croon now. "Diana of Ephesus, is that who you are? Stepping right out of the pages of mythology in all your fantastic beauty? Well, do me some magic, goddess, if that's who you are. Do a miracle for me, just a little one." The angry edge was back in his voice. "Turn that tree into an elephant. Turn me into a sheep, if you can. What's

23

the matter, Diana, you no spikka da English? All right. Why the hell should you? But how about Greek, then? Surely you can understand Greek."

"For Christ's sake, Charlie—"

He ignored me. It was as if I wasn't there. He was talking to her in Greek now. I suppose it was Greek. It was harsh, thick-sounding, jaggedly rhythmic. His eyes were wild and his face was flushed with fury. I was afraid that she would hurl a thunderbolt of blue-white light at him, but no, no, she just stood there through all his whole harangue, as motionless as those statues of her in the little museum, listening patiently as my furious brother went on and on and on at her in the language of Homer and Sophocles.

He stopped, finally. Waited as if expecting her to respond.

No response came. I could hear the whistling sound of her slow steady breathing; occasionally there was some slight movement of her body; but that was all.

"Well, Diana?" Charlie said. "What do you have to say for yourself, Diana?"

Silence.

"You fraud!" Charlie cried, in a great and terrible voice. "You fake! Some goddess you are! You aren't real at all, and that's God's own truth. You aren't even here. You're nothing but a fucking hallucination. A projection of some kind. I bet I could walk up to you and put my hand right through you."

Still no reaction. Nothing. She just stood there, those faceted eyes glittering, that little tongue flickering. Saying nothing, offering him no help.

That was when he flipped out. Charlie seemed to puff up as if about to explode with rage, and went rushing toward her, arms upraised, fists clenched in a wild gesture of attack. I wanted desperately to stop him, but my feet were frozen in place. I was certain that he was going to die. We both were.

"Damn you!" he roared, with something like a sob behind the fury. "Damn you, damn you, damn you!"

But before he could strike her, her aura flared up around her like a sheath, and for a moment the air was full of brilliant flares of cold flame that went whirling and whirling around her in a way that was too painful to watch. I caught a glimpse of Charlie staggering back from her, and I backed away

24

myself, covering my face with my forearm, but even so the whirling lights came stabbing into my brain, forcing me to the ground. It seemed then that they all coalesced into a single searing point of white light, which rose like a dagger into the sky, climbing, climbing, becoming something almost like a comet, and—then—

Vanishing.

And then I blacked out.

It was just before dawn when I awakened. My eyes fluttered open almost hesitantly. The moon was gone, the first pink streaks of light beginning to appear. Charlie sat beside me. He was already awake.

"Where is it?" I asked immediately.

"Gone, bro."

"Gone?"

He nodded. "Without a trace. If it was ever up here with us at all."

"What do you mean, if?"

"If, that's what I mean. Who the hell knows what was going on up here last night? Do you?"

"No."

"Well, neither do I. All I know is that it isn't going on anymore. There's nobody around but me and thee."

He was trying to sound like the old casual Charlie I knew, the man who had been everywhere and done everything and took it all in his stride. But there was a quality in his voice that I had never heard in it before, something entirely new.

"Gone?" I said, stupidly. "Really gone?"

"Really gone, yes. Vanished. You hear how quiet everything is?" Indeed the town, spread out below us, was silent except for the crowing of the first roosters and the far-off sound of a farm tractor starting up somewhere.

"Are you all right?" I asked him.

"Fine," he said. "Absolutely fine."

But he said it through clenched teeth. I couldn't bear to look at him. A thing had happened here that badly needed explanation, and no explanations were available, and I knew what that must be doing to him. I kept staring at the place where that eerie being had been, and I remembered that single shaft of light that had taken its place, and I felt a crushing sense of profound and terrible loss. Something strange and weirdly beautiful and utterly fantastic and inexplicable had been loose in the world for a little while, after centuries of—what? Imprisonment? Hibernation?—and now it was gone, and it would never return. It had known at once, I was sure, that this was no era for goddesses. Or whatever it was.

We sat side by side in silence for a minute or two.

"I think we ought to go back down now," I said finally.

"Right. Let's go back down," Charlie said.

And without saying another word as we descended, we made our way down the hill of Ayasuluk, the hill of St. John the Apostle, who was the man who wrote the Book of Revelations.

Mr. Gladstone was having breakfast in the hotel coffee shop when Charlie and I came in. He saw at once that something was wrong and asked if he could help in any way, and after some hesitation we told him something of what had happened, and then we told him more, and then we told him the whole story right to the end.

He didn't laugh and he didn't make any sarcastic skeptical comments. He took it all quite seriously.

"Perhaps the Seal of Solomon was what was on that marble slab," he suggested. "The Turks would say some such thing, at any rate. King Solomon had power over the evil jinn, and locked them away in flasks and caves and tombs, and put his seal on them to keep them locked up. It's in the Koran."

"You've read the Koran?" I asked, surprised.

"I've read a lot of things," said Mr. Gladstone.

"The Seal of Solomon," Charlie said, scowling. He was trying hard to be his old self again, and almost succeeding. Almost. "Evil spirits. Magic. Oh, Jesus Christ!"

"Perhaps," said Mr. Gladstone.

"What?" Charlie said.

The little man from Ohio or Indiana or Iowa put his hand over Charlie's. "If only I could help you," he said. "But you've been undone, haven't you, by the evidence of things seen."

"You have the quote wrong," said Charlie. " 'The substance of things hoped for, the evidence of things not seen.' Book of Hebrews, 11:1."

Mr. Gladstone was impressed. So was I.

"But this is different," he said to Charlie. "This time, you actually saw. You were, I think, a man who prided himself on believing in nothing at all. But now you can no longer even believe in your own disbelief."

Charlie reddened. "Saw what? A goddess? Jesus! You think I believe that that was a goddess? A genuine immortal supernatural being of a higher order of existence? Or—what?—some kind of actual alien creature? You want me to believe it was an alien that had been locked up in there all that time? An alien from where? Mars? And who locked it up? Or was it one of King Solomon's jinn, maybe?"

"Does it really matter which it was?" Mr. Gladstone asked softly.

Charlie started to say something; but he choked it back. After a moment he stood. "Listen, I need to go now," he said. "Mr. Gladstone—Timmo—I'll catch up with you later, is that all right?"

And then he turned and stalked away. But before he left, I saw the look in his eyes.

His eyes. Oh, Charlie. Oh. Those eyes. Those frightened, empty eyes.

The Face of Sekt

STORM CONSTANTINE

I am the lioness. I speak with her voice. I look out through her eyes. I am
she. I doze in the hot bars of sunlight that come down through the temple
roof. I breathe in the scent of flowers. Priests come to me and ask questions
so I will talk. It doesn't matter what I say, because all the words of the goddess
have meaning. They prostrate themselves and then Meni, the high priest, will
raise himself before the others. "Oh mighty Sekt, beloved of Aan, queen of
fire, lady of the red flower, hear our petitions."

Aan, I might mention, is my husband, whom I have never met. He lives
in another temple somewhere. They say his face is beautiful, but the chances
are I will never find this out for myself.

"Speak," I say, yawning.

The questions are too tedious to relate. I have to let my mind go blank
so the answers will come. Say this prayer, do that ritual task, cast scent, rake
the sand, spill blood. It's all they want from me.

The crown of the goddess covers my head, my face and rests upon my
shoulders. It is fashioned from beaten leaves of gold, shaped and painted.

Wearing it, I resemble the black basalt statues of the goddess that line the courtyards and populate the darkest niches of the temple: lioness-headed women. The mask was put upon me in my fifteenth year, a decade ago, and comes off rarely. No one may see the true face of the goddess. My hand-maidens withdraw from my chamber before I remove it to sleep.

There are no mirrors in my chamber. If I looked upon myself I might die, for the body that carries this goddess is still that of a woman. It is frail. I dare not even touch my face for fear of what my fingers might explore. When the mask was put upon me, Sekt entered my flesh. I wash myself in a sacred fountain, so that only the water may touch my face and hair.

At one time, our land was a province of the sacred kingdom of Mewt, and although those empire days are but distant memories, our culture is still saturated, if subtly, with Mewtish things. Originally, Sekt was a goddess of war, whose fierce countenance gazed down from the banners of Harakhte the conqueror. The temple he built here is a labyrinth of immense chambers, full of shadows, and tiny shrines where a priestess might mutter in the dark. It is called the Sektaeon.

As a representation of Sekt on earth, I am privileged above all other women. I have no secret yearning to escape the temple, or even this mask. I can bask in the sun all day if I want to. Long ago, my people embraced Sekt as a national goddess. At first this may have been due to fear, but later it was because they saw her power to work for them. She listened to their prayers, and very soon afterward Harakhte was killed in battle by the king of Cos, and Jessapur regained her independence. She has never lost it since. I like this irony. I believe Sekt loves us.

But every day, priests and priestesses in fire red robes walk the temple from end to end, renewing the magical seals over every entrance, however small. This is to keep the ancient spirits at bay, the djinn of the arid wilderness beyond the city and its fertile girdle of land. The djinn are born of fire and are therefore attracted to a goddess of that element. They desire also to wear flesh, and who better to steal a body from than a priest or priestess of fire? Sometimes, I think the djinn are long dead, and the precautions are only tired old ritual, but at other times, when the wind blows hot through the long reaches of the night, I hear a voice from the wilderness, in my heart rather than my ears, and it unnerves me.

Meni, my high priest, came to me this morning, in my solarium, which is actually a shady, green place. He glided between the lush trees and plants, dappled by the sunlight that found its way through the waving fronds of the vines. I was reclining upon some cushions, surrounded by lionesses, who lay licking their paws at my feet. We were being serenaded by the water garden. The rivulets conjured different notes as they ran through the various mechanisms hidden among the ferns. I was not in the best of moods as, during the night, the wind had blown with exceptional passion from the wilderness, carrying with it a scent of burning meat. I had turned restlessly, woken up from a dream of smoke. The darkness in my chamber had seemed watchful, almost sly. A flavor of the haunted night remained with me. I wondered whether it was a portent, and perhaps it was, for the high priest clearly hid a certain agitation beneath his serene and flawless countenance.

Meni stood before me and bowed. "Your reverence, there is a matter for your attention."

I have nothing to do most of the time, so it really perplexes me why every possibility of action seems only an irritant. "Oh, what, Meni? Can't you see to it?"

He bowed again. "Your reverence, it is a matter of importance. King Jaiver himself has requested that you turn your divine face toward it."

"What matter is it?"

"It concerns the Prince Reevan. He has a malady."

One of Sekt's aspects is a goddess of plagues, but she is equally adept at averting human illness. "I shall burn a pouch of incense for the boy and direct Sekt's healing force in the direction of the palace."

Meni paused. "It is rather more than that," he said. "The king has requested your presence."

That made me sit up. "Indeed?" I did not have to go. I was a goddess, who obeyed no one, yet I was intrigued as to why the king desired my physical presence. Was the prince so desperately ill? But that did not make sense. The most ailing of royals were generally carried to the temple, where they could be nursed by the priestesses, close to the presence of Sekt. "What is the nature of this malady, Meni?"

He shrugged. "I have not been told, your reverence. All I know is that Jaiver humbly requests your presence and has already made a sizable donation to the temple treasury."

"Then prepare my litter."

Meni bowed and departed, and presently a retinue of servants came padding to my garden, where they attended to my needs. They washed my hands and feet, and rubbed the palms and soles with red ochre. They applied cinnamon perfume to my wrists and throat, and veiled me in scarlet voile from head to foot. Beyond the temple, I would be concealed behind the curtains of my litter, but sometimes in the labyrinth of the city, strange winds can arise, which might blow the curtains apart. We have to take precautions so that common people never behold the face of the goddess.

The tasseled litter was carried by four eunuch priests. Before it marched a dozen priestesses in the red and gold robes of Sekt. They scattered petals of scarlet poppies before my path. At the head of the procession, Meni rode upon a beautiful nut-colored horse. Behind my litter strode three priests who also acted as my bodyguards. And behind them was a company of neophyte priests and priestesses, on hand to collect any spontaneous donations onlookers might wish to make.

Thus we processed through the faded grandeur of old Madramarta. I love my city, although I rarely get to see it. It is like a ghost of what it used to be, yet still beautiful. The ancient palaces are now tenement buildings full of low-caste workers, or else they have been turned into bazaars. The temples of forgotten gods stand rotting amid jungled gardens. In the dusty streets, forlorn peacocks trail their tails in the dirt, crying plaintively for the ordered landscapes of their ancestors. Everywhere there is evidence of a past opulence, now lost. As a province of Mewt, we prospered, for the Mewts loved the idea of sacred blood—such as the ichor that runs in the veins of our aristocratic families—and honored our country. They were not harsh governors and shared with us their knowledge of arts both occult and scientific. Now, in a time of independence, internal politics ravage the heart of Jessapur. The lowborn have turned our palaces into warrens. They spit on the idea of divine providence and seek power for themselves. The king still reigns, but just. His palace is a citadel.

We passed through the first series of gates and towers, into open parkland, where pale deer run. In the distance, we could see the ghost of the white palace shimmering in the heat. It is called Jurada, which means home of the high god. Only as you draw close to it can you tell it is not a mirage. Trefoil lakes surround it, and mock temples, and ornate gardens. Even though so many of the ancient houses have fallen into disrepair, Jurada still gleams as if new. It is said the entire remaining wealth of the country is divided between the upkeep of the temple of Sekt and that of the royal palace.

My party had to walk for nearly an hour along a shady avenue to reach Jurada. We came to a halt by a pool full of exotic fish in front of the main entrance. A scrum of servants ran out from the cool depths of the hall and laid down a carpet of ferns for me to step upon. I was offered saffron water and a piece of sugared coconut, which I accepted with grace. Meni went ahead of me into the palace and the rest of my retinue surrounded me protectively. The priestesses sang in rapturous high voices while the priests hummed an accompanying undertone. I put my sacred feet upon the ferns and walked the short distance to the hall. I left scarlet footprints.

The king was waiting for us in his throne room, which seemed a little inappropriate to me. I felt we should have been conducted directly to the royal family's private apartments, where the prince must lie in his sickbed. Was this a subtle affront? I was alert for strangenesses. A memory of my dream of smoke came back to me. Queen Satifa was present, magnificent in cloth of gold with a diadem of emeralds upon her regal brow. She sat on a golden throne beside the king, who was surrounded by courtiers in dark robes, the magi who counseled him. The chamberlain, chief conjuror over this clutch of demons, stood imperiously to the left of the king's throne. There was no sign of the crown prince, nor indeed of any of the other royal children or wives. The king's expression was grave.

He inclined his head to me, as I did to him, my hands raised, palms together, before my breast. "Oh mightiness, you have called for me. How may I aid you?"

The king made a nervous, abrupt gesture with one hand. "I am grateful for your presence, revered lady. My concern is Prince Reevan. He is sorely afflicted."

"Take me to him. I will assuage his hurts."

"It is not that simple."

I narrowed my eyes slightly, although no one would be able to tell because of the mask. All they'd see was the snarling face of the goddess, dimly through my veil. "Please explain the difficulty, your mightiness." I glanced at the queen. Her head was lowered. She would not look at me.

"A demon has possessed him," said the king.

I paused. "A demon, mightiness?" This would explain, then, the reluctance to bring the prince to the temple.

He looked slightly uncomfortable. "Yes. That is the diagnosis."

"By whom, may I ask?" I turned my head toward the vizier so he'd be sure I was looking at him.

"A wise man has come to us," said the king.

"A wise man?" I said haughtily. Who was it making diagnoses of royal ailments—indeed possessions—before I? "Are you sure his appraisal of the situation is sound? There are old legends concerning possession by demons, but now our more enlightened understanding is that in most cases when people were said to be hag-ridden, they were in fact afflicted by a malady of the mind. You must tell me, your mightiness, of your son's symptoms."

"This I will do," said the king. "Then you may see him and reach your own conclusion. But first, I must inform you of the events that led to it."

Eight days before, I was told, news had come to the court of a master magician who was creating something of a stir in the tearooms of the more affluent corners of the city. His illusions, it seemed, were so convincing they could inspire terror, obsessional devotion and dark hatred. He claimed he could drive people mad with his magic, mad for love or envy, mad for despair. The illusions themselves were so astounding, so beautiful, that many were moved to tears. One man said he was transported back into the most golden day of his childhood, when he had become aware in his heart of the spirit of the sky—a moment he had never before recaptured. Another man spoke of how his long-broken heart was healed of hurt as the woman who'd sundered it came to him and asked for his forgiveness. There were many stories such as these. It was all illusion, of course, but it touched people, and word of it came to the king. "Send for this man," he'd said. "Let him show the court his expert trickery." And so the magician was sent for.

As I was told this story, I could picture the man's charlatan's garb, all flouncing colorful robes and extreme hand gestures. I listened patiently while the king described the wonders this paragon of tricksters performed for the court. "It was all the usual fare and more," he said. "Not only could he make serpents dance to the music of a flute, but they would come out of their baskets and choose dancing partners from among the ladies. Then they would turn somersaults, before tying themselves into a complicated knot and flinging themselves back in their baskets."

I nodded. "Mmm."

"Then, he filled the air with flowers that turned to bubbles when you touched them. He made a servant boy climb up a rope he flung into the air, and which stayed there taut. The boy came down again and told us all of a magical land he'd found at the top, where the sky was red and the trees were bright yellow. The magician then took the hand of my old mother and turned her back into the girl she'd once been. The effect lasted for over an hour, and my mother has not stopped weeping since." The king raised his arms. "I have never beheld such wondrous magic. He is a powerful man indeed."

"Indeed. Does he have a name, this man?"

"He calls himself Arcaran."

"I see. How is his arrival connected with your son's illness?"

The king tapped his lips with restless fingers. "Ah, well, the two events go together, but not in any way you'd imagine. On the morning I sent for the magician, Reevan seemed out of sorts on awaking. He felt tired, listless. He could barely move. When my physician examined him, Reevan spoke of bad dreams, a night during which he had been hunted by demons through a strange and terrifying landscape. The experience had exhausted him. The

physician proclaimed that Reevan had a slight fever which had caused hallucinations in the night. The prince was given a posset to soothe him.

"But the illness only became worse. It was as if his life was draining away,
and it happened so quickly. In the space of a day. I decided Reevan must be
sent to the temple, but Arcaran intervened at this point. He came into the
sickroom, unbidden, and there made a terrible hissing noise, all the while
drawing symbols in the air around him. I was naturally aghast and affronted
and about to order him out, but he said to me, 'Great king, you are familiar
with the stinging salamander?'

"I can't remember how I answered this bizarre and inappropriate question, but Arcaran raised his hands against my bluster and said, 'There is a
stinging salamander on your son's back. It is feeding upon him.'

"I could see no such thing and said as much, although I remember my
flesh went cold.

" 'Oh, it is there,' said the magician. 'It is an elemental being, the cause
of the prince's torpor. It must be removed, and quickly, for it is already laying
eggs.'

"When I heard these words, I went utterly cold. It was as if I could smell
something foul in the room, something evil."

The king shook his head, and would have continued, but I decided it
was time to interrupt this preposterous narrative. "Eggs? Salamanders? Perhaps it is time I saw the phenomenon for myself." I paused. "I trust no action
has yet been taken to remove this alleged elemental?"

The king shook his head. "Indeed not. Arcaran was most insistent that
your aid should be sought first."

"How polite of him," I said. Quietly, I wondered why the charlatan
showed such consideration.

Accompanied only by his vizier, King Jaiver led Meni and me to the
prince's bedchamber. Here, dark drapes were drawn against the heat of the
day, so that the light was brownish. I saw the boy lying on golden pillows,
covered by a thin tasseled blanket. His body gleamed with sweat, but I sensed
that should I touch him, his flesh would be cold. I could tell at once that
this was more than a fever, but I could not credit the idea of unseen parasites.

I walked around the bed for a few moments, sniffing the air. The strange thing was that I could not smell sickness. The air was dry and faintly redolent of smoke. They had been burning an acrid incense in there. I forcibly repressed a shudder. "I really think he should be moved to the temple," I said. "He needs light and air."

"But the demon creature," said the king. "You should not carry one across the threshold of the Sektaeon. Surely that would be dangerous?"

I made my voice cold and harsh to indicate that my patience was fraying. "I and my priesthood are quite capable of dealing with any eventuality."

The king bowed. "Great lady, we have no choice but to obey your word, but I have to say that your decision distresses me greatly. In the temple of fire, the elemental could acquire great strength and take what is left of my son's life."

"You must trust me," I said.

Then, a faint hiss and a dry rattle emanated from one of the dark corners of the room and a man emerged from the shadows. He had, of course, been present the entire time, but for whatever reason had concealed his presence until now.

He bowed slightly and extended his arms in an expansive gesture. Such theatre! "Great lady, you must not take the boy into your temple."

I put as much sneer into my voice as I could muster. "Ah, you must be the *physician* who diagnosed the case. Your presence is no longer required. I am here now."

The magician stole forward. He was not garbed in the flamboyant robes I'd expected, but in dark, close-fitting garments, such as those worn by nomad warriors of the wilderness. "You are skeptical," he said mildly, "and that I understand, but perhaps if you and I could be alone with the prince for a short time, I could show you the nature of the affliction."

"Now is not the time for illusions," I said briskly. "We can all see the prince is gravely ill. Now, if you will step aside, my priest will carry his highness to my litter."

"No," said the magician, and for a brief moment his strange dark eyes burned with an amber spark. He held my eye for a while, almost as if he could see through my mask, and during that time it was as if he and I were the only people in the room. I had never encountered such an intensity of gaze. Within it, I saw passion, fire and knowledge, but also a fierce kind of tragedy. It shocked me.

"I am an illusionist, yes," said the magician softly, "but not just that. There are times for illusions and there are not. I am aware of the distinction, lady."

I hesitated for a moment, then said, "Leave us. Everyone."

There were murmured assents from the king and his vizier, but forthright protests from my high priest. "Your reverence," Meni said in a strained voice. "Is this wise?"

I turned my head to him. "There is nothing to fear. Please, leave. I will call you shortly."

Alone, Arcaran and I faced each other across the bed, where the prince moved feebly, uttering sighs.

"I appreciate this," said the magician. "You will—"

I interrupted him coldly. "Do you know who I am?"

He frowned briefly, then bowed again, smiling. "You are the avatar of Sekt, the goddess on earth."

"Yet you speak to me with little respect. It's clear to me that the king dances to your tune. Who and what are you? Why are you here? What is your aim in this?"

He continued to smile, apparently unflappable. "I appreciate your curiosity and concern. Here are the answers you seek. I am what you perceive me to be. I am here because I was summoned. My aim in this is to heal the prince."

It was clear he sought to charm me, yet there was something—*something*—utterly compelling about this man. Merely being in his presence seemed to inform me he had seen many wonders of the world, that he possessed great knowledge. Perhaps he, too, wore a mask. However, I would not let him win me over that easily. "You prey upon the rich," I said. "You dupe them of their riches with your illusions."

He grimaced, head tilted to one side. "That is a sour depiction of my profession, but not without some basis of truth. Still, I am a creature of many facets. Not all of them are based upon deception."

I made myself totally still. "Show me this parasite, then. No tricks. The truth."

Without further words, he leaned over the prince and gently turned him onto his stomach. He drew down the blanket. Reevan's flesh appeared sallow in the dim light, the sharp ladder of his spine too close to the surface of his skin. The magician lifted the prince's hair from his neck. "Look closely," he said. "To see it, focus beyond the prince's skin. Try to look inside him."

"I am not easily suggestible."

"This is no illusion. Do as I say. You are Sekt. You must be able to see this creature."

For some moments, I concentrated as he suggested, blurring my sight until my eyes watered. Then, it came. I saw nothing with my physical sight, yet, in my mind, I sensed pulsing movement, many legs and a presence of malevolence. If it had a form at all, it was a filthy smoky suggestion of a shape. I drew back, uttering an instinctive gasp. Even then, I was aware of the power of suggestion. This did not have to be real simply because I'd perceived it, yet there was no doubt an evil odor of malice oozed upward from the bed. It was like being in the presence of a crowd of people, all of whom hated me utterly. I made no comment, confused in my own thoughts.

"You see?" said the magician.

"I *see* nothing," I replied carefully. "But I sense something. This may, of course, be an illusion emanating from you."

"It is not," said the magician softly. "Come now, great lady. You are Sekt, a goddess. The goddess perceives all, does she not?"

It came to me swiftly then how wrapped up I was in the trivia of mundane life. I lived fully in the corporeal senses, lolling around in the sun, uttering the first words that came into my head. And yet I was supposed to be divine, to see and sense all. Perhaps I had been too much the lazy lioness. "There are ancient rituals in the temple library," I said slowly, "which are designed to deal with possession by bodiless entities. It would perhaps do no harm to perform them." I stood up straight. "I must summon my priest."

"No," said the magician.

"It is not your decision."

"I have another suggestion. Will you hear it?"

"Very well."

"I have traveled in many lands and have seen many strange things. My knowledge has been gathered from every corner of the world. I have seen cases such as this before, and once a fire witch taught me how to treat the condition. The prince is afflicted by a spirit of the wilderness, a creature of fire. The people of this city have mostly abandoned the old ways, and while, in some respects, this ignorance has weakened the ancient spirits, in other ways it has made the people vulnerable to them. They have forgotten how to protect themselves, how to fight back."

I remembered the dreams I had had, the smell of burned meat around the temple. "I have always believed that new gods drive out the old. Sekt is mistress here now."

"Yes, a goddess of fire. She is not that different. Like calls to like. What reason would she have to drive out her own denizens, only because they are known by a different name? This is why *you* can remove this parasite. In a way, it is your servant."

I stared down at the prince. If this was true, I felt no kinship to the thing on the boy's back. I could barely sense it. I realized then that the priesthood of Sekt had lost a lot of their magic. We were fat and domesticated lions, dozing by pools, licking our paws. Where was the lioness of the wilderness, breathing fire? Did she still exist within me? I had no doubt the magician had also thought these things. Perhaps he despised me for what I was: a mask with nothing behind it. "What was the suggestion you had to make?" I said.

"That you and I take the prince out into the wilderness, where I will teach you what the fire witch taught me."

"Why to the wilderness? Why not here?"

"We need the elements around us. We need to tap their power. Too long have you hidden behind stone, my lady. I am offering you a great gift. If you are wise, you will take it."

"You are importunate!" I snapped. "I am Sekt."

"Are you? Then banish this creature of fire now. Take it by the tail and toss it from the window." He stood back with folded arms, appraising me.

I was breathing hard. My veil fluttered before my face. Meni would never allow me to venture out into the wilderness alone with this man. He would not let me be so foolish and, if necessary, would physically restrain me. Yet I felt a wild desire to take what the magician offered me. I sensed he spoke the truth. I wanted to be alone with him, buffeted by hot winds beneath an ardent canopy of stars. I wanted to conjure fire spirits, be the lioness of the desert. "It would be regarded as unseemly for me to venture out with you alone," I said.

"Do they watch you so stringently?"

"Are you suggesting deception? How will you spirit the prince from his bed without detection?"

He smiled and I realized he was beautiful, like the sky is beautiful, or the raging of a storm. I had met no one like him before. "Remember what I am," he said.

"When? How?" I asked, breathless.

"Tonight," he said simply. "Why delay? Will you be able to get away?"

I thought about the sleeping temple, the dozing guards, the great air of torpor that hung over its colonnaded halls from dusk until dawn. I could slip like a wraith from shadow to shadow, leap the wall like a lioness, land without making a sound.

"I know what you are," he said. "You are a goddess, yes, but are you not also a woman? Are you not also a lioness? You crave adventure, even the hunt. You crave the ecstasy that freedom brings. Indulge yourself, my lady. Who will ever know?"

He was a friend to me. I had known him many lifetimes. In the night, in the wilderness, he would be a black lion, gliding at my side.

Once the king and Meni returned to the prince's bedroom, I told them that I would perform the ancient rituals the following evening, that I would need a day to prepare. Meni seemed a little bemused by my decision, and I knew that later he would quiz me about it, but he was loyal and did not voice his concern in public.

Outside the palace, back in my litter, I felt dizzy, almost sick. What was I doing? How had I become so infected with these alien feelings? The magician had conjured illusions for me, but I knew they could be real, because they did not involve magical ropes, phantom flowers or even bittersweet memories. They were possibilities, a revelation of what could be. I had never craved freedom, yet now it seemed the most heady thing on earth. I had never felt the stirrings of desire for a man, nor even curiosity, yet here it was, hot and burning in my belly.

I should have known then, sent word to the king, had the magician drowned or beheaded. Yet, instead, I lay back among my cushions, swooning like a lovesick girl.

I could not wait to dismiss my servants from my presence that evening. The air was full of a tension only I could feel. Candle flames bent into a wind that was not there. Incense smoke curled to the side. Even now, I entertained a dangerous hope. I thought of Aan, the husband I had never met, he whose face is beautiful. Had he found some way to escape his temple? Had he come to me wearing the face of a man? How could I think such things? And yet, I did not find myself thinking about the fate of Prince Reevan, or even about what the magician would show me tonight. I thought only of his face, of being near him, of the vast expanse of wilderness around us, the infinite sky above. I ran my fingers over the mask that shrouded me. The gold felt hot like fevered skin. I felt it might crack like the skin of a serpent and then I would slither out of it, reborn. If he did not wither before me, he would be the one, but dared I take that chance?

At each hour, boy priests sang litanies to the goddess and her heavenly entourage. At the hour after midnight, when only the young priests were awake, I slipped from my bed, took up the mask and placed it over my head. I dressed with speed and covered myself with a dark hooded cloak that I wear to walk through the gardens in the rainy season. As an afterthought, I clasped around my neck a golden chain, from which hung a lion's-eye stone, striped dark crimson and gold. Perhaps instinctively, I sought to provide myself with some kind of protection.

The temple was quiet, and yet I thought I heard in the distance a rumble of thunder. For a moment, I wondered whether I would ever return, and such was my excitement that at the time I did not care.

It was as if I were invisible. I hurried past the open doors, beyond which lay sleeping servants. I undulated like smoke past guards who lounged at their posts, their eyes wet slivers that looked only upon dreams. The gardens were held in a humid caul of air. Lionesses sprawled beneath the trees, some upon their backs with their paws curled over their chests. I ran among them and none stirred. Lightning scratched across the night, but there would be no rain. The sky was a robe of stars.

Then the garden wall was before me. I yearned to leap it, but it would not be necessary. Flights of steps run up to the top of the wall at regular intervals, so that guards can patrol it or else temple staff might sit there and watch the life of the city. I chose one of these flights at random and ran up, then stood for a while on the wall, looking down. The city was spread out ahead of me, a mass of dim glows and hulking shadows. Now I had to jump, for there were no steps on the other side of the wall. It looked so far, yet I knew it was not. I glanced behind, fearful for a second that someone was watching me, but the temple and the gardens were still and silent, as if enchanted. I drew in my breath and leapt.

I landed on all fours on the short wiry grass and, for some moments, felt I should continue my journey in this manner, that I had discarded the body of a woman altogether. Then I stood up and saw that, yes, I still had arms and legs and that running on all fours would be both ungainly and slow. Quickly, I ran to a grove of tamarinds near the road, which was a glaring pale ribbon in the darkness. The wilderness was very near. I had only to follow the road for a short time, then take a narrower track to the east. The wilderness is always there around us. If people should abandon the city, it would soon revert to a strange and tangled waste, dry and tough and desert-colored.

I had arranged to meet Arcaran at the edge of the waste, by a forest of broken towers, which were all that remained of a city older than ours. Their shattered fingers cast eerie shadows on the ground and I was sure that ghosts lingered there. For a while I could not find the magician and ran about in circles among the looming ruins. Then he stepped out of the shadow of a tower in front of me. He was a creature of night, yet I could see his face clearly: its sculpted planes, the faintest breath of dark beard about the jaw.

"I am here," I said. "Where is the prince?"

"I have hidden him in the ruins. I thought you were not coming."

"Take me to him."

"We must venture farther from the city. We are too close here."

Prince Reevan lay with his head resting on a broken column. He looked young and vulnerable, his eyes staring blankly at the stars. I thought for a moment that he was dead, then he made a small sound and a thread of drool fell from his lips. I was alarmed by his condition and knelt at once to place my hands upon him, but Arcaran cried, "No, don't touch him."

"Why?"

"The parasite could transfer itself to you. We are not yet prepared."

I stood up. "Then we should proceed quickly."

Arcaran lifted the prince in his arms and began to walk away through the ruins. I followed, looking about myself. I did not feel afraid, or if I did, the sensation felt pleasurable. It did not cross my mind that I was essentially, despite my title and status, a young woman alone with a strange man far from my sanctuary. I had always believed I was a goddess, but in truth did I really possess a goddess's powers? I did not know how to smite a man if he should attack me. I did not even know how to defend myself with human strength. Yet there I was, following him. It seems senseless now.

Beyond the ruins was a rocky valley, surrounded by high spiky cliffs. We went down into it and there I saw that a fire had been built and already lit, flames leaping hungrily at the sky, shedding showers of sparks.

The magician laid the prince down on the ground and I awaited the preparations for what I was convinced would be some arcane ritual. As he arranged the prince's limbs, the magician said, "I have spent a lot of time in Mewt, my lady. I have visited the great temples there of Sekt and of her sister, Purryah, the cat goddess. The priests revealed to me some of their knowledge. It is a wisdom that never came here. For a century, your people have had an incomplete belief system."

"The original priestess of Sekt in Madramarta was trained by Senu, High Priestess of Akahana," I said. "How do you know what we have or have not learned?"

"I know because you are unaware of what to do now. A true avatar of Sekt would know."

"And so, presumably, do you."

He nodded, squatting before me, his long, expressive hands dangling between his knees. "I do, and I will tell you, but it may alarm you."

I stood stiffly before him, wondering what would be said and whether it would be true.

"You must expel the breath of Sekt into the boy," said the magician. "You must conjure it. Do you know how?"

I wanted to answer that I did. I wanted him to think I was something more than just a mask, but I couldn't answer, because I didn't know.

He ignored my silence and said, "First you must remove your mask."

"No! It is forbidden. I may only do so when I'm alone. You should know that." But, in my heart, that leap of hope.

He looked at me steadily. "The mask should be removed for certain types of work. This is one of them. Don't you know why you are masked?"

"Because I am the goddess and her presence in me has changed me. I am too terrifying to look upon. I would wither you."

He laughed softly. "It would take more than that to wither me. Do you think you are hideous beneath it, a gorgon to turn me to stone?"

Again, I could not answer. "It is the law," I said.

He stood up and came toward me. He drew back the cloak of my hood and put his fingers against the hard skin of the mask. Beneath it, I burned. It was I who was turned to stone. "I can see your eyes," he said. "I can see your mouth. You wear this mask to contain your power. The High Priestess in Akahana wears hers only for state occasions, but you are bridled here, held back."

I felt I would die from suffocation. I could not breathe. The mask constricted me. I was more aware of its presence than I'd ever been.

"Take it off," he said. "I am not afraid. Nor should you be. Claim what is yours, what you've never truly had."

My hands moved automatically. I had no choice. He took a step back and watched me as I lifted the mask from my head and shoulders. Immediately, the wind felt too hot on my skin. My hair was lifted by it. His expression did not change. I felt exposed, impotent. Was all of my courage contained within the mask? I had no strength now. He came toward me, put his hands upon my face. I expelled a cry, for his touch burned me. "I know you," he said. "I have always known you."

Some instinct made me pull away. I glanced down at Prince Reevan and saw that his entire body was covered in a crawling black smoke. It was as if he was being devoured by a swarm of insects. The magician's face looked black too, yet his eyes burned wildly. They were blue now, yet surely only a moment ago, they'd been dark?

"Don't be afraid," he said. "Accept. You can see now, *truly* see."

I gulped the searing air. My eyes were weeping tears of flame. "The prince," I managed to burble.

The magician laughed and with a flick of his hand made a gesture. "The brat doesn't matter. He is only a decoy. Watch." At once, the enveloping darkness rose from the prince's body into the air. He cried out; his limbs jerked. "It is done," said the magician. "Simple. The salamander was my creature. I put it there. It was you I wanted. It was always you."

I backed away from him, incapable of thought, of reason.

He stalked me. "You people are pathetic," he said. "You were given a power you could have developed. You did nothing but lie complacently in the temple until the power fell asleep from ennui. I can wake it, lady. It is already mine. I have come for you. Do you understand? For all it has atrophied, something was created here in Jessapur. I smelled it. It drew me. You are more than Senu ever could have been, yet you do not know it." He drew himself up to his full height and it seemed to me as if his flesh was smoking. I could smell charred meat again. His eyes were smoldering blue flames. "Do you know what I am?"

I knew. Part of me, a part of me that should have been greater, had always known. "Djinn!" I said. Hungry, envious of flesh, full of guile.

"They let me in," he said. "You let me in. Look at you. A gargoyle. The *mask* has more life in it."

I put my hands to my face and all I could feel was a frozen snarl, made of ivory. I had the wedge-shaped muzzle of a cat, a cat's sharp teeth. If ever I had been a normal woman, now I truly was a semblance of Sekt, lioness-headed, a statue made flesh. Hideous. Monstrous. This was the secret the mask had hidden. Now, the lioness had been released, but she had no strength. She had been domesticated.

"You have the potential power of the red fire, the white fire," said the magician, "that which is stronger than the orange fires of hearth or altar. You are most powerful free of your mask, lady, but also, paradoxically, most vulnerable."

Arcaran made a sudden movement and grabbed hold of my arms. It was strange, because there was no substance to him. He was smoke, yet I could not escape him. From the waist down he had transformed into a boiling column of darkness. He dragged me toward the fire and I could hear the song of the sparks. The flames leapt higher as if in anticipation. "We shall be one," he said. "I shall have Sekt's essence. You do not deserve it."

He was never flesh, I can see that now. Even his body was an illusion. He wanted mine, and the gift of fire that lay slumbering within it. To him, I was naive and stupid, a posturing child with no true understanding of the goddess's power. Perhaps he saw himself as a denizen of Sekt and sought to reclaim her, release her. But most of all, he wanted my body. I knew that when I returned to the temple, I would no longer be me, and that a prince of djinn would hold sway in the hallowed precincts. No one would ever guess.

The flames licked at my clothes. Soon, it would be over. I could not help but fight, even though I felt my predicament was helpless.

Then she moved within me. I felt a flexing in my muscles and bones, a great sense of outrage. A voice roared from my throat. "I am Sekt!"

I breathed in the flames, and expelled them in a gust of bloodred sparks. Arcaran uttered an inhuman scream and fell backward into the fire. The leaping hot tongues enwrapped him and he lay there staring up at me in fury. I snarled at him and he snarled back, but he was no longer the one in control. "Do not presume," I growled. "Don't *ever* presume."

Then I turned my back on him and put my hands against my face. I was no longer snarling. I felt pliant flesh, slightly furred. The golden mask stared up at me from the ground. It was a lifeless thing. I sensed him move behind me and turned round. He looked like a man again, a beautiful man, although his long hair was smoking.

"You cannot have this flesh," I said. "It is mine. I have provenance over this land."

"Sekt," he said, "you misunderstand. I sought only to wake you."

I snarled at him again. "Fool! I know what you sought—a way into my temple, and thus to create your own reign of fire over the land and its people."

"It has already begun," he said. "You cannot stop it, but should join with me. Look at this land. It is dying. The divine kings are shorn of grace and power. My influence smokes through the streets of Madramarta, inspires its slaves to revolt."

I shook my head. "You are deluded. You were banished once, because you could not, or would not, help the people of Jessapur against their conquerors. You have no true might, merely a sneaking creeping insolence that finds a home only in the hearts of the ignorant and debased."

"The greatest changes will always be born in the darkest gutter," said the magician. "What happens in a noble court or an enclosed temple affects only the privileged few. That is not change, but indulgence."

"Perhaps there is some truth in your words," I said. "But now the people have me. I will serve them here as I served them in Mewt. I always will."

"Brave words," hissed Arcaran. "It is most likely that all you will do is fall asleep again. You need my influence."

I snarled and stamped my foot, and the ground shook for a great distance around us. "Smite you!" I hissed.

He raised his hands. "I am already smitten, as you pointed out. Is there to be no peace between us?"

"There cannot be. You cannot be trusted."

His face twisted into an evil leer. "Go back to your temple, then. Be alone. But rue this day, Sekt. Remember it. It will haunt you."

I stared at him unblinking for some moments, then turned away. I went to the prince, who lay unconscious near the fire, and lifted him in my arms.

"Sekt," said the magician. "You cannot contain me. You will return. You will call for me. You know you will. Like speaks to like. I woke you."

For some moments I considered his words, then I carefully placed the unconscious prince back on the ground. Arcaran was sitting amid the flames of the fire, the most beauteous sight I could imagine, the most treacherous. I lifted the lion's-eye pendant in one hand and held it up before my face on its chain. "I will never be without you," I purred. "I both love and hate you, and will hold you forever against my heart."

He grinned at me, confident.

I dropped my jaw into a smile and spoke in a voice of command. "I call upon the light at the center of the universe!"

"What are you doing?" said Arcaran. The smile had disappeared from his face.

"Great powers, attend me!" I roared. "Hear now the voice of Sekt! Give me your power of compulsion!"

"No," said Arcaran. The features on his face had begun to twist and flex.

"Yes," I answered softly, then raised my voice once more, arms held high. "By the power of the creative force, I compel thee, prince of djinn. I command thee. Enter into this stone. I am Sekt, queen of fire. You will obey."

A searing wind gusted past me, pressing my robes against my body, lifting my hair in a great tawny banner. Sparks fountained out of the fire.

Arcaran expelled a series of guttural cries and his body writhed amid the flames. I do not know whether he felt pain or not, but very swiftly, he reverted to a form of smoke. I sucked his essence toward me, then blew it into the lion's-eye pendant. It felt hot for some moments, and glowed with an eerie flame. Then it went cold and dark. I placed it back against my breast once more. He would always be with me, but contained, a genie in a stone.

I lifted the prince once more and glanced down at the golden mask lying nearby. Already ashes from the fire had drifted over it. I would not wear it again. There might be another mask, and sometimes I would wear it, but it would be of my own design and I would don it through choice.

It seemed my altercation with the djinn had taken only minutes, but as I walked back toward the ruins, I saw that already the light around me was gray with dawn. Soon the pink and gold would come, the morning. As I walked, I breathed upon the prince's face. His eyes moved rapidly beneath their closed lids. He would recover swiftly from his brief ordeal. I had breathed the white fire into him. He was mine. I would make a true king of him, for all the people.

Near the temple, I passed a peasant woman with her children taking fish to the market. When I drew near, they fell to the ground before me, their hands over their heads. "I am Sekt," I said to them. "Look upon me."

The woman moaned and uttered prayers, but even so, raised her head.

"You are blessed," I said. "Carry word to the city that Sekt walks amongst you. She is unmasked and awake. Remember her face."

Now, I am home. I can sense Meni awaking in his chamber. I will go to him, show myself to him. I am Sekt.

The Goddess Danced

LOIS TILTON

The traditional Brahmin rites were never neglected in Meena's family when she was a child. The small shrine with its images of the gods was the center of the household. Besides daily prayers, it seemed that every week there was a festival, some special ceremony to perform. On those days, her mother would fast while she made the preparations: purifying the house, cooking the special foods for the feast, carefully drawing the sacred *rangoli* images on the wall with colored rice powder.

Meena's mother was a special devotee of the goddess, and all her favorite stories had the same theme: if a woman was virtuous and performed the proper rites, then the goddess would ensure that her husband would love her, her sons would thrive, and all her sufferings would be requited. With the favor of the goddess, even the dead could be revived, if you could believe the tales. But a woman must always ask for the sake of others, never for herself.

Savitri, the king's daughter, had vowed to marry her lover Satyavan despite the objections of her father the king, for a prophecy foretold that Satyavan would die within a year.

So it came to pass. But when Lord Yama came for Satyavan's soul, Savitri would not let her husband go. She followed Lord Death until he turned around and told her to go home.

"How can I go without my husband?" Savitri asked, and Lord Yama was so pleased by her devotion that he offered to grant her whatever she would ask—anything but her husband's life.

"Will you give me a son?"

Lord Yama granted her one hundred sons. Then he continued on his way with Satyavan's soul, but when he turned around, Savitri was still following.

"Woman, I've already granted you one hundred sons, why are you still following me?"

Savitri answered, "Lord, I am a virtuous woman, how can I have one hundred sons without my husband?"

Then Lord Yama was so impressed by her devotion that he returned Satyavan to life.

Savitri, Meena's mother had explained to her, was really an incarnation of Parvati, consort of Lord Shiva. The goddess had many incarnations: virtuous Sati, fierce Durga, and even Kali, the black one, the destroyer. But Meena thought Kali was too bloodthirsty and cruel. She loved Savitri's story, though, and her feast was her mother's favorite holy day in all the year, because she was named Parvati, after the goddess, the model for all loyal and loving wives.

Yet when she died giving birth to her third child, no goddess intervened as Lord Death took her away, despite all the family's prayers and offerings. Worst of all, the baby was another girl. It was supposed to have been a boy, another son, a long-hoped-for blessing of the marriage after a series of miscarriages. Instead, it was the end of it.

At age twelve, Meena's childhood was over. Now she had to leave school to take care of the infant sister her father would barely acknowledge. She'd always done well in her classes and hoped that one day she might be able to go to nursing school if she could somehow get a scholarship. But there was no choice. Her family was too poor to afford a nursemaid or a servant, and had no one else, no grandmothers or aunts, who could help out.

"You can always keep up by helping your brother with his schoolwork," her father said. "Maybe one day, after you're older, you can even go back to school."

Meena could only hope so. And she was glad that at least her grieving father had no intention of marrying again and bringing a stepmother into the house. She was sure the family was better off as it was, without a stranger who could never love another woman's children. So Meena did everything she could to take her mother's place, all the housework and cooking as well as caring for the new baby. She also made sure not to neglect the household worship and performed the rites just as she remembered her mother doing, fasting and making the proper offerings at the household shrine.

By the time she was sixteen years old, one by one her former classmates were getting married, starting to have babies of their own. There was little talk of Meena's marriage, though. She was still needed at home. Who else could make the dinner, make sure Dinesh did his schoolwork, keep the house in order? "You made the *khir* just the way your mother used to," her father would tell her. And sadly, "You look more and more like her these days, now that you're growing up."

He never said those things to Abha, never spoke to his youngest daughter at all if he could help it, for he had always blamed her for his wife's death. Meena supposed that someday, when Abha was older, when her sister was finally in school and could take care of herself, then maybe it would be time for Meena to think of her own wedding. She could wait; there was plenty of time.

"You won't have a hard time finding a good husband, you're so pretty," her best friend Shanti declared. The girls were all together at the village washing tank that day. Meena didn't see her friends very often since she'd left school; she was always so busy in the house. She was glad her family wasn't rich enough to have their own clothes-washing machine, so she had to do the laundry the old-fashioned way, out in public where she could meet people.

Meena's face heated with embarrassment at all this talk of getting husbands, and she shook her head. "You're the pretty one, with that fair skin, Shanti. And Lalita has such good teeth, no wonder she smiles at all the boys." Yet despite her modesty, Meena did like to think she was pretty, and she always made sure to comb jasmine oil through her thick black waist-long hair before she braided it every morning. She was too shy to smile at the boys the way Lalita did, though, and she knew her mother wouldn't have wanted her to linger with the other girls once the laundry was done, or wander through the marketplace after school buying hot fried *pakoras* or sweet colored ices from the vendors, the way her friends did.

"Don't you want a husband?" Shanti demanded.

"Of course I do!" What girl didn't want a husband? These days her friends seemed to talk of nothing but weddings and wedding feasts and the gorgeous wedding saris their fathers would buy them. And boys—which ones were the best-looking, or were going to college, or had the most expensive clothes. Meena was too shy and virtuous to look much at the boys, but she did have her own dreams of marriage. She longed for that special bond she remembered seeing between her parents when her mother was alive, the quick looks they would pass each other, which held promises and secrets that a child wasn't supposed to know about, and which made her blush to think about now that she was old enough to understand.

If Meena was too modest to stare at the boys, they suffered from no such inhibitions. One young man in particular, whom all her friends seemed to admire exceedingly—he had a gold watch and a red Vespa that he drove through the village streets with reckless disregard for the general safety—had recently noticed her.

"Look! Ramesh is watching you!" Lalita whispered loudly, giggling and looking backward to flash her famous smile in his direction.

Leering at her was more like it. Meena's face went hot. She would have pulled the *pallu* of her sari down to hide it, except that she had her hands full with the laundry. Instead, she looked down at her feet and called to Abha to hurry and catch up, they needed to be home to start dinner. She'd known this Ramesh in school. He might be good-looking, but she could remember how he used to torment the younger boys Dinesh's age and steal their pocket money after classes. He had an uncle who was a policeman and so he could get away with it. She wanted nothing to do with him now.

"Meena, that man is calling you!" Abha piped up.

She shushed her sister, "A good girl doesn't talk to men on the streets, haven't I told you? What would Amma say if she could see you acting like that, bringing shame on us all. Don't even look at him!" As she scolded Abha she worried over the fact that Ramesh knew her name, that he assumed he knew her well enough to call after her in public on the streets. What would people say?

Her worries proved well-founded. The next few weeks, it seemed that every time she ventured out of the house, Ramesh was there, loitering at a corner she had to pass, or following after her. If she stopped at a market stall, he was at her elbow, crowding up too close to her, offering to buy her some pistachios or an ice cream. Then the game turned less innocent one day when he leaned down to Abha and whispered in a voice meant to be over-heard, "Tell your mother she should be more friendly to me."

"My Amma's dead!" Abha insisted, but Meena's shock made her jerk the child almost off her feet as she pulled her away. Now she understood why Ramesh persisted in treating her the way no man should ever treat a decent girl. He thought Abha was hers—her bastard child, not her sister!

In desperation, she asked Dinesh to say something to him. He was barely fourteen, but that was what a brother was supposed to do, wasn't it? But Dinesh only came back that evening with a bloody nose and angrily accused her of talking to men on the streets and getting a bad reputation.

Meena wept all that night. She couldn't tell her father what was happening, she'd be so ashamed! She knew she hadn't done anything wrong—she was the most virtuous girl in the village, all her friends said so. How could anyone believe such lies?

She decided finally that there was only one thing to do. "You have to come with me," she told her friends. "I can't go talk to him by myself."

They giggled. They didn't understand what she meant to do. They thought she was just going to flirt with him, like another girl might, a girl who didn't care about her reputation or what her mother would say. Together they went to the street where the movie theater was, where the boys liked to hang around the corner and watch for girls. A group of them were there as always, loitering near the ice cream stand. The sight of the three girls made them all stand up straight and preen. Meena flushed with embarrassment.

"You go tell him," she pleaded with Lalita, "I can't do it. Tell him I have to talk to him."

Lalita protested that she couldn't go by herself, but it didn't take too much persuasion to make her change her mind. Meena saw how the boys all looked at her when Lalita delivered her message, and she wanted to sink into the earth. Then Ramesh came up to her alone, and Meena knew she had to say what she'd come here for.

"You have to leave me alone," she told him desperately. "You have to stop following me around. People are starting to talk."

He laughed. "Let them talk, what do you care?"

"I care! My family cares! My brother told you—"

He said scornfully, "That kid!" He reached for her arm. "Why don't you and your friends let me take you to the movie tonight. We'll have a good time."

"No!" She tried to pull her arm away, but he wouldn't let go.

"Leave her alone!" Shanti cried in alarm, but he just laughed again.

"Why should she act so holy and virtuous, a girl like her?"

The tone of his voice, the implication in it, made Meena so furious, she swung her other arm and slapped him.

"Oh!" cried her friends, and there was laughter from the group of boys across the street.

Shoving away her arm, Ramesh rubbed his face and said viciously, "You'll be sorry for that. You'll see."

The girls hurried home, frightened. Lalita was whimpering, "I knew we shouldn't have talked to him. I hope my parents never find out! They'd kill me!"

Meena was too appalled and frightened to speak, but she was thinking the same thing: *I could never face my father if he finds out about this. I'd have to kill myself.*

A week or so later came the annual feast of misrule called Holi, where society turned upside down. Caste differences were ignored on Holi, and people flung colored water at each other until everyone was stained with bright colors and looked like they worked at a dye factory. Bands of boys and young men in particular would pursue girls in the streets to toss dye at them, taking advantage of the normally forbidden liberty.

Dinesh, of course, had been anticipating the festival for weeks and had accumulated a large store of dye packets with which to stain friend and stranger alike. He was out the door before sunrise to take full advantage of the day. Abha, too, had been looking forward to the holiday, but Meena hesitated to take her out. Ever since that terrible encounter outside the theater she'd avoided the streets and kept to the safety of the house, but of course Holi was a religious feast in honor of the god Krishna, and there would be processions carrying the holy image. And Amma had always loved the tales of Krishna.

"I suppose we can go," she finally decided, making sure that Abha was wearing her oldest clothes, for they were likely to be ruined by the end of the day.

It was early yet, but the village streets were already crowded and riotous with groups of boys in particular running wild and uncontrolled. "I don't know," Meena started to say doubtfully, but Abha pulled hard on her hand and said, "I hear a parade!"

Meena allowed herself to be towed toward the center of town, where they watched the procession passing by, men carrying the image of the god and singing cheerfully. She could remember when she'd been Abha's age and had stood here in the same place holding her mother's hand, hearing the same songs as the god passed by. "There," she started to say, "we've seen the procession, now we can go back home."

But just then a crowd of young men came running by, splashing everyone with bright colors. She thought she recognized—

At first, for an instant, she couldn't understand why she couldn't see, what was wrong with her eyes. Then, as she put her hands to her face, the first message of pain got through, and she started to scream. *Acid!* He'd thrown acid in her face!

THROUGHOUT her ordeal, Meena never entirely lost consciousness. They took her to the hospital, they wrapped her face and hands in gauze, but no one would answer her questions: "Am I blind? Will I be able to see?"

She wept tearlessly behind her bandages and prayed with all her heart to the goddess, promising her worship and offerings if she could only see again.

But hospitals were expensive. After a day, her father took her home, still in bandages, still in pain, to lie in her own bed and wonder what was going to happen to her, how she was going to live. Further treatment, plastic surgery—that was out of the question for such people as they. Her sister brought her meals and did everything a four year old could do to help. Her father and brother barely spoke to her. They'd pressed criminal charges against Ramesh, they said, but nothing was likely to come of it. The police never did anything in these cases, when it was a woman attacked. And there was that uncle of his.

After several more days the bandages were cut away, and Meena found that her prayer had been answered: she could see! The acid had destroyed her right eye, but the left one was spared.

"Want to see . . ." was the first thing she said, though she could barely form the words with her raw, acid-ravaged lips, ". . . mirror."

Her father shook his head, forbidding it. Not looking at her. Then Abha came into the room and saw her for the first time without the bandages covering her face. She screamed shrilly, and Meena knew it must be bad, very bad. She tried to remind herself that the goddess had granted her prayer, that at least she could see. Blindness would have been worse than any disfigurement. Wouldn't it?

"I want to go on a pilgrimage," she said a few days later. "To a temple of the goddess. I promised . . . if I could still see."

This, too, was wordlessly forbidden.

They'd taken all the mirrors away. Even her own mirror, the one that had been her mother's, was no longer in the house. She endured it a few days, not knowing, imagining what she must look like, a face made so hideous none of her family could stand to turn their eyes in her direction. She couldn't help seeing how her father and brother would always look away whenever they came into the room.

Finally she forced Abha to bring her something to see her face in. "I can't!" the child protested at first. "They told me not to!" But Abha was used to obeying her older sister, and she finally came to her with a small mirrored disk that had been sewn onto a dress. Meena had to see it, had to know the worst, hoping it wasn't really so bad.

It was worse. Worse than she'd been able to imagine.

The acid had flayed the entire right side of her face, down in some places to the bone, where her forehead and part of her scalp had been laid bare. Below, the eye socket was a red, gaping crater, and half her face was raw flesh. The acid had eaten away the side of her nose and even her lips, so that her exposed teeth grinned in the ruin of her face like a corpse's.

A corpse's face! A living skull!

Meena threw the mirror away and pulled the sheet over her head, to hide it. She never wanted anyone to look at her again.

YET she healed. The raw flesh became scar tissue, almost as livid as the original burns. The exposed skull grew white. The side of her nose never quite closed up, her scarred lips drew back even farther from her teeth, and the cavity where her eye had been was deep and dark, making the right side of her face even more skull-like.

After a few weeks she was able to resume her work around the house. Since that first moment after looking into the mirror, Meena had kept her face covered with a veil. She assumed she'd stay here in the house for the rest of her life, hidden away from sight. To look at her, veiled, no one would know that anything had ever happened to her, that anything had ever changed. Marriage, of course, was out of the question now, but maybe it wouldn't be so bad, maybe her life wasn't entirely over.

This possibility of even a little happiness ended one day when her father came to her (not looking at her; he never looked in her direction these days, not since it happened) and said, "You have to know, the hospital bill was more than I could pay, I had to go to the moneylender for it. Everything I'd saved for your dowry, that's gone."

It doesn't matter, she wanted to say, *I'll never marry now, who would have me, like this?*

He went on without letting her speak, "Of course it was hard, the way things are now, finding you a husband, but I did. He won't mind the way you look. He's blind."

"No!" she protested desperately, "I can't get married, I can't leave home! What about Abha? Who'll take care of her if I'm gone?"

He shook his head, dismissing her objections. "That one is old enough now to take care of herself." He'd never called Abha by her name, not once in her life, only "her" and "that one." He'd never looked at her if he could help it. And Meena suddenly realized that her father kept his eyes averted from both of them now, from both his daughters. *He doesn't want me here anymore! He can't stand to see me here!*

She sobbed bitterly. It was her own fault, it had to be. A girl could never be too careful, her mother had always said. If only she hadn't gone that day to confront Ramesh! Her whole life had been ruined in that moment, everything that she cherished lost. And her father's love—that was what hurt the most. Her father's love for her was dead.

MEENA's wedding was almost a furtive affair, as if it were something to be ashamed of: hardly the wedding that a girl was supposed to dream of all through her childhood. People in the village said her father was doing well to marry her off at all under the circumstances, that it was a wedding much better than such a girl deserved. And to think people once believed she was so virtuous!

But if there were few guests at the wedding, nothing proper to the ceremony had been omitted, the feast was spread, and the presents, her meager dowry, lay displayed on the table. Meena had to wonder how he'd managed to pay for it all, after the hospital bills. But he was a man who would always do what was right, despite his poverty, no matter what it cost him. His oldest daughter was disfigured and disgraced, but he'd done what was proper for her, and no one could accuse him of doing otherwise. She knew she shouldn't be ungrateful.

And now she was no longer his concern. Now she belonged to her husband.

That husband he'd found to take her from him sat next to her on the wedding platform, the ends of their shawls tied together to symbolize their union. She wasn't his first wife, Meena had learned. He was an older man, in his thirties. His name was Arjuna. A hero's name, so very incongruous for this oily-skinned man with his round face and sagging belly, his eyes hidden behind dark glasses as her whole face was hidden behind her veil. *My husband.* The words made no sense. Her mind rejected them.

But when, at the end of the feast, she stood to leave, it was this man she had to go with, her husband and his old parents, not back with her own family to her own home.

Her new family lived two hours away, a miserable journey on the lurching, crowded bus. Meena suffered in the heat and the close atmosphere, pressed uncomfortably against the fleshy body of her husband, his damp, sweaty body, his thigh pressing hers in a way that her mother had warned her a modest girl should never permit—but this was her husband.

And in the seat in front of them, her in-laws. Her mother-in-law had a sour countenance even at the wedding, and her frown on the bus was impatient, as if she were waiting for the first opportunity for complaint. Meena was glad of her veil, that she could hide behind it and no one could tell from her expression what she was thinking, or if she was shedding any tears.

Meena knew they were poor. Her own family was poor. Her parents had always told her: "We're poor people, we can't afford a servant . . . a modern washing machine . . . tuition for college."

Yet it wasn't her in-laws' poverty that so appalled her when she finally saw her new home, it was the squalor of the *bustee* where they lived, the tenement which seemed to exhale an odor of stale urine and rancid cooking oil, of too many humans in too small a space. The flat was only a single room, and ragged curtains afforded all the privacy possible in such quarters. The notion she'd secretly cherished, that she might be able to bring her young sister to live with her, died at the first sight of it. *How can I live in this place?* she wondered in disbelief. *How can I keep house here?*

But it was made clear to her right away that she wasn't wanted here as a housekeeper at all. Almost as soon as the door shut behind them, the old woman turned on her. "All right now, let's see what we've got."

Meena was too slow to understand, too slow to protest. The veil was snatched off her head, exposing all the horror of her face. She flung up her hands to cover it, but instead of recoiling from the sight Meena knew was so hideous, the old woman clicked her tongue in satisfaction. "Yes! That'll do very well!"

"Please!" Meena begged, reaching for the veil.

The old woman let her have it back, saying, "No need for us to have to look at it, not in here. Out on the street, though, that face will make us a fortune!"

Meena didn't understand.

"With a bowl in your hand, you ignorant fool!"

A begging bowl! They meant her to beg! To beg in the streets, where everyone could look at her, could see her ruined face. Where they'd stare and point, scream or laugh. Meena was so appalled she protested, "No!"

But her mother-in-law snapped, "You'll beg if you're told to! Why else do you think we agreed to this match? For your beauty? For your virtue?"

Meena refused. She wouldn't do it. She couldn't. They didn't understand—she couldn't let people look at her. She'd clean, she'd cook, she'd do all the proper duties of a daughter-in-law, but not what they were asking, no.

"We'll see about that," said the old woman grimly. "Hand me that broomstick," she ordered her husband. "This new daughter-in-law needs to learn a lesson."

Meena's father had never beaten her, or her mother. Now she bent under the blows of the broomstick in her mother-in-law's hands, warding it off as best she could with her arms, trying not to cry out and let the people in the nearby apartments hear her humiliation. Later, she learned it would have made no real difference—a dozen times a day the tenement was used to hearing the screams of someone beating a wife or child.

When her mother-in-law finally threw the stick down and snapped, "This had better be the end of your foolishness," Meena could only sob, but she knew the beatings would happen again and again, until she obeyed. And was it not a wife's place to obey?

But there was another place that a wife must occupy, and her new husband had been impatient for it all through the bus ride back to the city, as she'd known from the way he'd pressed himself against her. Now, even as she was sobbing and helpless, he took her there, dragged her behind the curtain where an unmade bed was waiting. Heedless of her bruises and her cries, he pushed her down on it and started to pull up her clothes.

"Don't try to fool me with that false modesty," he said roughly, shoving away her hands as she tried to cover herself. "I know all about that kid your family calls your sister."

"It's a lie!" she cried, but he paid no attention to her denials. Blindness was no handicap to him in bed. His knowing hands roamed across her body, stroking and probing her most intimate places.

"I'm lucky I don't have to look at your face, they say, but at least you're a woman where it counts," he said ungraciously.

Meena tried not to cry, not to fight him as he forced himself into her. This was her husband, they were married, he had every right. But he was rough and impatient, and it hurt her. He was surprised at that, and didn't seem particularly pleased to know he'd been wrong and his bride was a virgin, after all. "Well, I'll get you used to it soon enough."

Then she fully realized, as she lay under his heavy, sweating body, that she belonged entirely to this man now, to these people, that any attempt to resist them would be futile, would only bring her more bruises and pain.

So the next morning she made no more protest when they took her out to beg. The whole family were beggars in a way, she learned. The old father, with his bald head and ascetic's hollow belly, peddled religious trinkets on the streets. The son, her husband, used his blindness to try to earn charity from the pilgrims, as the family planned now to use Meena's ruined face.

They took her to the porch of Kali's Temple, where, it seemed, bribes had bought a place for her to sit and solicit alms from the goddess's worshippers. The old woman snatched away Meena's veil and balled it up in her hand. "And don't you go covering up your face with your sari, either," she warned, "or you'll be sorry tonight. I'll be watching you, don't forget it."

Meena was too humiliated to reply, exposed this way to public view. She would rather have been blind. Her misfortunes, she'd decided, could only be the punishment for some terrible sin in a past life. The gods couldn't be so cruel otherwise.

The old woman, as a manager of beggars, knew her business. The shocking sight of Meena's face in front of Kali's Temple made many worshippers reach to throw her a coin or two, almost as if she were some incarnation of the goddess of destruction. By the end of the day, the mother-in-law was satisfied that the new member of her family would be bringing in her share of income.

She never had to beat Meena again. She escorted her to the Temple every day and lurked on the outskirts to make sure she didn't desert her post, but Meena obediently kept to her place, and the coins piled up in the skirt of her sari. At day's end the old woman would take them, return the veil and lead her daughter-in-law home.

At first, Meena suffered every minute she had to sit exposed to the stares of passersby, and she kept her eyes cast down so as not to see the people who gasped in shock at the sight of her, and sometimes tossed their coins. All day she waited for the moment when she could veil her face again.

Yet the home she had to return to was no refuge. Her mother-in-law was a mean-spirited and miserly woman who begrudged her anything more than a single handful of rice to eat. Her husband expected her to serve and wait on him, then used her brutally in bed at night, complaining, "This is what they give me, a bride so ugly only a blind man would take her. I'd rather have a whore." If she wept at his cruelty he beat her, then forced her to perform the shameful and disgusting acts that gave him more pleasure than the normal union between man and wife.

Meena knew that many wives endured such things. Husbands were brutal, mothers-in-law were cruel, and there was nothing to be done. Yet she hadn't expected there would be no household shrine in her new home, no altar where the gods were honored. A dusty shelf in one corner held a cheap framed print depicting the god Shiva, and that was all.

She'd always honored the goddess, and she was determined at least to set up a shrine where she could worship as her own mother had. The old mother-in-law called it a foolishness and a waste. She objected even to a few grains of rice to offer the gods, let alone the milk and butter to anoint the images, or expensive camphor to burn. In this, though, Meena found an unexpected ally in her father-in-law. The old man overruled his wife and even brought home a chipped statue of the goddess for the shelf, which Meena cleaned up and made into a proper shrine, as well as she could.

Every day when she came back to the flat she prayed there, offering the goddess what little honor she could, pleading to be released from the torment and humiliation of begging in public, exposed in her shame to the stares and mockery of all the world.

The goddess answered, perhaps, in her own way. For gradually Meena began to feel the degradation less sharply. Little by little she was able to raise her head and look around her at the Temple where she was forced to spend her days. For who could not notice the wonder, the splendor of Kali's Temple? There'd been no such place of worship in Meena's village. Until now, her prayers had been confined to her own home.

The Temple, when she finally allowed herself to look at it, made her heart swell with awe. Every inch of the stone was ornamented or carved with figures related to the stories of the goddess. At the top of the gate Kali was depicted in relief dancing on the prone corpse of her consort Shiva, for she was the incarnate power of the god, who destroys the world so it can be created anew. There were images of the goddess as she came bursting from the forehead of Devi, battling the demons, even battling the gods. Inside was the great statue of the goddess, as tall as five men: her face was fearsome, with exposed fangs and a protruding tongue. Her naked body was skeletal and black. In her four hands she held a noose, a trident, a sword and a demon's severed head, and there was a necklace of skulls around her neck.

Meena had always venerated the goddess in her benevolent aspects as consort and mother, particularly as Parvati. Yet as everyone knew, Kali was also the holy mother. *She is black and hideous, but we worship her.*

Everywhere in the Temple there were marvels to be seen. Each column of the porch was topped with a skull, and every skull was different. The tower had nine tiers, every tier covered with sculpture, every figure representing some character associated with Kali. Meena recognized the terrible demons Canda and Munda, both slain by the avenging goddess. Here was the fearsome demon Raktavija—every drop of his blood that struck the earth produced a thousand more demons like himself, but Kali lifted him high on a spear and drank every drop before it could hit the ground. Here was the army of a hundred thousand evil-souled Asuras defeated by the goddess. Each sculpture was unique, each more hideous and demonic than the last, too many of them to count.

Meena began to have the notion that in one of the demon-faces she would discover her own image carved in stone. What this might mean, she wasn't quite sure, but she struggled with the question for some time, even finally purchasing a small hand mirror so she could see exactly what she now looked like. She'd grown gaunt on the scant rations her mother-in-law allowed her, and the bones of her skull were more prominent than ever beneath her scarred flesh. The scar tissue had puckered and twisted her mouth into a permanent, lipless snarl. *A demon,* she thought. *A demon in flesh.*

As the weeks passed and she continued collecting alms at the Temple, the mother-in-law gradually relaxed her watchfulness. As long as Meena returned home every night with a large enough handful of coins, the woman was satisfied. At the same time, Meena's husband started to spend less time on the streets begging. He liked to sleep late and have his mother bring him tea in bed. He was always in bed when Meena left for the Temple, eager not to miss the morning sacrifice.

There finally came a day when she dared use a few coins to purchase a small offering to honor Kali at her altar. She discovered that as long as she continued to bring home enough to satisfy her mother-in-law, she was free to do what she wished with any amount over that. From then on, she made her offerings daily, and the greater her zeal for the goddess grew, the more she collected from the worshippers.

She never neglected the household shrine and continued her devotions there in her mother's memory, but now her true place of worship was the Temple. Here she was surrounded by the power of the goddess made manifest, here she could witness the rites and pray:

> O Goddess, you who dispel the sufferings of those who come
> to you for shelter, have mercy!
> O be gracious, be gracious O Mother of the world!
> Queen of the universe, be gracious and protect us.

As the years passed, there was little change in Meena's life. Her husband began to use the coins she brought home to visit prostitutes, complaining that his wife was so hideous even a blind man couldn't stand the sight of her. The only intercourse he had with her now were those acts she always found so degrading. The mother-in-law continued as mean and grasping as she'd always been, except when it came to her son, for whom she prepared special treats, the spicy fried dishes he gobbled down hot and fresh and dripping with oil.

Meena never complained. She obeyed her husband and his mother, but she suffered less and less from their cruelty, and became increasingly detached from it. She had her refuge and consolation at the Temple of Kali. Whenever she looked up at the tower, with its hosts of gods and demons, she knew that she belonged, and nothing else really mattered.

Then her father-in-law suffered a heart attack. The old man had always been an enigma to Meena. He seemed to subsist on an ascetic's diet of plain rice and was supposed to make his living as a sort of holy beggar, but she'd long suspected he must be some sort of fraud, for there was no sign of religious observance inside his home. He never performed the daily prayers and there'd been no household shrine until she came into the family. Yet now he lay dying in a state of serene detachment that was almost saintly.

His wife and son were distraught. Her husband slapped Meena, screaming, "What kind of daughter-in-law are you? Make my father some tea, some rice!"

She did it ungrudgingly. The father-in-law had never intervened to stop the others from abusing her, but he'd allowed her to worship the goddess. When she knelt at the side of his bed and lifted his head so he could swallow the tea without choking, he met her eyes and whispered to her, "Be careful, daughter, at the cookfire. Accidents, you know, can happen."

She stared at him with a sudden question that she was afraid to ask: How had her husband's first wife died? She knew, as every bride knew, how often an unsatisfactory daughter-in-law might meet with an accident while crouched over a cookfire, and burn to death. It happened in particular when the daughter's family failed to make the payments on her dowry—cheaper and quicker, people said, than a divorce. Was this what the old man was trying to tell her?

But he never spoke again, and that night he died.

His death changed more than Meena would have expected. For one thing, it seemed that many years ago he'd held a job in a government office and taken out an insurance policy which now provided his widow a small stipend every month, enough to pay most of the household expenses. For another, his wife and son began to think on immortality and the fact that Arjuna had no sons of his own, no children.

This, of course, earned Meena more slaps and curses as a barren wife; in such matters, it was always the wife's fault. She didn't bother to protest, to argue that for years her husband had only used her in ways that could never produce a child. Once, a son would have been the greatest blessing she could have imagined, but how could she ever ask a child to look at her face and love it? No, matters were best as they stood, and she'd long since grown indifferent to such concerns. She lived only for the goddess now, and was detached from worldly cares.

But Meena was soon reminded of former ties to the world. One day, returning early from the Temple and approaching the door of the flat, she could hear her husband and mother arguing, and it made her pause to hear her father's name: "If old Chatterjee had ever paid up—"

She entered the room as if she'd heard nothing, and all that night there was no more said between the mother and son. Whatever they'd been discussing, it involved her family in some way, she knew. They wanted her father to pay—something. Her dowry? Had they been demanding more money? She recalled her father-in-law's last words, his warning, and couldn't help suspecting the worst. Fortunately, the flat was on the ground floor in the back, and the next morning, pretending to leave for the Temple, she was able to slip into the alley and crouch to listen below the room's single small window.

The two of them had already recommenced their quarrel, which was, yes, about her.

"If you hadn't made me take a wife so hideous no other man would touch her, maybe you'd have a grandson by now!"

"You're a fool! That face of hers is worth a fortune in the right place! And what do you care about her face anyway? It's not like you need to see it when you're between her legs!"

They continued to reproach each other, whereby Meena learned that ever since the wedding they'd been threatening to starve her to death if her father didn't pay more dowry. When no more money was forthcoming, her husband had wanted to kill her and look for another wife, but the old woman was too greedy to give up the coins Meena earned begging. Only now, desperate for a grandson, would she consider it.

But there was more. The mother had consulted a marriage broker to find a new prospect as a bride. "They say she's fourteen years old. Her name is Abha."

68

Below the window, Meena almost gasped aloud. *Abha!* Could they mean her sister?

Meena's shell of detachment crumbled away. For years, cut off from her family, she'd put them out of her heart; it hurt too much to remember when she was happy and loved. Now it all came rushing back: her father, telling her how she made the *khir* just like her mother had. And Abha, the little sister she'd raised since the day she was born, as dear to her as a daughter could ever be.

Now her horror mounted as she heard her husband. "You think Chatterjee will let us have his other daughter? After we get rid of this one?"

"Fool! Who says he has to know how she died? Say she was hit by a truck in the marketplace, say she had a miscarriage and died, say anything. Then we offer for the other girl. From what I hear, he'll be glad to get her off his hands. They say she's a bastard, and her horoscope is nothing but bad luck besides. He wants to get rid of her, and he'll take the first offer he gets."

Abha, no! They can't do this to you! I won't let them! A hot rage possessed Meena as she burst into the room, crying, "You won't have my sister! I won't let you have my sister!"

Mother and son were startled, but they fought back against the fury of her attack. The old woman had been frying *puris*, and she splashed the hot oil into Meena's veiled face. While Meena struggled to remove the veil, the mother-in-law struck her with the iron pan and shoved her toward her blind son, screaming viciously, "Hold her!"

The can of kerosene — the old woman flung it at her, the fluid soaking her sari — the volatile fumes choking, blinding — the cookfire —

Meena ignited in a single rush of flame. The thin, kerosene-soaked fabric of her sari burned away in an instant; her hair blazed. Her face without its veil was a skull, her naked body skeletal like death, and black.

Kali Ma! She was black; her eyes were blazing red, her teeth bloody fangs. No evil could withstand her, no enemy could escape her terrible anger. Like the flame that devours the flesh of the dead, she was pure destructive energy, the terror of demons, the annihilator of worlds. *Kali Ma!*

The goddess incarnate threw back her head and laughed, exulting in her power. She seized her tormentors, one in each pair of hands. She raised them over her head, dancing as the flames raced up her arms to devour them, dancing and laughing as they writhed and screamed, dancing and singing as they burned.

> How we praise you, Divine Kali!
> May your fearsome trident, with its barbs of flame,
> Destroyer of all demons, guard us from danger.
> Dripping with demon blood and fat, ablaze,
> May your sword be triumphant!
> O Fierce Goddess, we bow to your power!

The Grotto

KATHRYN PTACEK

Ceil Uccello Wallace had always wanted to visit Tuscany. It was a shame that she had returned to her ancestral home only now, when she was dying.

Ceil slowed her pace, then detached herself from the tour group that she'd been following all morning and wandered down a narrow cobblestone street, so angled and steep that she thought if she fell she'd just bounce, much like a pinball, off the thick stucco walls all the way down to the vineyard below the walled town. She chuckled.

The tour group was out of sight now, heading toward the town's unassuming church; otherwise she was the only person out and about this close to one. Overhead the sky was a stark cerulean, and a faint spicy smell wafted from the profusion of bright flowers blooming in window boxes. A black and white cat sitting in a doorway yawned as she passed by.

San Damonio, northwest above Florence, had been her family's home for more generations than anyone could count. Local tradition held that her family, the Uccellos, and a handful of others were Etruscan farmers who had migrated to this valley some three thousand years ago.

Ceil thought that was a fanciful story, fabricated to satisfy history-hungry tourists.

Tourists, like herself, she thought ruefully. In a single day she'd played the role: checking the cluster of shops—none with the usual tourist knick-knacks, which she found refreshing—as well as visiting the church, a most unpretentious structure with nothing of value to offer: not a single marble statue, lofty bell tower, stunning mosaic or fresco, or even a worthy *cappella* or chapel. In fact, she had never seen such a boring church. It was almost as if the place were unused, and yet she had seen some townspeople going inside. Hadn't she spotted a priest earlier . . . ?

Actually, as she thought about it, there was very little in San Damonio of interest to visitors. On her map the town appeared as just a tiny dot, and when she'd tried to find out more about it, she'd met with a dead end.

San Damonio wasn't famous for its nondescript church, nor was it known for the wine from its vineyards—in fact, what she had glimpsed of those fields on her way into town seemed sadly insignificant compared with the vast and renowned vineyards she had seen in Chianti, south of Florence. Surely, though, the town must have *something* of note.

As she reached La Rondine, the town's one and only inn, a flock of birds wheeled overhead. She shielded her eyes with one hand and peered upward into the bright sky. The flock dipped, barreling straight toward the street, then abruptly changed direction and flew out of sight.

Were they swallows, she wondered, or just common sparrows? She didn't know if there had actually ever been swallows in the area to give the inn its name.

Still, for all that, it was a pleasant place, and the staff seemed quite friendly.

She headed straight for the dining room. It was close enough to lunch-time, if the slight rumbling in her stomach was to be believed. Besides, she'd had only a cup of tea before leaving that morning.

"*Buon giorno,* and how did the *signorina* sleep last night?" Arturo Ventaglio, the owner of La Rondine, asked in English. He was an older man, his hair dusted with gray. Marco, the teenaged morning desk clerk who also served as the dining-room waiter, smiled widely, revealing a few gaps in that handsome expression.

"Quite well, thank you. It's so restful here." Ceil thought Signore Ventaglio was being quite diplomatic, referring to her as a young woman. She wasn't old at forty-one, but then she guessed she didn't fall in the young woman category, either . . . not anymore. Still, it was flattering.

Ventaglio bobbed his head. "Very soothing, *si?*"

Marco nodded, too. "Very healthy, too!"

"Yes, so I understand," she said with some irony. "The climate is certainly ideal."

She was grateful both men spoke English, because her Italian was rusty. Her parents had fled the village during the ravages of World War II and settled in New York City and then later, as the family grew, moved across the Hudson to Kearny, New Jersey. But always when they spoke of "home" it was the Tuscan village. Once Ceil started school, her parents insisted that they speak only English. Sometimes, though, her father and mother reverted, and Ceil and her brother and sister picked up the language that way.

Her parents had died before they could return, and so Ceil had taken it upon herself to go to San Damonio. Year after year, though, she canceled her plans, with one decade dissolving into another. Her sister and brother were to accompany her, but early in the year Michael had died in an army training mission, while Lucy had been killed by a drunk driver at 2 o'clock one afternoon. Shortly after that, Ceil and her husband of two years separated, and it was the following month that she had had the wake-up call of cancer. In that moment she knew she had to go "home."

She'd told no one of her coming; she wasn't even sure any family remained. If that were so, then that made her journey all the more poignant— she was the last of the Uccellos.

"More sightseeing today?" Signore Ventaglio asked, escorting her into the dining room.

"Yes," she said. He drew out the high-backed chair with a flourish, and she smiled.

He did tend to fuss a bit over her, but as she scanned the dining room she didn't see many other guests—a retired couple, by their appearance, and a man about her age. Perhaps Signore Ventaglio just felt the need to hone his hospitality skills.

"Ah, good. There are many ruins north of town. Very old. Who knows how old, *si*? And you must visit the vineyard—tell them that Arturo Ventaglio sent you, and they will give you a bottle of their best *vino*."

"And the *grotta*," Marco called as he headed toward the kitchen to get her tea. She noticed that he walked with a marked limp.

Signore Ventaglio scowled at Marco. "*Si*, the *grotta*, although that is a difficult climb for most. Straight up." He gestured with both hands. "Much better for a *capra*." He saw her confusion. "A goat."

Interesting, but her guidebook hadn't mentioned a grotto, not here in this out-of-the-way village. "Tell me more, *signore*."

The man shrugged. "The *grotta*. It isn't very spectacular. Damp. Dirty. Not a place for a lady such as yourself."

"No, no, no," Marco said, shaking his head. He was back with her pot of tea. "Not a place for a lady."

She smiled. "I'm hardly a lady—I'm a historian who's been on many archaeological digs. I've gotten dirty with the best of them."

The innkeeper's frown deepened. "It is not a place for a lady such as yourself," he repeated, then took Marco by the shoulder and shoved him back into the kitchen. The door swung shut behind them as Ventaglio's voice rose, loud and angry. She heard the word *imbecille*. She felt sorry that Marco was in trouble because of her.

But, she told herself, she'd done nothing. The boy had volunteered the information. She read the menu, forcing herself to ignore the shouting. A few minutes later Marco returned, a chastised expression on his face. He stood by her chair, waiting for her to make up her mind.

"Just an *antipasto*," she said. He nodded and shuffled back to the kitchen. Her appetite had decreased over the past few weeks; she knew she should eat more; it was just that nothing tasted or smelled good. When her doctor had told her of the cancer, she'd panicked—wanted to run from the exam room, as if she could escape her fate. She'd stayed, though, and listened to him, noted his recommendation for an oncologist. The next few days remained a blur—the cancer specialist saw her; then he gave her the prognosis. Yes, he could fill her body with chemicals and radiation, but it wouldn't matter; nothing would help at this late stage. She was dying. It was just a matter of time.

Curiously Ceil remained somewhat aloof from all this; it was as if it were happening to someone else. The specialist said he would sign her into the hospital that afternoon to start the therapy, but she said no; she thanked him, then dressed and returned to the university where she'd taught for the past decade. She typed out her resignation, handed it to her bewildered depart-ment chairman—summer classes were in session—waved to her fellow his-tory lecturers, packed up the few personal items in her office, and went home.

There, she unplugged the phone and crawled into bed fully dressed, burrowing under the covers. She lay there for nearly twenty hours before finally emerging. She hadn't slept much, just dozing here and there. All the time she did little but think. Mentally she felt like a mouse in a maze . . . her mind running down first one corridor, then another, and all of them dead ends; there had to be some way out, she told herself, some corridor that didn't dead-end. She did know, however, that she didn't have enough time left to lie around the house and feel sorry for herself. She showered, dressed in her favorite pair of jeans and shirt, and called a travel agent. Then she called a real estate agent who was a friend and had the house put up for sale; funds from that sale—she would take the first offer, she said—were to be wired to her. Of her belongings she took only what she would need for a prolonged visit. Everything else she donated to charities.

Four days later she was on her way to Italy.

Anytime, the specialist had said; she could die anytime. It could be a week from now, a month . . . a year; it could even be longer . . . or not. She had medicine for the pain that the doctor said would come later. Mostly, though, she just felt tired.

As she poked at a pepper on the *antipasto* plate, she realized that she still hadn't cried about it. Of course, what good would that do? Crying wouldn't cure her. Besides, she had too much to do yet, so much to see. Better for her to focus on that.

For the past month she'd toured Venice, Rome, Naples, and Milan, leaving Florence and the surrounding Tuscany countryside to the last.

And now that she was here . . . she didn't know. She didn't feel like she'd come home; she didn't feel much of anything, besides a certain curiosity.

She speared an olive as she gazed out the window. The same black and white cat she had seen earlier lounged on a bench opposite the inn. He yawned and rolled over, exposing a white belly to the summer sunshine. A shadow spread across the dozing cat, and the animal sprang to its feet and darted into a shop. She peered up, saw nothing. An eagle or a hawk, perhaps. Did they have eagles here? she wondered, and reminded herself to search for a book on the local flora and fauna; the guidebook was certainly useless in that respect.

"Excuse me," said a smooth baritone voice.

Startled, Ceil dropped her fork onto the plate.

"I'm sorry to have frightened you." It was the man from the other side of the dining room.

"You didn't," she replied somewhat crossly. She picked up her fork, then set it down. "I'm sorry. That was bad manners. Please, sit down and join me."

"I could not help but overhear your conversation. You expressed interest in the *grotta*."

"Yes."

"I could take you there, Signorina. . . ."

"Uccello. Ceil Uccello." Until this moment she had been going by her husband's last name. It was time to change, she thought; time . . . and how much more of that did she have? Would she stand up after this meal and simply drop dead? Would she just not wake up one morning? She forced herself to concentrate on what the man was saying.

"Ah. Did you know that your last name means 'bird'?"

She nodded. "My parents told me when I was small."

"Ah. But yes, about the grotto . . . it's close to the villa up the hill."

"I see." Ceil wasn't sure about this. The man spoke with a slight accent, almost English.

"I am sorry again. My name is Laurence San Damonio."

She arched a brow. "The same as the town?"

The corners of his thin mouth lifted ever so slightly. "The very same. My family has been here for a long time — but as to whether we were named after the town, or it after us, no one can say. My mother, though, was English; as a child I lived in Kent; when I was old enough I came home."

"I see." She was repeating herself, and chastised herself over what a dunce he must have thought her. "And you're a tour guide now?" she asked lightly.

He laughed, a rich sound. "Hardly. A businessman. A little of this, a little of that."

Oh swell, she thought, a ne'er-do-well. And yet he hardly looked the part. His clothes, while casual, seemed expensive, and he was well groomed. Maybe, one part of her said, he was a mass murderer — a local one — and he was waiting to get her alone before he stabbed her seven thousand times. Go ahead, another part of her said; who cares?

Who cares, indeed? Ceil wondered, and realized she did.

"Okay. When?"

"Tomorrow?"

"Fine." If she lived that long. Ceil, Ceil, stop it, she told herself. Stop, stop, stop.

"I'll meet you here around noon then." He stood and bowed ever so perceptibly, then returned to his table.

Ceil finished her *antipasto* and set down her fork, and Signore Ventaglio approached, as if he had timed his entrance to that very moment.

"Signore San Damonio is quite a gentleman," Ventaglio said as he whisked her plate away. "Very charming, indeed?"

"Indeed," Ceil said, trying hard not to smile. "Very continental."

"*Si!*" He beamed at her. "And would there be anything else for you?"

Yes, a new life. Aloud: "Not today, *grazie*." As she started to leave the dining room, she noticed for the first time a terra-cotta medallion to one side of the door. The bas-relief appeared quite worn in places, as though many fingers had rubbed it. "What's that?"

"Janus, the god of the Sun and of all portals, doorways, and thresholds," the innkeeper said.

A grotesque, she knew, was an architectural decoration, a fanciful creature or representation of a person . . . commonly found on old architecture. Did this date from some ancient temple? "Oh, yes, of course—Janus, the Roman god!"

"The *Etruscan* god," Signore Ventaglio corrected politely.

Of course. Rome's authority lessened the farther north she went. Here, the Etruscan influence remained strong.

Interesting. Perhaps there was a book about the Etruscan gods . . . if she could find a bookshop. All these books she was buying . . . when would she have time to read them? She had the rest of her life, she reminded herself, then nearly laughed aloud at the idea.

She could have gone to her room for a nap, but she wasn't tired, at least not yet; and besides, wouldn't she have time enough later on to rest . . . ?

It was close to 3:30 now, and the shops were just beginning to reopen. Ceil nodded to an elderly woman sweeping the stoop in front of a grocer's. Several times she thought she was being watched, but when she turned around she saw no one—only another black and white cat. Or was it the same one? Always a magnet for animals, she wouldn't have been surprised if this one had adopted her. She'd seen few animals in the village, which was odd because in other towns she'd visited she'd seen dozens of roaming dogs and cats.

At a fruit vendor's, she selected several oranges. A few steps away she discovered a store filled with antiques. Many of the pieces, she realized after she stepped inside and greeted the owner, weren't more than a few decades old. But still . . . there might be something she just couldn't live without.

She paused, an ironic smile on her lips. Sometimes . . . for a moment or two . . . she forgot. Briefly tears threatened to sting her eyes; she bit her lower lip and moved away so that the owner couldn't see her.

"What is this?" she asked, holding up a bronze object, one of many on a table. It was shaped almost like a bowl, the center a sun face, with an outer circle of moons.

"Etruscan lamp," the proprietor answered, her dark eyes solemn. "Very, very old. From two thousand years ago. It comes from the tombs. A sepulchral lamp. Very famous."

Ceil studied the lamp. The vessel was filled with olive oil, upon which a wick floated. The lamp might well date from the time of Christ, she thought, but if it was a copy it was well done. She ran her fingers along it, the bronze cool against her skin.

"I'll take it." She paid for the lamp, tucked it into her oversized purse, then stopped at the threshold. Another terra-cotta medallion hung by the door. This one depicted a youth wearing a cape and helmet, his right hand holding a lance. The carving was so lifelike that she reached up to touch the rounded cheeks. "Mars?" she guessed.

"Laran."

"The Etruscan version, I see."

By the time she arrived at the vineyard, she was hot, dusty, and extremely thirsty. She traipsed into the winery's restaurant and ordered a glass of wine. "On the house," the man said, proffering a glass of Chianti. She thanked him and asked if it was all right to wander through the vineyard. He nodded toward another door.

Outside again, she strolled up and down the orderly rows, she wasn't sure why—she scarcely knew anything about wine. Some wines were white, some red, some sweet, some dry, French, Italian, Californian, New York. That was the sum total of her *vino* knowledge.

Here and there olive trees intermingled with the vines. The trees were gnarled, old, perhaps even ancient. How many decades—centuries—had they grown? she wondered. These trees would be here long after she was dead. She marveled at the age of everything in this town; Americans, with a history of only a few centuries, could not comprehend something thousands of years old.

Insects buzzed around the fruit—the only sound. She paused under the shade of an olive tree. A dusty haze hung over one end of the vineyard;

perhaps, she thought, someone was working there. With the heat of the sun and the droning of the insects, she felt drowsy now.

Suddenly something moved a few rows away from her; she'd caught a glimpse of it out of the corner of her eye. She stepped back into the sun and peered around a fat bunch of grapes. Nothing. Her skin prickled, and again she sensed being watched. Surely there were workers—pickers? harvesters?— out here. But as she glanced around she saw no one.

She returned the glass to the man and thanked him. She checked for a terra-cotta medallion—surely the winery had one. In the tasting room she found it: a man in his middle years, his smiling face surrounded by grapes and grape leaves.

"Bacchus?" she asked, pointing.

The man shook his head. "Fufluns, the God of Wine. Of vitality." He winked.

"Ah." So, she mused, it would seem that, at least in the townspeople's version of things, the Roman gods could all be traced to the Etruscan gods. That made sense; the Etruscans were the first to settle this area, and it was the tongue of Tuscany, after all, that was the basis of the language of the country.

She wondered if any of the shops sold the medallions. She would ask Signore Ventaglio about it; he would know. The lamp, the medallion . . . what would she do with all these things she was suddenly adding to her life? She could always send them to her husband . . . her soon-to-be ex-husband; the divorce proceedings hadn't started yet. Perhaps he would be curious as to why she wasn't around; perhaps not. And she wished with all her heart that she could turn back the clock, return to the moment she'd met her husband and change that chance encounter—find someone who would truly love her.

She shook her head sharply. Enough.

"You are sad," the man said. She shrugged. "You are so young yet, you must live."

"I wish," she said bitterly, and left the winery. She took her time returning to the inn; it was all uphill now and sometimes quite steep. Exhausted, she paused only to wave to Signore Ventaglio and climbed the stairs to her room.

She wanted a bath badly. The minute she reached her room she started stripping clothes off. She ran hot water until the tub was half-filled, then eased into the warmth, and almost immediately the aches of the day began to fade. She closed her eyes. She would rest for a moment or so.

When she awoke, the bathwater was cold. She finished bathing, toweled herself dry, then slipped into a long T-shirt that served as her nightgown. Checking her watch, she was shocked to see that it was after nine. She had been in the tub over an hour. She considered going downstairs for dinner, but just the thought of talking to someone seemed too much of a strain.

She had her oranges; she'd dine on those. And perhaps if she got ravenous later, she'd ask whether a tray could be delivered to the room.

She sat on the bed, peeling her first orange carefully, and flipped through the guidebook, reading about all the places she hadn't visited yet. She finished the orange, then selected another, but when she realized she was doing more yawning than peeling, she put the orange down and washed her hands. She wobbled back across the room, turned out the light, and fell into bed.

Almost instantly she drifted off to sleep.

It seemed like only a moment later that she opened her eyes, but she knew she'd been asleep for some time. Had a noise awakened her? She listened hard, but heard nothing. As she moved her legs she touched something furry, and she yelped, leaped up, and switched on the light. The black and white cat lay curled on the mattress. It blinked at her, then yawned.

She laughed nervously. "Just how did you get in here?" The window—wide open. She had forgotten to latch it. "I suppose you can stay!" She flicked the light off and crawled back into bed. The cat shifted, its head resting on her shin. She closed her eyes.

And woke again much later. She reached out to touch the cat, but it must have moved. The air seemed thick, almost like velvet, and she could scarcely breathe. Sitting up, she shivered. The room was pitch dark, but outside there seemed to be a faint light. She rose and crossed to the window and saw a full moon in the inky sky.

Faint lights, like the flames of candles, dotted the slope above the town. In the street below a flame bobbed along. It paused beneath her window, and she saw a face—horribly disfigured—and then realized it was a mask, one of a grinning youth, whose nose was so long and sharp that it nearly met with its equally pointed chin.

Whoever was behind the mask stared up at her. Quickly she stepped away from the window; surely she couldn't be seen. Her heart pounding, she waited until she thought it was safe, then sneaked a glance out the window. The man in the mask now stood farther up the street, but he had turned and was watching her even now.

She gasped, stepped back, and latched the window, then drew the curtain across the rod. She ran to the bed, pulling the sheet up over her head. She was shaking, and she lay there, too fearful to lower the sheet. After all, she asked herself, what if she peeked out and saw the masked man inside her room?

Don't be ridiculous, Ceil, another part of her said. She was being silly. It had probably just been a trick of light; whoever it was couldn't see her. But still . . .

She closed her eyes, but all she could see was that hateful mask and the way it had looked at her.

WHEN she finally woke again in the morning, she ached all over. The cat, seeing she was up, started purring and rubbing its head against her. The purring intensified as she scrinched it behind the ears. She didn't want to move, didn't want to get up and bathe and dress. She didn't care. She would stay in bed all day. She wasn't even hungry. She closed her eyes. Was this how it was to be? No, she wouldn't give up, not yet at least. She peered at her wristwatch. Almost 11:30.

Suddenly she leaped from the bed, startling the cat, who hissed. She was meeting that man at noon! She had almost forgotten! She jumped into the tub, scrubbed briskly, washed her hair, threw on her makeup and clothes, peered into the mirror at her pale face and the dark circles beneath her eyes, sighed, then grabbed the cat and left the room.

She arrived in the dining room just as San Damonio sat down. Breathlessly, she rushed to the table.

"You've brought me a cat?" he asked, his tone droll. "How kind."

"It slipped into my room last night." She set the cat down, and immediately, purring loudly, it began threading its way around her legs.

"You have a friend."

"And I haven't even fed it. But perhaps someone in the kitchen could."

"Perhaps. Are you ready?"

"Yes."

"Do you want me to drive or do you want to walk?" he asked.

This was a test, she figured . . . let's see the lazy American in action. "Walk. It's not really that far, is it?"

"A few miles. Uphill."

"I'll manage." And she hoped she would.

"Good. I'll point out some sights along the way."

San Damonio set off briskly; Ceil hurried to catch up.

They encountered no one else on the rugged, cypress-lined road, and as for interesting sights, there were few. Once, he stopped by a ruin, which was only tumbled blocks now.

"This was the abbey," he explained. "It was abandoned several centuries ago." He kicked one of the blocks, knocking a sizable chunk off. It rolled down the slope a few yards, then stopped when it hit a tuft of grass.

"And the Church didn't rebuild?"

"The Church never cared about San Damonio."

"Oh." They started walking again. "I saw lights last night—up here, I think. Was there a festival or something?"

"Lights?" He shrugged.

That gesture could mean anything. He hadn't said no, there weren't lights; but he hadn't said there were. He seemed far less friendly than the day before, and for the first time she wondered at her eagerness to follow a man she didn't know to an isolated spot.

This is Italy, Ceil reminded herself, not the United States. But still . . . she wasn't being very careful.

And once more she had the sense of being watched. Pausing, she scanned the hills. Nothing. But of course it would be so easy for someone to hide from sight. She glanced back and saw a small black and white object.

"Oh-oh."

"What?" San Damonio asked.

"The cat from the inn is following me."

He glanced back at the animal. "Ridiculous beast."

A curious way of putting it, she thought, and more and more she felt uneasy. Yet they weren't that far away; she saw the villa pressed up hard against the hill, almost as if the earth had tried to swallow it.

Overhead birds, dark against the sky, wheeled in lazy patterns. She wondered what kind they were, and when she glanced back at the cat, she saw that it had flattened itself against the ground, as if it feared being attacked.

They reached the villa. Once grand, it had obviously not been maintained for years now. Here and there Ceil saw missing roof tiles, and the windows all looked curiously blank. Like dead eyes, she thought with a slight shiver.

Instead of escorting her up to the double front doors, San Damonio led her around the side to a huge stone arch, under that, and into a modest-sized courtyard, paved with slabs of volcanic rock. A marble fountain, long unused, sat in the center. Blue wildflowers grew now where water had once splashed.

"This is lovely. It's too bad it's fallen into disrepair. Is this yours?" Ceil asked.

San Damonio nodded. "I live here."

"Oh. I'm sorry, I didn't mean—"

He cut her off. "It's all right. The family has fallen onto hard times, as you Americans say. I've closed off most of the villa, and this is one part we haven't repaired yet. We'll get to it. Soon."

She studied the courtyard walls for the first time. Dozens and dozens of medallions—like those she'd seen in the town below, but of bronze—were set into them.

"They're beautiful! The workmanship is marvelous! These must be worth a fortune."

"Or two," he said wryly. "There," he said, gesturing to one high up on the left. "That's Horta, the Goddess of Agriculture. That one is Losna, the Etruscan Moon Goddess."

Losna's medallion reminded her of the sepulchral lamp, only the inner face was of the goddess, the outer ring showing the moon in its different phases.

"Who's this naked fellow?" she asked, indicating a bearded figure over San Damonio's shoulder.

"The God of Fresh Water—Nethuns." In quick succession he rattled off a dozen names that swirled in her head: Juventus, Menrva, Mlukukh, Picus, Summamus, Zirna, and more. Gods and goddesses . . . some of them long forgotten, some evolved into familiar Roman deities: Minerva and Diana, among others.

"And this?" she asked. One medallion had caught her eye even more than the others, for the goddess depicted was part animal, part human, part bird, with snakes entwined in her hair and along her arms. There was something about the fierce stare of the goddess that alarmed her, and she took a step back, bumping with San Damonio.

"Tuchulcha. The Goddess of Death. There is no other goddess like her anywhere in the world. . . . Even the Romans, who took so much from us, did not corrupt her. She's partly of the sky, partly of the earth. . . ." Running his fingers across the medallion now, San Damonio traced the outline of Tuchulcha's visage, caressed the stone snakes.

Shivering, Ceil edged away. She rubbed her hands along her bare arms. It was hot today, but suddenly she was cold.

"The grotto?" she asked.

"Come this way." He led her through another arch, smaller than the first, and down a flight of crumbling steps. As she peered back toward the fountain she thought she saw something move. She was getting creeped out; perhaps they should postpone seeing the grotto. And yet they were almost there . . . and it *was* a long hike, one that she didn't want to repeat. She was so tired now.

Down and down the couple went until finally they reached an old wooden door. San Damonio pulled the door open, and they stepped inside.

The blackness swallowed the light from the doorway. It was indeed damp, as Signore Ventaglio had said. Again the skin on her arms prickled and she rubbed the skin hard, trying to warm up.

Abruptly San Damonio stopped. She couldn't see his face now. "What's wrong?" she whispered.

"You must go on by yourself now."

"I don't understand."

He pressed something in her hand. A sepulchral lamp, just like the one she'd bought. Or was it the same one? Firmly San Damonio gripped her by the shoulder and pushed her past him. "Go on. You must go alone."

Inside her chest her heart fluttered like a panicked bird. "No, I think I want to go back now. Take me back to the inn!"

"It's too late."

"What?"

Ceil struggled to get away, but he held her easily, though not unkindly, and suddenly over his shoulder she saw the doorway crowded with other people, all of them silent. She knew she could never push past them.

She realized that they were wearing masks—or were they? There was so little light, and yet wasn't that Veive, the god of Revenge? Cautha, Janus, Summamus . . . all those that she had seen in the village and out in the courtyard.

Who were they? The villagers? Something more? Wasn't that Signore Ventaglio with the Janus mask? And that had to be Marco, limping, under the Laran face? What were they doing here? Why had they followed her?

One of the watchers held the black and white cat, which, seeing Ceil, leaped to the ground and ran to her. She scooped the animal up with one arm and retreated, as San Damonio and the others silently pressed forward.

Realizing that the lamp was burning, she nearly dropped it. She glanced back, saw those staring faces in the flickering light, and stumbled away.

The blackness pressed down on her, threatening to swallow her, and she tried not to whimper. She had never been afraid of the dark . . . until now. She prayed that the flame of her lamp would not be extinguished.

Deeper into the grotto she went, and it seemed that the walls, so confining here, were carved with strange animals and figures, all of them grotesque. They seemed to stare at her, to watch her, and she ducked her head.

From time to time Ceil glanced back, afraid the others were still behind her, but she was alone. She didn't understand what the villagers wanted . . . didn't know why they were acting so strangely. Perhaps there was another way out. She'd find it, and she'd leave—with the cat, of course—and she'd run back to the village, and in no time at all she'd be back in Florence. She almost laughed aloud at the thought—it was so easy!

Overhead, the grotesques acquired identity, and as she walked on, Ceil saw her father's face, her mother's, that of her sister and her brother. There was her friend from the third grade, Amy, who had died from a burst appendix. Peering over Amy's shoulder was Danny, Ceil's boyfriend from high school who had died during the first Tet offensive. Her grandparents were there, her great-aunt, the young man she had dated during college, students from classes she had taught, and ringing them all were the pets of her childhood: the abandoned birds she'd brought home to tenderly nurse, only to have them die; the stray cats and dogs . . . all of them dying after only a few years.

Dying . . . as everyone in her life had. Dying . . . as did everything—everyone—she touched. She wondered that her husband had survived; perhaps it was only a matter of time for him.

The walls fanned out now, and above her she saw still more faces, more and more fanciful, some part animal. The cat jumped to the ground and trotted after her.

Ahead, Ceil heard rushing water. The tunnel widened into an immense cavern with a fast and wide river. The grotto proper. On this side of the waterway a man in a boat waited. Cautiously, she approached him.

Charon. Or Charun, as the Etruscans knew him.

Wordlessly Charun beckoned to her and, not knowing what else to do, she climbed into the boat and handed him the lamp. He blew out the flame, and yet Ceil could still see. The cat jumped in beside her, and Charun pushed away from the riverbank. From the tunnel the grotesque faces watched.

Ceil didn't speak to Charun, nor he to her. The cat, trembling, crawled into her lap; she tried to calm it by petting it, but her own hand was shaking. Silently they floated across the river, and there on the other side, Ceil saw a woman waiting . . . no, something more. A goddess.

Tuchulcha, she recognized with a stab of cold fear. The Goddess of Death—part human, part bird, part animal, with snakes in her hair and curled around her arms. The goddess looked at her, and Ceil felt the ice grow inside her. Above them the dark birds circled, their cries echoing in the grotto's vastness.

Ceil wanted to cry out; she wasn't ready; not yet, not yet. But would she ever be ready for death? Would she? She who had brought so much death in her life?

She hadn't meant to! She wanted to cry it aloud. She hadn't wanted any of them dead. But they had all died, had left her . . . left her to die alone in this cold cavern.

Somehow Ceil found herself standing on the shore, still clutching the cat. Already Charun was halfway across the river. She tried to call to him, but the cold of the underground stole the words from her.

She faced the goddess, who reached out to her with her long fingers.

Ceil squeezed her eyes shut as the fingers and snakes spiraled around her arms, drawing her and the cat closer. The animal struggled, and she murmured words of comfort to it. She shivered, feeling both hot and cold. Once more she saw her parents, her sister, her brother, Danny, all the others of her life, one face after another, their features melting to reveal the masks beneath . . . all grotesque.

It had been a long journey, she thought, but she had come home. Home to this underground grotto. And all of them here had known, had waited for her. A feather brushed her cheek.

Then abruptly the exhaustion she'd fought for so long was gone. She was no longer cold. She opened her bright bird eyes. She gazed down at the snakes curling and writhing around her arms, at the soft black and white fur stretched across her abdomen. And she finally cried, grief mixed with joy.

The Eleventh City

GENE WOLFE

April 18, 2003
Franklin A. Abraham, Ph.D., Chair
Comparative Religion and Folklore
U. of Nebraska Lincoln
Lincoln, NE 68501
Estados Unidos

Dear Frank,

I am in the little town of San Marcos del Lago, in the province of Córdoba. You can write me here *poste restante*. I have asked that my mail be forwarded from Buenos Aires, but you never can tell. E-mail should reach me if phone service is ever restored.

This is the happy hunting ground of the folklorist, exactly as Adolfo promised—not only is there the rich folklore of the Native American tribes of the Chaco (who are actually inclined to be rather closemouthed with a stranger) but Spanish folklore and Spanish-American folklore, which is often a strange mixture of the two. Every day I rove the town or range the countryside on horseback, a method of operation I find much more effectual than driving around in my rented jeep. At night I haunt the *cantinas*, nursing a *cerveza* or three and buying one for anybody with a good story. The plentiful fruits of my labors you shall read when my book appears. What will follow in this present letter is somewhat different. I give it to you now in the hope of obtaining your advice. To tell the truth, I do not know what to do with it. Is it American or Spanish-American? Is it folklore at all, properly considered? Advise me, Frank, if you have any counsel to give.

From time to time I have seen an elderly man, quite well dressed, drinking in the *cantina* closest to this house. Somebody or other told me that he was a *gringo* too (he is from St. Louis originally, as it turns out) and so I made no effort to engage him in conversation. He is generally quiet, pays cash, and keeps to himself. His name is Wendell Zane, he asked me to call him Dell, and for the present that is all you need to know about him.

As I was riding past the old Catholic cemetery yesterday evening, I was accosted by a madwoman. The sun was low, the shadows were long, and the incident was unsettling to say the least. She shouted at me in a language that was neither Spanish nor English, shrieked like a banshee, and tried to pull me off my horse; and when my horse bolted, she threw stones at us in much the same way that a rifle throws bullets. If this were some tale of romance, no doubt she would be beautiful. Believe me, Frank, she is anything but.

In the *cantina* that evening I mentioned the incident to the barman, suggesting as diplomatically as I could that she be confined for her own protection. He shrugged and said that it had been tried many times and was perfectly useless. "Soon she gets away, *señor*, always." He glanced at the man I had been told was a fellow American as he spoke. "She is so strong! Nothing can hold her."

Later Dell introduced himself. My recorder was on by that time, so I can give you his story as he told it:

I'M a civil engineer, Doctor Cooper, and I came down here when they were running the new line to Tucumán. I was pretty close to retirement already, and I made friends here and got myself a young wife—that's why I'm in San Marcos—and what with one thing and another, I never went back. The trains here run over a couple of bridges I helped design and build, and I could say the same thing just about anywhere north of La Pampa.

Anyway, it happened the second year I was here. Or maybe it was the third, I'm not sure anymore. I was ready to pack it in after a long day on the job when I heard a funny noise way down the track, and all the men stopped work to cross themselves. I asked about it, and they said it was *el jabalí encadenados*, the pig-in-chains. They said it ran up and down the tracks all over the world and brought bad luck wherever it went. Well, I told them I'd done a lot of work around railroads in the States and I'd never heard of it. And they said maybe it hadn't gotten there yet, because it had been looking around their country for a long time.

Next day we lost Pepe Cardoza and two more. It was one of those damned stupid accidents where the plans say you've got to build A before you even start on B, but somebody decides he'll go ahead with B anyhow, because A is waiting for parts. The welds cracked and the beams fell, like any damned fool could have told you they would. And they fell right on three good men. That night I heard the noise again, and I—well, I got out of bed and got my clothes on and went out on the line to have a look.

After a while the girl I was shacking up with then caught up with me. This wasn't my wife, you understand. I hadn't met my wife yet when all this happened. This was just a girl, not bad-looking, who had slept around some. A friend had told me to buy her a couple of drinks and she might show me a good time that night. So I did, and I sort of hooked onto her, or she hooked onto me. Her name was Jacinta.

Anyway my shutting the door woke her up, and she thought I might be sneaking out to see another woman. So I told her about the pig, a sort of ghost pig according to the men I'd talked to, and she said she'd heard of it and she knew a woman that was real good with ghosts, she'd talk to her tomorrow but it would probably cost me money. I said all right, we'll try her if it's not too much.

So this old witch was there waiting for me when I got back the next day. I told her about the pig-in-chains, everything the men had said, and she said there were a lot of things like that and she'd have to find out. She threw her head back and sang to herself without much music in it, drumming on the table. That lasted a long time. I remember Jacinta and I about did for a pack of cigarettes waiting for her to stop it and tell us something.

Then she shut up. It was dark out by that time. This is going to be sort of hard to tell you about.

[Here I assured Dell at some length that I would give full credit to whatever he might tell us.]

It got to be too quiet. Usually you could hear somebody singing in the *cantina* down the street, and street vendors, and so forth and so on; but there wasn't any of that anymore. Just quiet little noises that told you there were other things in the room that you couldn't see. It was like rats in the walls, only you knew it wasn't rats. There was an electric light over the table, just the bare bulb, we used to have them all over, and it got dim. It didn't go out, but it didn't give near as much light as it should have either. It was like the voltage had dropped.

Then the witch got to talking to the things we couldn't see. Some of it was in Spanish, and I remember her saying, *"Qué busca él?"* over and over. A lot of it was names, or at any rate that was how it seemed to me. Funny names, and maybe they were Toba names. I don't know.

Finally she came out of it. You're not going to believe any of this, and I didn't either. But this is what she said. She said that back when Christ walked this earth he had put devils into a bunch of pigs, and the pigs had drowned themselves to get rid of them. The men who owned the pigs had tried to save them, and they had saved this one, pulling it out of the water before it died. After that it couldn't kill itself anymore, because the devil inside wouldn't let it. The whole story's in the Bible somewhere. I looked it up and read it once, but that was a long time ago.

[As did I, Frank, after Dell and I separated. Slightly condensed from the Fifth Chapter of the Gospel According to Mark:

Now a great herd of swine was there on the mountainside, feeding. And the devils kept entreating Him, saying, "Send us into the swine, that we may enter into them." And Jesus gave them leave. And the devils came out and entered into the swine; and the herd, in number about two thousand, rushed down with great violence into the sea, and were drowned.

But the swineherds fled and reported it; and people came out to see what was happening. And they came to Jesus and saw the man who had been afflicted by the devil sitting clothed and in his right mind, and they were afraid. And they began to entreat him to depart from their midst. . . . And he departed and began to publish in the Ten Cities all that Jesus had done for him. And all marveled.]

This pig, she said, was still alive. The devil inside wouldn't let it die, and because that devil was in it, it knew more than any man. People had tried to catch it and pen it up and they had even fastened big chains around its neck, but it had broken all those chains and run away, always looking for somebody that would free it from the devil Jesus had put into it. It brought bad luck, naturally, because it carried that devil with it wherever it went.

I asked her if she couldn't do something about it, and she said she'd try but she'd have to have a piece of the blessed sacrament to work with. She said the priest would never give her one because he didn't trust her. Jacinta said she'd get it, steal it some way.

To make a long story short, Jacinta did it the next Sunday, and the witch tacked it onto a long cross she'd made out of two sticks that she could use about like a leveling rod. After that we'd make a date, her and Jacinta and me, and wait along the tracks someplace at night, usually for three or four hours. It must have gone on like that for about a month before we finally got it.

It didn't look like a pig, not to me anyway. There was a green glow, with something dark behind it that I never could see right. But it stopped when the witch stepped out onto the tracks with her cross, and she talked to it a little and the dark thing said, "Cast me into the woman." I had never heard a voice like that before, and I've never heard another one like that since. I don't want to, either.

There was a lot of talk about that between Jacinta and the witch and me. But eventually the witch did it, putting it into Jacinta like it wanted. After that, we never heard the pig-in-chains again, and I don't think anybody else has heard it, either.

And that's all there is to tell, Doctor Cooper. You saw Jacinta today, so you know the rest.

THAT was his story, Frank. I asked him whether she had consented; and he said she had, that the witch had promised her she would be wiser than anyone alive and would live forever, and she had believed her. I did not ask him how much he had paid the witch or what had become of her, but he volunteered the information that she had died not long after that. He did not say how, but there was a certain dark satisfaction in his voice when he talked about it.

As I said earlier, Frank, I would appreciate your advice. Is this folklore? The madwoman is real enough—I saw her and was stoned by her; I still have the bruises. If it is folklore, is it Spanish-American? I heard it from an American in this godforsaken little town in Argentina, and I suspect that I might have heard much the same tale from the barman if Dell himself had not been present.

Should I put it in my book or just try to forget about it?

I trust that everything is going well back in Lincoln. Give Joe and Rusty, and the whole department, my regards and tell them I will see them again in the fall and regale them with my adventures. Although I should not say it, I can hardly wait to get out of this place.

Sincerely,
Sam Cooper

P.S. I spent most of this morning wandering around the town, but this afternoon I rode out to the cemetery to look for the madwoman. I did not find her; but between the road and the closest grave markers someone had sculpted a surrealistic and truly horrible pig from mud and straw, with padlocks and broken chains lying at its feet. That was Jacinta's work, I believe; no sane person could have done it and remained sane. I have photographed it.

Heart of Stone

LAWRENCE WATT-EVANS

When they came for the wizard and dragged him from his little house of carved stone and wood, carrying him away to the gallows, she was lost in dreams, unaware of the outside world. It was not until they began to smash equipment and furniture that she awoke and swam to the surface, where she looked out of the wall upon chaos.

None of them noticed her arrival, and she stared in horror at the frenzy of destruction. Jars of precious herbs brought thousands of miles across sea and mountain were shattered on the floor; pages were torn from ancient books of lore that had survived centuries of careful use, and flung upon the wind.

"Smash it all!" a man in a black robe shouted. "Unclean, all of it!"

She stared in silent shocked stillness as the villagers obeyed.

At last there was nothing more to smash, and the dozen men stood, panting heavily, their clothes damp with sweat, their booted feet awash in the wreckage of the wizard's life, and glanced at each other and around the room.

One of them caught sight of her and stared. He pointed.

"What's that on the wall?" he asked.

The others looked.

"It's just a shadow," someone said.

"I thought it moved."

"It doesn't look like a shadow to me."

"An image in charcoal, perhaps?"

She let herself sink back into the stone in terror until she could barely see the villagers, until they were just vague shapes seen dimly through the thick gray of the wall.

". . . gone now," she heard, faintly. And then came the crackle of flame, and heat and light penetrated dimly into the stone.

She cowered, safe within her wall, for a long time. Then, when the stone was long cold, she cautiously drifted back up to the surface and looked over the ruins.

There was nothing left but bare stone and rubbish. The glass was gone from the room's one window, and harsh sunlight shone unfiltered on a layer of ash and debris.

She wondered what had become of the wizard, and why the men had come and destroyed everything. The wizard had told her that people feared him—it seemed plain they had not feared him as much as he thought, or they would never have had the courage to do this.

Or no—perhaps their fear had become unbearable, and they had resolved to destroy it the only way they could?

Whatever the exact truth might be, she did not think the wizard would be returning. Even if he yet lived, even if he had somehow escaped their fury, what was here that would be worth returning to? All his precious belongings were gone. The books were burned to ash. The bell jar that had held the homunculus was smashed, the creature itself gone. The scrying glass was shattered.

Only she remained—and she did not think the wizard would trouble himself about her. After all, he had created her in the first place, and if he were lonely wherever he might now be, he could always make another. It was not as if he could take her away with him to some new home; she was bound within the stone of the wall, an image brought to life.

But what was to become of her, then? She could not leave. She needed neither food nor drink; the wizard's spell sustained her, so she would not starve, nor age. She would not die—would she?

She was unsure how long the wizard's magic would last without the wizard himself present. But clearly, since she was still alive, it had not faded yet. He had gone away for weeks at a time in the past, and she had not suffered from his absence. . . .

Or rather, she had not suffered physically; she had been very lonely indeed during his travels.

And of course, she had always known he would return in time. He had been alive somewhere in the world. This time, she was fairly certain he was not.

No one to talk to, no wizard to watch as he went about his studies and experiments, ever again—perhaps in time she would die of loneliness.

She stared forlornly from the stone and wept at the thought, fine drops of moisture trickling down the cool stone. Then she could not bear to look at the chamber any longer, nor that fraction of the outside world she could see through the shattered window, and she let herself sink down into the wall, where she could neither see nor be seen, where the cool substance of the stone strengthened her and gave her rest. She sank down to the heart of the wall, where it rested upon the earth itself. And hours later, as she lay deep in the stone, she found herself wondering whether she could pass down beneath the wall, into the earth, and thus be free, to roam the world and find new companions.

For the next few days she spent most of her time deep in the stone, digging downward with fingers and toes and thoughts, trying to pierce the earth, to make an opening between the magical substance of the enchanted wall and the magical substance of the greater world. She made no perceptible headway, but she did not give up—after all, what other choice did she have?

And then she heard footsteps upon the flagstones. Joy burst into bloom in her heart, and she leaped upward—the wizard had returned after all! He still lived!

But when she reached the plaster surface, when her face appeared as a shadowy outline and she looked out at the dusty, wind-scoured ruin of the wizard's chamber, the two men she saw there were strangers.

"Look at this!" one of them said, as he stirred the ash with his foot. "They left *nothing!*"

Thieves, she realized—they were just thieves, come to steal the wizard's treasures, and disappointed to find none.

But of course, one of the wizard's treasures did still remain, and wanted to escape. These men might be worthless scavengers, but they were still men, people she could talk to. They might be able to answer her questions, tell her what had become of the wizard, help her get free—or perhaps, if they couldn't free her, they would stay to keep her company. She pressed up against the outside world and watched them for a moment, gathering her courage before speaking.

But the shorter one looked up just then and saw her image sharpening into detailed clarity. He slapped the other on the arm and shouted, "Look!"

"What?" the taller man asked, looking first at his companion, then at the wall. He saw her face, and his jaw sagged.

"That wasn't there before," he said.

She hesitated, unsure what to say.

"It's magic," the shorter man said. "The wizard must have left it."

She smiled at him, and started to open her mouth.

"It's *moving!*" the taller man barked, cutting her off.

She blinked in surprise, and her mouth closed again as she tried to find the right words. Of course she was moving.

"A guardian spell," the shorter man said. "Let's get out of here!"

The taller man nodded and took a step backward. "I think you're right," he said.

Then both men whirled and hurried toward the door, as she finally found her voice.

"Wait!" she cried softly—her voice had never been as loud as a real person's, for the wizard had liked peace and quiet.

If the thieves heard her, they paid no attention—unless it was to hasten even more. She stared helplessly after them.

"Wait," she whispered, but they were gone.

She stayed at the surface for hours, staring out at the stone walls and the darkening evening sky outside the window, hoping they would return, but they did not, and at last she let herself sink back into the stone.

For a night and a day she sulked and mourned, but at last she gathered herself together, telling herself that she would do no one any good with such behavior. She debated whether to resume her attempts at digging out the bottom of her home—her home, which had become her prison—or whether she would do better to stay near the surface, where she might catch the attention of any further intruders.

Eventually she decided to do both, in alternation.

She was pressed up against the surface, her eye to the slight imperfections in the wall to get the sharpest angle, trying to see through the door to the narrow little entryway, when she heard voices. She swallowed—or rather, did her immaterial equivalent—to be better ready to speak, and listened closely, hoping the speakers would approach.

This time, she promised herself, she would not wait—she would call out as soon as she could to assure any visitor that she would not harm him. She strained to hear.

The voices had been approaching, but now she heard one say, "I'm not going any closer! Duin said there was a monster in there, guarding the old wizard's treasure!"

It was a high-pitched voice, plainly audible through the glassless window, though she could not see the speaker. She had never heard a child before, but she guessed that this was a child.

"Duin's a liar," the other voice, another child, replied. "Would the wizard have let the priest's men catch him and burn all his things if he had a monster?"

"Maybe the monster was sleeping," the first voice said. "*I* don't know.

But Duin said he saw it—it had the face of a beautiful woman, but the body of a winged serpent, and it came right through a stone wall at him."

"And you believe him?"

"Maybe," the first said, a little less certain. "But believe him or no, I'm not going in there. Even if there's no monster, there could be traps."

"Or just snakes," the other said. "Maybe that's what Duin *really* saw, a snake in a hole, and he made up the woman's face so we wouldn't know he was scared of a mere snake."

"So are you going in to see if it's a snake?" the first speaker challenged the second.

For several long seconds there was no reply, and she held perfectly still, listening intently.

"No," the other said at last. "I guess not. It might be dangerous. I don't believe in snake-women, but I guess there could still be *something* in there."

And then they turned away, and spoke of other things, as she called desperately after them, too quietly to be heard, "I am no serpent! I'm just a woman, alone in here, trapped!"

They didn't hear her, and then they were gone.

She strained against the surface for several long minutes, but at last sank back into the stone, weeping in frustration.

She lost track of the days after that. The sun rose and set, rain came and went, and in time the cold winter winds blew in through the empty window frame, bringing white flakes that danced briefly in the air before settling into pale streaks in the dark ash on the floor. She struggled fruitlessly against the limits of her home, but could not break free; sometimes she sank into silent depression for days or weeks at a time. She often called out, as loudly as she could, but received no answer.

And then one day, when the wind howled around the walls and snow was piling up on the sill, she heard a man's voice, cursing. It was barely audible over the storm, but it was growing louder. He was at the door of the house, she was certain.

Then he stopped cursing. "Hello!" he called. "Is anyone here? Am I intruding?"

She hesitated. Her voice could not be heard over the wind, she was certain. She waited, at the very surface of the wall, plainly visible should he come inside the house and up the two steps from the entryway to the room that had once been the wizard's home and study.

She wished she could go down into the entryway to greet him, but the walls there were not of stone. They were mud and wood and plaster, and she could not enter them.

"It would appear not," the man said, more quietly. She listened, struggling to hear over the wind's complaints.

And she held very still as the man came inside—she could not hear his boots on the stone floor, but she could hear the difference in the wind when he pushed shut the broken remains of the exterior door that had hung open for so long.

And then he stepped into the room, scuffing at the ash and snow, looking about curiously. He was a tall man, heavily built, with a thick black beard and curly black hair, clutching a sheepskin cloak tightly around himself.

"Hello," she said, and she smiled nervously, as broad and welcoming a smile as she could manage.

He stopped dead in his tracks and stared at her, thunderstruck.

"You're welcome to stay here, if you like," she said. "I'm sorry it's such a mess."

He looked around at the empty window frame and the gray ash.

"It is, isn't it?" he said. Then he took a few cautious steps toward her, and stared at her intently. "What are you?" he asked.

She frowned helplessly, confused by the question. "I don't know," she said. "I'm *me*."

"Are you a woman, then? Or something else?"

She remembered conversations with the wizard, when he would reply to something she said with, "Of course you would say that, since you're a woman," or some similar remark.

"I'm a woman," she said.

"*Where* are you?"

Puzzled, she answered, "I'm right here, in the wall in front of you."

"You're *in* the wall? Inside it?"

"Yes."

"How did you *get* there? Is it magic?"

"The wizard put me here."

"The wizard?" He looked around, suddenly nervous. "What wizard?"

"The wizard who used to live here. The villagers came and took him away, and left me here alone."

He relaxed. "He's gone, then?"

"Yes."

"And you're trapped here?"

"Yes!" He understood!

He stroked his bearded chin. "Now, *that's* interesting!"

She hesitated, then asked, "Can you free me?"

She wasn't really sure what she would do if she were free; she didn't really understand how people lived, what they did with themselves, what would become of her if she were out of the wall and free to move about as other people did. Still, it seemed the best possibility—she was so very tired of being alone here, trapped in the tiny world inside the wall. She had some concept of hunger and cold and pain, though she had never experienced any of them, and she knew that if she were freed she would probably suffer all those and more, but she could see through the window, could see the wide world, the vast sky, the days and nights, the changing seasons, and it all seemed so open and glorious that she was sure it would be better to suffer betimes out there in the wide world than to endure her lonely and limited existence in the wall.

"I'm afraid not, my dear. I'm no wizard; I haven't the slightest notion of how to free you."

"Oh," she said sadly. "But will you stay here, then, and keep me company? At least for a little while?"

"Oh, I'll stay, have no fear," he said. He gestured at the window. "At the very least, I'll stay here until this storm ends."

"Of course," she said, embarrassed and grateful. "I'd offer to help make you comfortable if I could, but I can't do anything from in here."

"Well, you can talk," the man said. "Can you tell me where I might find firewood?" He gestured at the fireplace in the end wall. "I'd like to warm the place up a little."

"I'm sorry," she said. "I don't know. There may not be any left. The men who took the wizard away smashed or burned or stole just about everything."

"Just my luck," the man muttered, pulling the sheepskin cloak more tightly about himself. He looked around, then said, "I'll be right back."

She waited eagerly as he hurried down the two steps to the entryway, and out of her sight. She listened as he pried open the door, admitting the howling wind. A moment later she heard a distant crunching and crashing, then silence until he returned, stamping snow from his boots as he slammed the broken door.

He held up his prize, two lengths of damp wood, a streak of snow still clinging to one. "From the fence," he said. "Hope I can get it lit." He tossed it into the fireplace, then squatted on the hearth, pulled out a tinderbox and a wad of kindling from somewhere under his cloak, and began building a fire.

"It'll be good to have some heat," he said. "You must be freezing, in that light dress!"

"No," she said. "I can't feel the cold."

He looked up at her, startled. "You can't?" He turned his attention back to the fire. "Must be part of the spell. I suppose you don't need to eat, or drink, or breathe, while you're in there?"

"That's right."

He snorted. "Trust a wizard to find an easier way to keep a woman," he said. He leaned forward and blew gently at the smoldering tinder; when it was burning satisfactorily he glanced up at her. "What's your name?" he asked.

"I . . . I don't know," she said.

"You don't remember?"

"I don't *know*."

He considered her for a moment, then shrugged. "So be it, then." He turned back to the fire, tending it carefully.

She watched, fascinated. When the wizard had wanted a fire he had simply spoken a certain Word, and flame burst from wood laid in place by the homunculus. He hadn't had to worry himself with all this painstaking effort.

At last the man sat back, gazing critically at the small, steady blaze he had achieved. He held out his hands, warming them before the flame.

"What's *your* name?" she asked.

He looked over his shoulder at her. "Reuel," he said.

"A pleasure to meet you, sir," she said, curtsying—the wizard had always been fond of that effect.

"By the good Lord," Reuel said. "That looks *very* odd! It's as if your body fades away while your face bobs up and down."

"Oh," she said, flustered by this reminder that Reuel was not at all like the wizard.

He stared at her. "You can fade in and out, then? And appear anywhere on the wall?"

"Yes," she whispered.

He considered her silently for a moment, then said, "You asked if I could stay, to keep you company—you're lonely?"

"Very much so," she admitted.

"I think I might be persuaded to stay for a time, even after this storm has passed," he said. "And I think I may bring you some other people to talk to, as well, if you'll do as I say."

She blinked at him, unsure how to respond. Do as he said? She was trapped in the wall; what could she do?

"I'll try," she said.

He looked around. "I'll need to clean this place up," he said. "And a curtain would add to the effect...." He was talking to himself, not to her; she listened without replying, just enjoying the sound of a human voice.

The storm died away by mid-afternoon; by evening Reuel had swept the ash, dust, and debris from the chamber, leaving only bare stone. The fire burned cheerily on the hearth, warming the room somewhat and melting away the snow that had blown in, though the stone remained chill.

He stayed that night, and slept wrapped in his cloak on the bare stone floor in front of the fire. He talked to her before dozing off, telling her tales of lands he had seen, and listening to her own reminiscences about the wizard and his magic.

In the morning he arose shortly after dawn, washed his face with snow, then told her, "I'll be back soon," and departed. She listened longingly to the fading crunch of his footsteps in the crusted snow as he trudged away; when at last she admitted to herself that she could no longer hear him she sank back into the wall to think.

Would he really return? He had said he would, but she knew that men could lie.

At least they had spoken the day and night before; their talk had given her strength. He hadn't fled at the sight of her. Their conversation had been *different* from her conversations with the wizard, but in its way quite satisfactory. She was much reassured; even if he did not return as promised, she had hope for the future in the knowledge that others might yet take pleasure in her company.

Night was falling when she heard a distant scraping and rose to the surface. Something was approaching, but the sound was not exactly footsteps; instead it sounded as if something large and heavy was being dragged through the snow.

And in fact, when Reuel finally appeared in the doorway, it appeared he *was* dragging something large and heavy—an immense bundle. He began unwrapping it in the entryway.

She stared as he began hauling his treasures into the chamber.

Rugs, and draperies, and cushions, a bedroll, two folding chairs and a little table—in a matter of minutes the chamber was furnished once again.

It was nothing like the wizard's chamber of old; there were no bell jars, no crowded shelves, no books nor scrolls, no oaken bedstead, no elaborate workbench with its dozens of drawers and compartments. There was no homunculus nor mummified crocodile, no herbs nor alembics, no scrying glass.

Still, it was furnished.

"That's better," Reuel said, looking over his handiwork.

She clapped her hands silently. "It's lovely!" she called. "I'm *so* glad you're back!"

He smiled at her, and doffed the black cap she had not until then noticed, making a sweeping bow. "The pleasure is all mine, milady," he said. "I've spent every ducat I had, sold half my gear, and pledged my credit to the very limits of what the merchants would accept in order to equip this place appropriately, but I am *quite* certain that with your cooperation I shall swiftly earn back every bit of it."

Her own happy smile vanished, and she studied him uncertainly. "*My* cooperation? But what can *I* do, here in the wall?"

"You, milady, can tell fortunes. I have spread the word in yonder village that I am a holy man, drawn here by my mystical knowledge, and that I have found that the late unlamented wizard had confined spirits here, with whom I can speak. I propose to bring those interested in knowing the future here, where they, too, can be counseled by those trapped spirits—for a fee. *You*, milady, will of course play the part of the spirits." He clapped his hat back on his head. "It would be even better if in fact you actually *can* see the future, or judge a man's fate—can you?"

"Of course not!" she said. "Reuel, I am glad you're here, but I fear you've misjudged or misunderstood something. I am no wizard. *I* can't tell fortunes!"

"Certainly you can! It's easy; I'll teach you. You need merely speak in terms so vague they might mean anything, and then let the customer's own words lead you on to the specifics. They'll be so astounded by the wonder of speaking to an apparition such as yourself that they won't notice any errors."

She hesitated. She was not sure she understood him—though she feared she did. "But it would be lies and trickery," she said.

"In a way, in a way," he said, with a wave of dismissal.

"I can't do it," she said unhappily.

He frowned, then shrugged. "If you cannot, then you need merely appear on cue, speak nonsense or move your lips silently, and I will translate. That will be just as effective, I'm sure."

"But it's untrue!"

"Who does it harm? 'Twill bring us all we need, and do no one any hurt. You'll see, you'll see—we'll only be telling them what they want to hear."

"It's still wrong," she said, but with less certainty.

The argument continued for a time, but finally they both knew he had won, and that she would do as he asked.

That night he hung a curtain on the long wall, over the spot where she appeared most readily. She protested without effect. Her discomfort with his plans and with the presence of the curtain put a damper on their conversation.

In the morning he departed for a time, leaving the curtain open, but then he returned—and not alone. She heard his voice outside the window, telling someone, "Wait here while I prepare; I'll call you in when I'm ready."

"Reuel?" she called. Then she heard the door open—it creaked on its hinges now, in a way the wizard would never have permitted. Reuel's footsteps could be heard, and then he was there on the steps, a finger pressed to his lips.

She frowned at him, unhappy that he was determined to carry out his ruse.

"Listen," he said, "I want you to disappear, and then when I say, 'Spirits, come forth!' you appear. Move your lips, but do not speak aloud. That's all you need do this time. Will you do it?"

"I don't want to," she said.

He growled deep in his throat. "Do this for me, and I'll stay, and we'll talk in the evenings. Refuse, and I'll go on my way and leave you here alone. It's your choice."

She hesitated, and he demanded, "Well?"

"I'll do it," she whispered.

"Good!" He smiled broadly, not just with his mouth but with his eyes and cheeks and beard. "Then get out of sight until I call you."

She sank down into the wall, watching the gray stone close over Reuel's face like gathering clouds—and she saw him close the curtain as well, shutting out the light.

This was not right. And Reuel, while he smiled often and spoke freely with her, while he told fine stories, was not the man the wizard had been. He had not even thanked her for agreeing to perform on cue; the wizard almost always thanked her when she was of service to him.

She ached at the realization that she was beginning to not really *like* Reuel.

But what choice did she have? Reuel was the one who had come to her.

She could no longer see anything but cool darkness, but she could hear, faintly, as Reuel called out to someone, inviting him in. The two of them spoke for a time, and then light filtered in—the curtain had been opened again. Reuel began chanting nonsense—not true incantations that made the stone hum and the air tingle, like those the wizard had used, but childish babbling.

"Arkazam noggle-torp wicko da wicko pung dorpander . . ."

Utter nonsense, she thought; she could do better herself. But then, she had spent years as a wizard's companion, while her conversations with Reuel led her to suspect that he had never met a true magician.

"By the Unholy Powers I command you! Spirits, come forth!"

Reluctantly, she rose to the surface and looked out at the chamber that had once been the wizard's.

Reuel knelt on the carpet before her, arms spread wide, head bowed; behind him stood a well-dressed young man, staring wide-eyed over Reuel's head at her.

She had seen the stranger's face before, she was certain. "I know you," she said, before she remembered Reuel's instructions. Then she lowered her gaze and recalled what she was supposed to do.

She raised her arms high over her head, then spread them wide in what she hoped was a mystical gesture and silently mouthed, "Reuel is deceiving you, young man."

Reuel looked up at her face.

"The spirit speaks!" he said.

"Why do I know your face?" she asked silently, lowering her hands. "Were you one of the thieves?"

"She knows your heart, knows your future," Reuel proclaimed.

She shook her head; she knew him now. "No, not the thieves," she mouthed. "You were here with the priest, when my master was taken from me and all his precious belongings destroyed."

"She tells me that you are destined for greatness, Alberch, son of Alberin—you are to be a leader of men, a wise counselor to a score of followers."

"You are a hypocrite, Alberch, son of Alberin," she said inaudibly. "You destroyed a wizard because the priest told you his magic was unholy, yet here you are, seeking counsel from unholy spirits."

"She says you must leave your home soon, to seek out the destiny that awaits you."

"Then I . . . my destiny isn't *here*?" Alberch asked.

Reuel shook his head, and looked up at her, but she merely looked back, meeting his gaze. She had no more to say.

"No," Reuel said. "Your destiny is too great for a town of this size; you must find it elsewhere, in richer lands than this, in greater towns than this."

"But . . ."

She looked directly at Alberch, met his gaze, then slowly shook her head, left to right to left. She meant him to understand that he was not to believe Reuel's lies, but she knew he would probably not interpret her gesture so.

"I will have no more to do with this," she mouthed. Reuel was a scoundrel, deceiving this man—but Alberch was no better, coming here seeking magic when he had aided in destroying the town's *real* magic months before. She wanted nothing more to do with either of them just now. She sank back into the wall, vanishing from their sight.

"The spirits depart!" Reuel announced, as if Alberch could not see that for himself.

She stayed down in the darkness for a long time, refusing to listen as Reuel and Alberch spoke, then fell silent. At last she grew bored and curious, and returned to the wall's surface.

Reuel was sitting cross-legged on his red-and-gold silk prayer rug, gnawing at a hambone. He looked up.

"*There* you are!" he said. "Have you had enough of sulking, then?"

"I did as you asked," she said.

"You disappeared before I commanded you to begone," he said.

"I am not yours to command," she said. "*You* are in *my* home."

He grinned at her. "It's *my* home now, as well. We can live together in peace and cooperate with one another, or you can be difficult; the choice is yours."

She stared at him for a moment, then asked, "Why did you tell Alberch to leave the village?"

He shrugged. "It does a man good to travel."

"And he shan't tell anyone you've lied to him, if he is not here."

"That, too. But he doesn't know I've lied to him; I confess, you played your part well."

She had no answer to that.

"Do the same a few more times, and I can make a tidy sum."

"As you will," she said resignedly.

He smiled broadly. "That's my girl!" he said. "And I'll do my part in return. Have I told you yet about the day I came to the banks of the River Oullen, and wished to cross?"

She listened as he told his tale, and much as she hated Reuel's deceptions, and what she was beginning to see as his mistreatment of her, she enjoyed the flow of words, the images they conjured in her mind. The man could speak, and speak well.

How odd, she thought, to take such pleasure in his talents while she was coming to despise him.

In the days that followed, Reuel would leave each morning. Sometimes he would return by midday, accompanied by some trusting soul come to have his or her fortune told. Sometimes it would not be until late afternoon, and on those days Reuel was irritable and impatient. Whenever he brought a customer he would go through the ritual of calling upon the spirits, and she would appear, to mouth silent insults at him and his client that he interpreted as prophecies of happiness and good fortune.

And on some days he did not return until after dark, and he returned alone. On those days he staggered and shouted and fell asleep early, without his evening's full share of conversation. He was drunk, she knew, when he did this, and when he was drunk he boasted openly of his quick wit and his prowess at all the manly arts.

She came to see that even the tales told when he was sober held hidden boasts. In his accounts of his travels he was never bested by anyone; when he was wronged he always triumphed in the end, and he never wronged another unless it was plainly deserved and just.

Somehow, she doubted that he was such a paragon among men. Deceit came naturally to him.

A day came when he did not return until the next morning, and would not explain his absence.

"Were you lonely, then?" he demanded when she asked where he had been. "Well, so was I. Maybe it was a reminder of what you'll have to live with if I ever leave. I saw what you said the other day—I recognized the movement of your lips. You called me a liar in front of a customer. You do as you're told, and don't defy me, or I'll go."

She stared at him, but did not reply.

She had not been lonely that night, when he was gone; she had been relieved.

Still, she did not rebel openly. Instead, when he brought another customer, she simply recited over and over, silently, "I am no spirit. I am a woman. I am no spirit. I am a woman."

"That's better," he told her that night, when the two of them were once more alone.

For three more days he brought clients to have their fortunes told, and then on the fourth day he returned late, alone and drunk.

And on the fifth day he came back late in the afternoon, accompanied by a young woman. The wizard's creation sank down into the wall, awaiting Reuel's summons.

It never came; instead she heard sounds she did not recognize, whisperings and high-pitched giggling and animal gruntings, and at last she could resist her curiosity no longer. She emerged far enough to peer around the closed curtain and observe Reuel and the woman coupling on the hearth, lit only by the fire. The sight fascinated and repulsed her.

When they were done she heard Reuel say, "Now, wasn't that better than that boy Alberch?"

She did not wait for the woman's reply, but sank back into the stone.

There were no customers for several days after that, but the woman came and went frequently. The woman in the wall stayed out of sight much of the time.

And then one day the girl was gone, and Reuel was gone for a day, and then Reuel was back, without her. After that he returned to the old pattern.

And finally, one morning, she had had enough; as a plump old man stared goggle-eyed at her, instead of staying silent she said aloud, "I am no spirit summoned by this man—I am a woman, imprisoned here by the wizard who built this house. I do not prophesy; any words this man speaks to you are his own, not mine."

And with that she sank down out of sight, down into the stone, ignoring the old man's querulous demands and Reuel's desperate attempts at persuasion.

Then the old man was gone, and Reuel screamed at the blank wall, "Bitch! You worthless bitch! You think I'll stay here now? You think I'll forgive you? Never! May you rot in Hell, you faithless abomination!"

She let herself rest in the guarding darkness, drifting in and out of dreams, one part of her trying to forget that Reuel ever existed while another listened intently to the stamping of his angry footsteps as he stripped the chamber of everything of value and bundled it up, preparing to depart. And a third part, one surprisingly small and weak, screamed silently for Reuel to forgive her, to stay, not to leave her trapped and alone in the wall.

She stayed dreaming in the dark for a long time.

She was awakened at last by the sound of many voices, frightened and angry voices. She recognized one—the priest who had come for the wizard, so long ago.

"We should never have let this evil place stand!" he cried. "We do now what should have been done long ago. Let not one stone remain upon another!"

And then, before she could move from her resting place deep within the stones, she experienced something new, something she had never known before—a sensation, a pressure.

A pain.

And then another, and another, and she pressed toward the surface of the wall to look out and see what was happening, but the surface was already cracked and she could not see clearly, could not press herself too close.

Still, she could see the men with great hammers, the handles as long as a man's arm, the iron heads as big as a man's thigh, black against the late afternoon sunlight as they swung blow after blow at the carved stone walls of the wizard's house.

She screamed, and saw the men shiver and hesitate—but not stop. A hammerblow struck over her belly, and the pain was intense, overwhelming; defeated, she let herself fall back into the stony depths.

There was nothing she could do. The house would be destroyed, the wall would be destroyed—and surely, she would perish as well.

She did not want to die, but what was the use in struggling? She had never been able to touch the outside world, to affect it, and nothing she could do would change that.

Her tears slicked the stone, and splashed into nothingness as the hammers struck.

Death might not be so very terrible, she told herself, as she struggled to swallow her pain. No one knew what lay beyond death—the wizard had told her that, and she believed it, for the wizard had never lied to her. Death would mean an end to loneliness, an end to betrayal and neglect, and an end to pain.

She sank down into the stone and tried to return to her dreams, to die in peace, but the blows of the hammers rained down, breaking the wall and sending jabs of pain through her. She burrowed as deeply as she could, to the very foundations of the wall, and crouched there, curled up within herself, waiting for it to all be over.

And at last it was over, her consciousness gone—but after a time she became aware again, slowly, as if awakening from her dreams, and wondered: Was she dead?

She tried to rise up through the stone, but nothing happened; her will did not propel her. Panicky, blind, she raised her head, uncurled, flung her arms wide.

Stone cracked and split like an eggshell, and tumbled away. She heard the sharp rattle and felt the wafer-thin shards fall from her, a sensation like nothing she could remember. She looked up—and saw stars.

She stared.

She had seen stars before—a few at a time, glimpsed through the window. Now she saw thousands upon thousands of them, a glittering river across all the world, and she realized that the roof was gone, that she was seeing the entire sky for the first time.

A cold wind blew across her back, and she shivered.

She could feel the air and the stone, and realized that the wall that had always surrounded and protected her was gone. She was crouched in a hollow in the earth where the foundation of the wall had been, but the wall was gone; the men had smashed it all, broken away all the stone until only she was left, hidden in a thin shell, so thin she was able to break out of it, like a chick being born.

She was not dead. She was not blind. She was alive, and gazing up at the night sky, and she was out of the wall.

Carefully, she uncurled further and stood up, slowly and cautiously, sending a cascade of rocks and dirt from her back. She stood tall and straight and looked around, feeling the wind on her arms and face. Her hair, which had always draped elegantly across her shoulders, now snapped and writhed in the breeze, whipping across her face.

The wizard's house was gone—and the wall was gone. She was free, standing amid the scattered stones that had been her prison. The world was dark and colorless, lit only by the stars, but she could see more of it than she ever had before.

She was free.

She was cold and aching and alone, standing amid ruins in a thin, dusty dress on a cold night in early spring—but she was free. She could go where she pleased; she needed no longer wait for the world to come to her, for Reuel or the wizard to call upon her.

Joy bubbled up within her.

She was, she supposed, merely human now, subject to all the usual mortal ills—hunger and thirst, pain and disease, aging and death. The spell was broken.

That was, she thought, a more than fair exchange.

She looked around, at hills and trees and fields, and westward at the dim gray outlines of the village houses in the distance. She could find food and warmth there, she supposed—but she would also find far too many familiar faces.

Reuel was a wanderer, and had told her how he had adventured across many lands. If he could do it, she thought, then so could she.

She turned, and without another look back began walking to the east, toward where the sun would rise.

Cora

ESTHER FRIESNER

The manticore lived in an empty wooden crate in the back room of Brown's Emporium of Oddments. The crate had once held oranges from California, and the wooden slats were still disposed to offer up a ghostly fragrance of citrus and sunshine when atmospheric conditions allowed. The bottom of the crate was covered with a thick bed of pine shavings which the shop's proprietor, Mr. Edward Pandolfo Brown, changed twice a week with his own hands. He was known as a fastidious gentleman of the old school to those few souls who did know him, and to the rest of the world as a bit of a spinsterish fussbudget. Neither opinion mattered to him half so much as maintaining a workplace whose atmosphere did not advertise the presence of his more extraordinary wares. (Fishmongers' stores that smelled of fish were anathema to him as well.) Between the scents of freshly shredded conifer wood and ancient Sunkists it was virtually impossible to distinguish the smell of monster at all.

The monster in question was a compact abomination, about the size of an old lady's Chihuahua, small of stature but hugely tubby. Tradition stated that the manticore was supposed to have the body of a lion with the tail thereof terminating in a scorpion's sting. This was so, as far as it went. Tradition mentioned nothing to forbid the lion-scorpion amalgam from being a bijou sort of beast, a parlor horror suitable for cosseting in one's lap if a body were so inclined. Few were. It wasn't the matter of the deadly stinger alone so much as the fact that the manticore was simply ugly, and the wrong kind of ugly at that. It could claim neither the puissant ugliness of a dragon, which might appeal to the power-hungry, nor the poignant ugliness of gnome or kobold, which might allure the tenderhearted, nor even the comical ugliness of a mandrill's inflamed bottom, which might draw in that most dearly desired class of buyer, the type with more money than sense. Goggle-eyed, crook-snouted, snaggle-fanged, with a patchy green mane and a scrofulous pelt the color of old creamed corn, the manticore was ugly beyond the abilities of a hundred bards to describe or a hundred advertising copywriters to redeem. Mr. Brown called it Cora.

It had occupied its orange crate for well over fifty years, yet never showed the slightest sign of discontent or impatience with its accommodations. Fifty years was barely enough time to make the faintest of impressions upon such a creature. It was five hundred thirty-seven years old if it was a day, and also if you could trust the word of the wandering Coptic monk who originally sold the singular brute to Mr. Brown's thrice-removed great-aunt Irene when she was touring the Valley of the Kings back in '07. Of course the monk was quite mad—even a flibbertigibbet like Irene Woodsides could tell that much. His eyes were bloodshot, his tonsure frowzy and ill-kept, and his hempen sandals badly stained by the foamy ropes of saliva perpetually dripping from both sides of his mouth. Still, he did give her a good price for the creature, selling it to her under the mistaken impression that it was a corkindrill.

Well, of course it was *not* a corkindrill, although a genuine corkindrill (another of Irene's finds) had shared its crate for approximately fifteen years. Mr. Brown acquired the pair of them as an especial bequest from his great-aunt. He always was her favorite relation, no matter how many times removed, and when she heard that he had been utterly disinherited by his parents (a direct result of his expulsion from Harvard in '43 for practicing certain vices detrimental to the war effort), she rallied 'round at once to provide the poor boy with some self-perpetuating means of support congenial to his nature. The manticore, the corkindrill, a selection of bezoars and periapts, most of the books from her late father's collection of incunabula, plus as many mummies—human and animal—as she could spare, all were shipped to the modest shopfront in lower Manhattan where her disgraced great-nephew had betaken himself, Harvard banner, vices, and all. Thus, Brown's Emporium of Oddments was born.

Born, but born neither to thrive nor flourish. From its earliest days the Emporium showed itself to be a sickly, limping, pulling sort of venture, rather like its owner-administrator. Edward Pandolfo Brown was a wispy man with an outsized head that resembled a peeled onion, the sharp, canny stare of a raven, and hands long and white and soft as strips of cod fillet. He spoke with an affected quasi-British accent to which he had no birthright and he walked in a manner that made him seem as though he were always sneaking up on things sideways.

The years passed, and while the Emporium did not thrive, neither did it succumb entirely. Its marginal existence was helped by its fortuitous geographical location. People *expected* to find such places in Greenwich Village, and people were always willing to pay for a souvenir that might serve as proof that their expectations had been met. Tourists would enter the shop, stare stupidly at the old books, utter gasps and giggles over the mummies, and exchange delightedly scandalized whispers over some of the more priapic statuary. They would end by purchasing a deck of tarot cards or a skull-shaped candleholder or a book of love spells, the better to prove to their friends back in Iowa that they had visited such a den of dark doings as this. Mr. Brown did not grow rich on such custom, but he could survive on it. And once he learned to jack up the prices on the tarot cards, he survived very well indeed.

He never allowed the tourists to view the manticore. He knew better. A student of the Classics, he knew better because he knew himself, and this meant he also knew how poorly he would be able to stomach their reactions. Some would insist it was dead and stuffed, others would lecture their wives as to how it was all done with mirrors. A third group would take fear and flight, summoning official attention from the departments of Police, Zoning, and Animal Control which the Emporium (and the manticore) did not need. And leaving the worst for last, there would be those among the gawking throng who would feel honor-bound to stick their clumsy hands into the box and pat the monster.

That would not do at all. The manticore would sting them. It was a melancholy beast, sluggish and indifferent to its extended captivity, but it did not like to be touched. So the mad monk had told Mr. Brown's great-aunt Irene, and so she had in turn told him. He saw no reason to doubt this intelligence, nor to put it to the test. There had come into his possession, along with the manticore and the corkindrill, a certain piece of sculpture popularly known as a death mask. A plaster impression had been made of the face of one recently deceased, a likeness whose lineaments were frozen in an expression that was a visual symphony of pain, horror, and despair, performed in the key of madness. This, according to the message (in French) scratched into the reverse of the mask, was the face of the last person to have felt the manticore's sting.

There were some things Mr. Brown thought best to accept on faith. That was why he had never laid a hand to the beast. When he needed to clean its residence, he merely provided an upended cardboard box containing a dish of the manticore's favorite food, tilted the orange crate onto one side, and waited while the creature waddled leisurely over to feed. When he wanted it back in the crate, a second offering of food was used to lure it.

Cora's response to food was not natural. All the texts that Mr. Brown had ever studied on the subject of manticores agreed that the beast had no real *need* to eat in order to survive, nor to drink, nor even to breathe air after the fashion of commoner clay. By these lights, its several weekly defecations were also optional events, produced as a favor to Mr. Brown, in order to give him something to do. Taken all in all, it was a convenient monster. It had never tried to bolt for freedom. It had never given him any cause to fear that it might attack him while he worked on cleaning its accommodations. It treated him like a very clever and useful piece of furniture, which some might say was exactly the manner in which he treated it.

This was true, up to a certain point in time. However, this point had not yet been reached when Mr. Brown's great-aunt Irene took it into her head to meddle in his business affairs. The last of her husbands had passed away almost a year previous to this outburst of unsolicited officiousness, and she had no hobbies. It was to be the occasion of her final visit to the Emporium, although neither she nor Mr. Brown were prescient enough to know it at the time.

"Edward," she said almost immediately upon crossing the worn granite threshold of the shop. "Edward, my precious, however are you going to show anything resembling a decent profit if you do not sell something more substantial than these tourist gewgaws? Child, child, I am an old woman who has almost outlived her trust fund. Much as I would like to leave you a sizable inheritance, I fear it may not be. There is no need to tell me that I am your only hope of financial support within the family—I know it, to my everlasting regret. Oh my poor, dear Teddy-bear, what *shall* you do when I am gone?" And she caressed his cheek just as she had done so often in the old days.

True to his memories, Edward flinched away from the touch of the old woman's hand, although his mind still echoed with his mother's waspish exhortation for him to stand still and be grateful that he had found favor in the eyes of the family's richest, most barren relative.

"I assure you, I can manage," he replied. "Perhaps I am unable to sell any of the larger items, but think: They are not so much merchandise as stage dressing, and difficult to replace. They lend the Emporium its unique atmosphere; it would not be the same if I sold them off. Mummies don't grow on trees."

Great-aunt Irene clucked her tongue and laid hold of Edward's hand with fingers softer than his own. "Well, you ought at least *attempt* to find buyers for some of the midsized *objets*," she persisted. "Remember what a fine price you got for the corkindrill?"

"A fine price, and no possibility of repeating the sale, seeing as it was one of a kind. I will never be able to find another," he reminded her.

"Why should you want to do that? Living rarities are more trouble than they're worth. You ought to have sold the manticore ages ago. The same buyer I sent you for the corkindrill would have given you as good a price and better if you'd seen fit to retail them as a set. Why didn't you?"

All of Edward's face grew taut and cold as the skin of a drowned man. "I have become fond of the beast," he said stiffly.

"Pfaugh! Nonsense." Great-aunt Irene snorted, then doubled over around the cough that was destined to bring her death. When she recovered, she added: "What possible affection can there be between you? The monster only cares about having its wants met; an automaton could provide it the same services you do."

"I know this to be true," Edward replied, his voice still level and rigid as a good oak plank. "The years have provided me much experience of monsters."

"You are still a foolish boy." Great-aunt Irene coughed again, and rummaged in her purse for a wispy lace and linen handkerchief into which she primly spat a ladylike quantity of blood. "And to think how promising you were as a child! How prepossessing! It seems as if your common sense has departed along with your good looks. I tried to help you, to sustain you, to give you a firm footing from which your ambitions might spring higher than the stars, and what have you done with it? Stood there. Just *stood* there."

"Perhaps I am not yet ready to dare a leap so high," Mr. Brown said blandly. "Perhaps I have had experience of similar foundations, touted as equally reliable, which have crumbled out from under me the moment I thought to try their solidity."

Great-aunt Irene failed to see the humor, whether or not Edward was offering her any humor to be seen. "Words," she grumbled. "Games. This is how you waste the days allotted you on this earth. Someday you will realize how badly you've squandered a very precious thing."

"Aunt Irene, I don't like to displease you, but I must also remind you that it's been a long time since I was a child. My choices these days are my own."

She snorted again. "And welcome to them." With that, she rose up and departed Brown's Emporium of Oddments, nevermore to return.

She died on the following Tuesday—an impromptu demise stemming not from her declining pulmonary fitness, but from an unheralded encounter with a speeding taxicab. (However, since it was a violent respiratory spasm whose throes in mid-street prevented her from seeing and evading the fatal vehicle, it might be truly said that she perished of a hacking cough.)

She was buried from the Episcopal church on Fifth Avenue which the Woodsides clan had patronized for decades. Mr. Brown went to her funeral to make sure she was really dead. He was the only blood relation to attend the services, having had the happy chance of surviving those of his kindred who had been alienated from that gadabout gadfly Irene. He was therefore more than a little taken aback when, at the reading of the will, he learned that his only inheritance was to be the niggardly sum of five thousand dollars, a boxful of old photograph albums, and her full set of the Harvard Classics, nicely bound. The rest of her substantial estate she left to a young man named Herbert Pennyroyal of Knightsbridge, London, U.K.

Edward deposited the money in his business account at the Dime Savings Bank, sold off the Harvard Classics at a fair and fairly decent price, and tucked the old albums into the bookshelves above his bed, first removing a single photograph from its gummed black corner-holders for closer perusal. He sat there in the back room of the Emporium, his feet up on the edge of Cora's crate, studying it by the harlequin light of a Tiffany lamp. It was a photograph of himself at the age of five, taken on the lawn of Great-aunt Irene's old estate on Long Island, both sold ages ago. Hours passed. The manticore fidgeted and snuffled among its shavings. Edward told it "Hush" several times, but either the weather or some enigmatic quirk intrinsic to its nature was at work, for the creature would neither hush, settle, nor sleep.

At last Edward sat up straight, feet on the floor, tossed the photograph into the crate, and left the room.

It was six months after the reading of Great-aunt Irene's will that the beautiful young man came into Brown's Emporium of Oddments. He was tall and slender and fastidiously dressed in a shade of khaki guaranteed to set off his golden hair and ice-blue eyes to heartbreaking perfection. Although his clothing was cut to the style proper to an explorer of dangerous terrain and waste places, it took no more than a second glance (if that) to reveal that it had been procured from one of those catalogs whose peddling prose is far more exotic and romantic than the lives of the starved souls who patronize the same. From the manner in which he carried himself and the delicacy with which he placed his every footstep, it was quite clear that here was no doughty adventurer, but a youth whose greatest exploit to date had no doubt been maintaining a stiff upper lip when confronted with the horrific news that the local grocery had run out of his preferred brand of mineral water.

Edward Pandolfo Brown was already half in love by the time the visitor introduced himself as Herbert Pennyroyal.

The two men got along famously from the start. Setting aside the radical differences in their ages and looks, they discovered that they had all manner of things in common, Great-aunt Irene being the least of these. It turned out that Herbert had come to the States to discover why he had been chosen as Great-aunt Irene's chief heir, preferred even over and above her blood kin.

"That was very kind of you," Edward told him as they lay contentedly together in his bed.

"No it wasn't." Herbert sighed and snuggled himself in more comfortably before attempting to correct his new lover's misapprehension. "I never intended to *do* anything about it—anything like making amends by offering you some of the money. I just wanted to see what sort of person you were. I rather hoped you'd be a brute so that I could go back home again and enjoy my new wealth with complete peace of mind. Not *my* fault if you were horrid. Quite logical for you to be cut out of the will in that case, what? Couldn't expect the old girl to leave all that cash to a bally villain, now could one?"

"Of course not," said Edward, with a kiss.

"Yet here you are, a delightful chap. I'm quite torn. Shall I give you a fair share of the inheritance or shall I persuade myself that you're a beastly cad after all and keep it?"

"Why don't you stay here with me until you can decide?"

Stay he did. They soon became an identifiable couple, Herbert and Edward, and were frequently approached by others of their amorous inclination with invitations to parties, soirees, sporting events, picnics, and other social functions patronized exclusively by gentlemen who preferred . . . gentlemen.

These they declined, for another disposition Edward and Herbert held in common was their dislike for exclusivity of any sort. Since Herbert had come into his life, Mr. Brown had blossomed and now claimed an ever-widening circle of acquaintances of as many sexes as humanly possible. It was all very free, and very beautiful, and very tender. Of course it couldn't last.

Edward knew this. He was no starry-eyed romantic, not he, even though there were moments when he would stand behind the counter in Brown's Emporium of Oddments and burst into unsuitably fatuous laughter for no apparent cause. That Herbert Pennyroyal loved him was one of life's infrequent treats, bound to be as finite as it was rare. The only question was not *if* it would end, but *when*.

One year passed, then two, then three. The younger man spoke longingly of applying for United States citizenship, but his sweetly indolent nature did not prompt him to any specific course for actualizing that desire. There were times when Edward dared to hope he was wrong about the impermanence of his relationship with Herbert, but these fleeting, fool-hearted moments crumbled to so much mummy-dust the instant he paused to regard his ill-favored countenance in the mirror.

Not *if* it would end, but *when*. Yes, that was the question.

It was July. Herbert stood over the suitcase which he had laid open on the bed to facilitate packing. He gabbled promises of making this the briefest of brief visits, a long-postponed jaunt home to England to tie up loose ends before uprooting himself from that land entirely, but Edward was not to be gulled. No matter how often Herbert tried to reassure him, he knew that compared with forcing an *adieu* into the false shape of an *au revoir*, wrangling a sow's ear into a silk purse was child's play.

"*Why* won't you believe me?" Herbert demanded. "I've told you how much I care. What more do you want of me?"

"Nothing," said Edward.

"I say, if you're going to be this way, I won't go; that's all there is to it."

"Don't let *me* stop you."

Herbert flung a set of smallclothes into the suitcase and uttered a wordless exclamation of disgust. "You're being a beast about this! You don't trust me! I've given you my word that I'll return and it means nothing to you!"

Mr. Brown recalled other words that had been given to him, other promises made by other people whom he'd had every cause to trust:

You'll have such a nice time at Aunt Irene's house, darling!

There's my little Teddy-bear! Come climb in here with your aunt Irene and we'll play a lovely game.

Why are you crying like that, child? No one's done anything to you. And don't say I have; no one will ever believe it.

What do you mean, saying those awful things about Aunt Irene? Do you want her to be angry with us? She's a respectable woman of means; how dare you? You must've imagined it. Either that or you're a liar. Where do you get such nasty thoughts? Shame on you!

The ghosts hovered before him, their breath like the cool touch of a bat's wing brushing across his cheek. The mother he had loved and the father he had sought in vain to please blended their phantom forms with the milky apparition of Great-aunt Irene, a Cerberus whose two scowling countenances were not half so terrifying as its third, too sweetly smiling face.

Mr. Brown drew a deep breath and blew it out as hard as ever he could, scattering them all to wisps. "You'll have to forgive me, Herbert," he said heavily. "I love more easily than I trust. Perhaps you might understand—?"

Herbert sighed, a man who has reached his rope's end and found it to be buttered. "Not *that* again," he said, shaking his head. "I say, the old girl's dead; bury her and be done."

"I would like to."

"Then *do* it! My dear, dear man, she used us much the same, you and I, but you don't hear me still moaning over it."

"There were . . . differences. Our ages, for one thing. And at least she *asked* for your cooperation. *You* went with her willingly."

"How very kind of you not to add *and you were paid for it.*" Herbert's beautiful eyes hardened. "I went with her because it was better than starving and less dangerous than my previous means of support. Better the devil one knows and all that, even if it's a devil that reeks of stale violets. Tsk. Just listen to me: ingratitude! She took me from the streets, as she herself reminded me on a weekly basis." He paused for a time, growing thoughtful. "From the streets, from the streets . . . ," he repeated. "Silly me. Perhaps that's what's at the bottom of your distrust, Edward: My former profession doesn't enjoy a reputation for honesty."

"I don't want honesty from you," Mr. Brown said. "I'll settle for honor."

"What's *that* supposed to mean?"

Mr. Brown wordlessly absented himself from the room. Herbert stood there idle for a time, then shrugged off his lover's quirkery and went back to the task of packing. He was almost completely free of his labor when Mr. Brown returned. He was carrying a large cardboard box with the lid securely bound by tape and stout cord. There were no airholes.

"Take this with you," he told Herbert, "and bring it home again if—when you return. If you can."

Herbert eyed the crate doubtfully. "What's in it?" he asked. In all the time that he and Edward had been together, he had been denied this last intimacy: the revelation of the manticore's presence on the Emporium premises. Perhaps it was a precaution on Edward's part, one made from either prescience or pessimism, but certainly one determined with an eye to just such circumstances as these. It did not seem possible that he could have concealed the creature from Herbert for so long, yet he *had* done so.

Now Herbert's hand strayed toward the Gordian knot binding up the box. Edward slapped it aside lightly. "I had rather you returned this to me in the same condition as it leaves my hands," he said.

"But what *is* it?" Herbert persisted.

"That, my darling, is something you'll find out if you betray me," Edward replied, and kissed him on the mouth, and agreed to pay whatever extra freightage or customs duty the transportation of the box might entail. If he knew about the narrow questioning the airlines brought to bear upon people transporting boxes of unknown contents, or of the British laws governing the quarantine of alien beasts, it was plain that he had further private knowledge which allowed him not to give these a second thought.

"That box must hold the strangest chastity belt in Christendom," Herbert observed, somewhat peevishly.

"It is certainly the most effective," Edward countered.

So Herbert made a face over the whole matter, but he made no further arguments. When he left, he took the box with him. The next communication Mr. Brown had from his beloved was a telephone call to let him know that Herbert and the box together had enjoyed a tranquil flight and an uneventful passage through Heathrow Customs.

That was the last that Edward heard from Herbert for a good long time. Days passed, and in their wake sailed weeks, which dragged along behind them the roil of months and seasons. Edward saw autumn come in alone, and spent his winter evenings reading bad novels about Hollywood whores while he rested his feet on the edge of an empty orange crate that no longer needed to hold pinewood shavings.

And then, one day in early May, Herbert came back. He didn't look at all well. In fact, he looked quite as white as plaster and his eyes were the deep blue of a sky that means to birth thunder.

He came walking in through the front door of Brown's Emporium of Oddments at one o'clock of a Saturday afternoon. Tourists were everywhere. Ignoring them all, he walked up to the counter behind which Edward Pandolfo Brown stood haggling with a fat-armed female about the price of a desiccated monkey head. He let the box drop to the countertop and glared venomed daggers until the woman snorted and left. He proceeded to render the same treatment to every one of Edward's potential customers until the Emporium was as empty as the streets of Dodge before a showdown.

"Herbert..." Edward could not bring himself to say the name above a whisper. "It's been—I didn't think you were ever—It's so good to see—"

"It's a manticore," Herbert stated. He could not forbear a fleeting smirk on seeing the expression his words brought to Edward's eyes, but plainly he derived no enjoyment from it.

"But—but the box is still—" Edward looked from his lover to the package on the countertop. The tape sealing it was undisturbed, the complex knot still tightly secure in its original form. There were even a few fluffs of dust caught between the loops of cord. "How *could* you know?"

"I couldn't," Herbert replied. "I wouldn't, if it hadn't been for the gentleman I met one evening in the Strand shortly after my return to London. A most peculiar fellow. When one encounters a man who's obviously been dressed by Saville Row it's not customary to see him to drool copiously out of *both* corners of his mouth. Poor chap must ruin a fortune in Italian shoes that way. At any rate, he drew near and seized me by the shoulders, pressing his nose to my shirtfront, and sniffed with a bloodhound's intrusive eagerness. I fended him away, only to hear him cackle triumphantly, '*Manticora! Manticora!*' and in broken English stumble through a natural history of the beast. I found the whole experience to be more than somewhat disconcerting. It was when he mentioned the part concerning the practical uses of the monster that I stopped looking for a policeman and began paying him some small heed.

"It was hard going, making sense of his words—he claimed an Egyptian pedigree, though I can't see how he could sanely claim to be as old as he swore himself to be. Well, he might not have known the proper words to describe his age, but he certainly had them down pat when it came to describing manticores. Did you know that the manticore is a dismally torpid creature? It can go for long periods of time without food or water or even air." He glanced at the box between them and added: "What a silly question. Of course *you* knew that. Yes, just as you knew that it can bear almost anything, with one exception: the betrayal of the one it loves best in all the world. Then it stings."

Edward rested one hand atop the box and looked shamefaced. "It was because I loved you," he muttered.

"It was because you'd rather see me dead than out of your hands," Herbert corrected him. "It was also because you thought I wouldn't waste any time in betraying you. I haven't had your advantages, Edward, but I know an excuse when I hear one."

"Can you blame me?" Edward cried. "You know what I've endured; can you wonder if I question anyone who becomes close to me?"

"You've suffered, I can't deny it. You've been robbed of things you can never hope to recover this side of the grave, but what have you done since then? Invited the thief into your home, kept her with you, held her close. Why? I know you'll never be rid of her entirely, but at least you might have shown her to a door that leads *out* of your house instead of one that brings her even farther in." His mouth quirked up at one corner, a joyless parody of a smile. "Even dead, she's a great convenience. How much else has she excused you from, Edward? What else have you done to suit yourself and blamed on her?"

Mr. Brown did not choose to hear these words. Instead he lifted what little there was of his chin with what little righteous indignation he was able to muster and declared, "You said you couldn't hope to be happy away from me. You said you wouldn't be gone long. You lied!"

"You never did say you wanted honesty from me," Herbert said. By this time his natural color had returned and his eyes were tranquil. "Merely honor. I stayed away longer than need be so that you might have the pleasure of seeing the proof of my chastity." He waved a hand over the still-sealed box. "And now, for my own pleasure, I'm going to leave you. Yes, forever. Take that expression off your face; you look like an electrocuted goldfish. While in England I used the time and Irene's legacy to create a comfortably reliable investment portfolio for myself. It may be that, in future, I will need to travel in order to look after my financial interests. Would you allow that unless I carried this with me?" He patted the box. "I doubt it. I am still more than somewhat fond of you, Edward, but I'd prefer to spare us both the strain of enduring another trial-by-monster."

He left. The door had almost closed all the way behind him before Edward recovered the use of his voice, and then it was only to vent a hoarse, inarticulate cry of rage. His second breath brought back the gift of speech: "Come back here, you bastard! You can't just walk out on me! Do you think *that's* not betrayal? God help you, you've brought this on yourself!"

He snatched up a pair of scissors from the countertop and sheared away the cord binding the cardboard box, then stabbed the open blades downward, slashing the sealing tape open. The flaps fell wide apart, loose and limp as the petals of a blown tulip. He plunged his hands into the darkness.

He screamed when the manticore's sting touched his hand. It was not a scream of pain. His cry was something utterly other, a gasp whose jagged edges melted into tears as he drew out the pitiful bundle of bones barely overlaid with skin. The stinger's tip was gone, leaving only a rotted black cavity stained with the residue of venom long since dried and virtueless. When he examined Cora's sorry little corpse, he found the place where the manticore had lodged its final sting. He touched the still-open wound at the base of its throat tenderly. Even in his grief he had to marvel that so podgy a creature was also lithe enough to thus deal its own deathstroke. He was carrying the bones and body with him into the back room, intending to lay Cora out for burial in the old orange crate, when he chanced to trip over the outstretched tail of a mummified baboon. He had just the time left as he went falling headfirst amid the manticore's bones to realize that the ancient Egyptians never preserved their sacred animals without first binding all such caudal entanglements close to the body. He had lived with monstrous impossibilities all his life: This last was not too much to bear. He fell heavily, crushing the manticore's remains to powder beneath his body, and he breathed deeply of the sickly yellow dust as he lay there on the Emporium floor.

By the time the next group of tourists jingled the bell above the doorway, the transformation was complete. The first one through the door was a retired automobile salesman from Natchez; his death made all the papers. His wife escaped, shrieking horribly. The police took one look at the monster crouched over the body, drew their guns, and decided not to trouble Animal Control after all.

Ascension

YVONNE NAVARRO

Mother, may I . . . ?
    Not tonight, niña.
Holy, holy, Mother of God and power and light . . .

THERE are deep alcoves evenly spaced behind the parapet of the massive cathedral, and the one in which I am trapped is on the northernmost side. The church dominates one end of our small Mexican village, the sun shining somewhere beyond the corners of huge stone blocks nearly three hundred years old; their edges crack and weather as the years pass, softening a little more with the turn of each season. In the summer the southern and western breezes never quite find their way into my darkness to warm the surfaces of my hardened skin, and the blistering sunshine is always beyond my reach. This is the land of undying heat, where sometimes the ground shimmers with a sort of mad, eternal glee and a man caught without water can die of thirst within a quarter day. There are no cold or freezing winter storms to make ice expand and contract; no water creeps into my curves and crevices and does its best to tear me apart and send me crumbling into the oblivion and freedom I so desire. I can only sit and watch and think, and wait for the day of discovery that must, surely, eventually arrive.

Mother, may I . . . ?

Not yet, niña.

I see everything.

Far below in shades of black and gray, the descendants of He Who Put Me Here visit the cathedral every Sunday, then again on the holiest of days. Perhaps these regal Spaniards believe this will elevate them to grace, but to my knowing eyes, the passage of centuries has not dulled the blood on their hands — it shows in stripes of shadowless black, like the oil I once saw spilling from the broken underside of an automobile that limped to the curb and sat, panting and coughing like a dying animal.

I thought the car was bleeding.

Now, of course, I know better. Mother may not let me move, but in Her infinite wisdom She does allow me to learn.

There, gliding up the steps of the magnificent cathedral built so many years before by his own family, is the great-great-great-grandson, hair gleaming and as black as the bloodlike oil I remember so well. He moves like a jaguar, sleek and lean, and even from my station far above I can see how his night-filled eyes glitter with heat and passion, an inherited internal fire passed from father to son six times over. How I yearn to touch that spark, to wrap my stone-tipped fingers around its source and squeeze until I can take it for my very own.

Mother, may I . . . ?

Not today, niña.

Like that spark, the sins of the father are also passed on, to son and daughter, son and daughter, ad infinitum. My hands, too, are tainted, but not with blood, though my sin was just as mortal. None is better than the other — once fallen, we are all to be trod upon by those who bear the guiltless blood of righteousness.

Ascension

It's just a matter of waiting your turn.

And I am patient.

I have no choice.

But I have not been bored. I have watched the passage of time, man, and machine with an imprisoned but predatory interest, like a caged wolf which instinctively believes—because it must—that it will someday be freed.

Mother, may I . . . ?

Later, niña.

In my monotone existence, the blood on my hands is not the telltale black of death, as that which washes the spirits of those upon whom my cold, eternal gaze falls. Rather, it is another shade of gray, deep and rich, the incriminating stain of lust still visible long after the man who awakened it in me has gone to dust on the frigid, snow-filled winds along the peak of the extinct Orizaba volcano.

Ah, but my trespass has no end, and thus no forgiveness. Even as I am, I have not lost the memory of his touch, of how his pale skin rested molten against mine upon the altar of the very church which rises like a majestic mountain beneath me.

I remember, too, the time before it became too late, the words of the people in my village as they cast their furtive glances in his direction—

Es diferente que su padre, some claimed in hushed voices. *Un monstruo.*

El diablo, whispered others.

—and it was that very sense of danger and forbidden desire that drew me to him, like an ant drawn to the sweetness beneath the edge of liquid amber. Night after night within his smoking embrace, steeped in ecstasy and unconcerned—*unbelieving*—as to the ever-widening chasm I created between myself and my God while I writhed in breathless delirium upon the most hallowed spaces of His place of worship.

And after our last act, *there,* upon the chapel's marble floor below the statue of Our Lady of Guadalupe and bathed in the glow of a hundred votive candles, was where I broached the subject of true unity. In my ignorance I made demands for things he could not, *would* not meet, items of earthly and insubstantial value such as vows of matrimony and procreation and sanctity—

I, a peasant Indian woman cursed with the timeless beauty of a Spanish aristocrat and a hunger for the worldly things so far above what destiny had decreed to be my lowly station in life.

How cruelly he laughed, my dark and depraved lover, his eyes hellishly reflecting what should have been the beauty of the candlelight. Never had I thought to hear such brutal words from the same lips that had covered mine and driven me beyond the threshold of pleasure and sanity—

Chiquita, you must know that I can never marry beneath my standing.

My pleas, my demands, my screams, my threats to dishonor his family and shame the bride-to-be he told me was on the way—all meant nothing to him. Only my tears seemed to soften the heart of rock within his fine chest, only those sweet signs of sorrow made him gather me tenderly and rock me like a troubled child.

Mi amor, he told me softly as I lay weeping within the coveted circle of his arms, *Let me show you the ultimate eternity.*

And for me, the end of our unblessed union came in an airless, bloodless embrace.

I felt it all as my life seeped away—the rigid strength of the same hands that had once explored every mystery of my body now gripped mercilessly around my throat, the creeping paralysis as will and strength eagerly fled the prison of fragile flesh and bone.

I died, yes.

But I never truly *left*.

My lover, my murderer . . . he never even cared to close my eyes as he gathered up my naked corpse and carried me to a hidden panel that slid aside at his knowing touch. Climbing then, up a concealed flight of stairs to a passageway known only to a few in his family and created, no doubt, as an escape route for the bluebloods should there be a nasty peasant uprising. Far behind the parapet in the tiny, shaded alcove where I could overlook the town but where those who lived in it would never have to look upon or notice me—there he placed my lifeless, naked remains. And finally, in a last, absurd act of affection, the only love of my short existence arranged my corpse so that I could see just over the rim of stone and down, far, far down, to the streets of the village and the warmth and love that I would never know again. . . .

Like the elements, time can be an enemy or a friend. Working together, they are comrades, and how quickly and hungrily the searing temperatures of that Veracruz summer robbed the moisture from my form, how judiciously the passage of years worked to solidify what remained. Flesh but not, the magic of self-petrification, stone but not quite. Trapped for eternity, immortal but immobile, yearning, always, for that which I can never have, unknown memorial to a dark and unrevealed deed.

My punishment has been long, but I have endured, and Mother has whispered that I will be repaid for my patience. Our Lady of Guadalupe has neither forgotten nor forgiven the transgression of my unholy lover; while his remains are long since moldered and lost, his soul still spins restlessly amid the heavy forest behind the church, yearning for freedom as I do, lonely and alone, helpless to warn or protect his ancestors.

Someday, I will not be so helpless.

Mother, may I . . . ?

Soon, niña.

THEY say that history repeats itself and that the seventh generation is a magical one.

Tonight the heat is unrelenting, the scant breeze that whispers through the crevices and halls of the cathedral no relief to the wilting villagers beyond its walls. What stirs the air above the rows of benches in the hours beyond midnight is neither Mother Nature nor magic, something, instead, more primal and deadly, the dirty taste of lust and pre-adultery as it slinks along the polished wood and ancient tiles, moves to caress a cross of gold and precious stones that has, since my death nearly two centuries before, remade itself in purity.

It will not be contaminated again.

Mother, may I . . . ?

Sí, niña.

Tonight, this one night only, you may.

Centuries unmoved, the silent release of an unknown alchemy of holy and unholy to at last work together—

—and petrified flesh melts away to become once again supple, joints, though bloodless and still earthen-cold, bend at last in response to my mental commands. I stretch not because it forces blood to dead muscles but because I finally can, reaching for the heavens I will never know. Dust and a thousand tiny stones fall in intricate patterns around me, artful testimony to my ageless patience as I push myself to my feet; I am awkward at first, gaining confidence only as my hands, the stain of sin still dark upon them, find the walls of my alcove and cling to them for support.

My descent is an odd mixture of awkwardness and grace, more like a skittish chameleon moving in fits and starts down the camouflaging gray walls of the bell tower. From five stories below, I can feel the emotions of a young woman, her reluctance and dismay at her lover-to-be's choice of trysting places, the battle of her convictions against the tide of passion his simple nearness elicits in her belly.

Like father, like son, six times removed.

But it ends here: there will be no seventh generation.

Tonight, I will again touch that spark.

Sounds echo through the cathedral's dome, soft footsteps, encouraging murmurs not yet consummated. Four stories, then three, then two, and now I am on the ground floor and easing inside, enjoying the sense of air slipping across my naked skin even though I know it is only temporary. For a long moment, I am awed by the beauty of this great building in which I have not set foot for nearly twenty decades. Then, across the expanse of the cavernous room, I see the reason for my resurrection: there, to the same hallowed spot behind the altar of Our Lady's chapel, the sleek and handsome ancestor of my ruthless beloved brings his future mistress, his future *victim.*

This time, Our Lady of Guadalupe will allow him neither.

Mother, may I . . . ?

Sí, niña. You may.

His thoughts are full of desire and his coming pleasure, with nothing to spare for the girl who so trustingly meets his eyes, no care for the havoc he inflicts upon her unsuspecting soul. His hands pull her to him and fumble for her clothes—

—while beneath my own dead but not dead fingers, a bench in the shadow-filled back corner overturns.

The sound makes them freeze and his hands drop to his sides; God forbid he should be caught not behind a hallowed altar in the village's cathedral, but with a peasant girl, a commoner without a drop of blue blood running through her Mexican-Indian veins. I run a languid fingertip along the edge of the upended bench, delighted at the power I feel in myself as the heavy piece of furniture slides across the floor as if it weighs no more than an ounce or two. The noise is horrendous in the nearly deserted church, escalating as it bounces from wall to wall—unmistakably the sign of an intruder, evidence that someone unseen watches what these two would do to defile this grand place of worship.

The scent of their lust turns to fear, sharp and intoxicating, fleeting to me because I cannot truly inhale. In a flurry of hushed words and feather-light footsteps, he sends the girl away—

"Wait outside, Chiquita. I will come for you when it is safe."

—and the silence returns, not quite complete to my sensitive hearing, as he stalks amid the polished pews like the great, dark cat to which I often compared him. His movements are fluid and smooth, fraught with danger and the fury of being interrupted; he will find the intruder and teach this person the error of interfering with his plans, of spoiling what would have been the first of many decadent meetings, the start of the eventual death and damnation of the girl.

He finds, instead, me.

We stare at each other. His gaze is disbelieving but curious, admirably free of fear. Mine is hungry for the sight of him, so much like the man six times removed whom I so desired. He is tall and lean, with fine black hair and marble-pale skin, the same depthless, oil-black eyes that I know can flame into sensuality at the merest of touches. To him I am a creature of mystery, a moving woman of stone worn practically smooth by time and heat in this savage tropical clime, a sculpture come to life without—he thinks—purpose.

I open my mouth, but no sound escapes.

Mother, may I . . . ?

No, niña.

Mother will not allow me to speak.

A pity.

I spring instead.

While it is not for me to tell him *why* he dies this night, mine still remains the power of justice, of a woman wronged long ago and granted one sweet moment of righteous revenge. There is no chance of escape for him, no hope for survival or rescue. My fingers are stone, my grasp as unbreakable as the one I learned so well from his long-dead ancestor.

So long to wait, and so short the moment of joy.

When my darkest deed is done, I tenderly strip the clothes from his cooling body and carry him up the stairs of the secret passageway, cradling him in my arms like the corpse of a lover freshly mourned. Though it will leave me dispossessed and exposed, his petrifying form takes my place in the alcove, settling comfortably into the unseen niche where for scores of years I waited for retribution. He is so beautiful there, with his arms and legs carefully arranged in the pose of infinite patience that he will soon find he needs.

I do not close his eyes before I leave.

THE children find my body in the morning, first staring in awe as they circle it, then singing songs to the strange stone statue that appeared out of nowhere and now sits in a pose of serenity on the edge of the village's water fountain, the one consecrated each Sunday morning by the priest so that the residents may bless themselves at their convenience with the water of God. Time has eroded what was once the sharp angles that evidenced my lust; now the curves of my breasts and the juncture of my thighs are rounded and soft and smooth, nearly featureless. To the unknowing eyes of the children and the priest they fetch, my form seems not naked but wrapped in a burial shroud of stone fabric. Only my palms are different: ever-outstretched in supplication, they remain inexplicably washed in a darker shade of gray.

It is a miracle, they say, a lost gift from God and Our Lady of Guadalupe, appearing out of nowhere. The priest nods his head in agreement and places me in the center of that same holy fountain, to sit and contemplate the passersby and to soak in the rays of the blazing Veracruz sun I was denied for such a long time.

But the village women look into my soulless gray eyes and they know.

They *know*.

Each morning at dawn they bring sweet-scented flowers and toss them into the holy water at my feet, then they kneel and pray to the Lady of the Lost to help them find those things that will be, as they were for me, eternally beyond their reach. I can hear their words and desires as whispers in my head, warm and deep and never-ending:

Mother, may I . . . ?

Mud

BRIAN MCNAUGHTON

I had spent two years in the trenches when a terrible truth was revealed to me: Jerry was merely the noisiest, most numerous and most vexatious tool of our real enemy, and that enemy was Mud.

In his proper state, a man walks upon solid ground, drinks pure water and breathes clean air. In the most improper state, into which we soldiers had been thrust, men crawled and fought and slept in the same foul substance they drank and breathed.

To call it by so plain a name can give you no idea of its capacity for mischief. It was no mere compound of earth and water like the honest mud of the countryside, but a complex organism of earth and water and blood and waste, seasoned with foul chemicals and thickened with the rotted flesh of men and beasts. This malign entity clutched us always in its soggy grip, seeping through our clothing, staining our bodies, flavoring our food, clogging our nostrils, stopping our mouths, fouling our weapons and ultimately claiming our lives.

I do not believe we created this being with our murderous war. I suspect we unwittingly freed it from a prison fashioned by far wiser men in the dim past, men who had most unwisely neglected to tell us what combination of words and actions, what volume of human corpses and human suffering was required to break the seals they had put on this Mud of primal chaos.

The war had nothing to do with some absurd quarrel among kings and ministers or some brainless tangle of treaties. No one understood why the war began or why it continued. No one could stop it. No one wanted it . . . except the Mud.

This revelation — so simple, really, so obvious — came to me one morning after an all-night barrage. Those of us who still could crawled from our dug-outs to see Jerry advancing through the mist. But were they in fact men? Their uniforms were not gray, their faces were not white. They were brown all over, brown as the ground they slogged through, brown as I was.

I looked about me. The formerly coherent lines and angles of the trench had been eroded, rounded . . . muddied. This amorphous mass concealed my absent comrades and fed upon them, gathering strength and size by a geometric progression. The surviving fools were all firing, hammering even more Huns into the Mud or falling into it themselves and being sucked down.

I wanted to explain my vision to Captain Bennett when he seized me by the shoulder and swore a blasphemous oath. "What are you playing at, sergeant?" he screamed in my Mud-clogged ear. "Shoot! For God's sake, man, shoot!"

One look at the crudely sculptured face of this brown Mud-man told me he would not understand. I gestured at the mound beside me: Wilkins, my feeder, who had tangled the ammunition belt when he sank. The captain retrieved the belt and fed muddy rounds into the gun. I fired and Fritz fell, a dozen, a hundred, two hundred. I couldn't miss them at this range. But why? Dead men made Mud.

The captain professed to believe that I had held my fire to lure as many of the enemy as possible toward my gun-position, and that my "steel nerves" had foiled their attack almost single-handedly. He later gave me a sealed message that, he said, contained my recommendation for a D.C.M., and he ordered me to convey it to the rear along with a small contingent of the wounded.

SUCH was my state of mind at this time that I suspected the message I carried might be an order to execute the bearer for having stumbled upon the truth behind the war. This may have been why I led my charges astray.

I believe, however, that I was beguiled by the unfamiliar song of a bird to investigate a sunken lane between flowering hedges, a lane of moist but solid earth that promised to lead to a dryer, cleaner place.

Surely neither reason would have consoled the two men who died, denied the treatment they might have received upon prompt delivery to a field hospital. But I don't regret their deaths, as we were able to bury them in the honest earth of a meadow. I thought they must have been grateful.

The bird continued to pipe its song as I recited the appropriate words over the shallow graves. I resisted an unseemly urge to cut short the ceremony and follow it. Its song was not unlike "La Folia," the weird folk-melody that bemused C.P.E. Bach, the elder Scarlatti, and so many other eighteenth-century musicians whose works I had played before I was thrown into the Mud, but it was not quite the same. As soon as was decently possible, I tried to whistle the tune and analyze the difference as we marched—more properly, as we hobbled along.

"That's a rum tune, Sergeant," Atkins muttered. "What is it?"

"That bird—," I began, but the bird had chosen to embarrass me by holding its peace. Atkins began to bleat a spirited version of "That's the Wrong Way to Tickle Mary," and the others joined in. I silently cursed them for scattering my concentration.

The lane led us to a medieval town of narrow lanes twisting between thick walls of stone, where nothing met our eyes that would have puzzled Scarlatti himself; although he too might have commented on the antiquity of his surroundings. The utter peace was seductive but disturbing. Without the cries of children and animals in the thickening dusk, without even the incessant, quarrelsome, Gallic jabber, with no smoke at any chimney nor light in any leaded window, the peace seemed less that of the civilian world than of the grave.

As an oppressed hush fell on the men's music-hall renditions, the bird sang again from a shadowed eve, but I was distracted by a new sound, an urgent clangor of human industry. At least two men were plying sledges against metal and stone with a vigor and rhythm reminiscent of the Nibelungs' workshop in Wagner's *Ring*.

The simile that came so readily to my mind may have been an omen, for no sooner had I thought of Wagner than I found myself face-to-face with a pack of Huns. They were a bigger and better-fed version of Jerry than one finds in the trenches nowadays, fitted with their new chamber-pot helmets, and with not a spot of the Mud on their loose, stormtrooper uniforms. I leveled my rifle and called on them to surrender, but I wadded myself into a doorway as I did so.

They seemed oddly *annoyed*, as if we were more of an irksome hindrance to their purpose than a dangerous enemy, but they were clever as cockroaches, and we were able to kill only three of them before they had vanished into previously unimagined nooks and crannies in the stone facades. For their part, they took down Williams, who had been blinded by a phosphorus-shell, and the stiff-legged Robertson, who had been guiding him.

I called on them once more to surrender, but was greeted by a snarling diatribe that outstripped my linguistic skills.

"What's the bugger on about?" I asked Collins, our scholar from Dublin, who crouched under a farm wagon directly opposite.

"Let them pass, he says, and they'll do the same for us, if we're foolish enough to go farther."

"Tell him that's not how war works," I said, but I delivered the message myself by loosing a round at an unsteady shadow where I had marked the voice, and was rewarded with a shrill cry of "Scheisse!"

I instantly regretted that, for Fritz marked my own position and opened up. I cringed against a stinging hail of stone splinters as bullets hammered the lintel. But my own men returned the fire—I believed there were no more than five on either side now—and Fritz soon forgot his special animus against me.

As in so many French towns, we had just turned a corner in a remote village and come upon a cathedral worthy of a capital city. It lay across an open square of hard-packed earth at the foot of the street, and it had apparently been the site of all that Wagnerian racket as the enemy looted artifacts or engaged in vandalism for its own sake. Guttural cries and sustained gunfire came from that direction as more of them emerged from the cathedral.

I believed we were goners then, but Collins, who had a better view of the square, called, "They're mad, Sergeant! They're after targeting their own men."

I thought at first this might have been a typical case of military confusion, but now the men in hiding returned the fire of those in the square, keeping up a lively dialogue all the while. We resumed firing, too, and the deadly crossfire soon brought that queer internal dispute to an end.

"Go away, Englishmen!" cried a voice from the square. "This is none of your concern."

"A peculiar attitude, surely," I remarked to Collins. "How many are there?"

"Three outside, an officer and two lads stripped to the waist."

"See if you can pick off the head Hun."

He missed, and the three vanished into the cathedral. Hugging the walls, we—only Collins, Liddell, Atkins and I now—descended to the square, where Fritz welcomed us with a burst of machine-gun fire. We found crowded shelter behind a stone trough. "Bloody hell, Sergeant, let's give it up!" Atkins said. "What's all this in aid of, then? Why are we even here?"

"Because God made us to share His everlasting happiness in Heaven, and because the King wants us to kill Huns. See if that lot were carrying anything useful."

Atkins may have thought my answer flippant, but it seemed true enough. The purpose of the war was clearer now that I could fight the enemy without making more Mud. It became dreadfully clear when, peeking out to survey piles of dirty laundry I had seen bandaging the base of the cathedral, I identified them as human bodies, men, women, priests in soutanes, even children that the beastly Alleymen had lined up and shot.

Atkins returned with five potato-mashers. One never knew about these things, but I doubted Jerry would have been carrying booby-trapped grenades. I hesitated only a moment before twisting the handle of one and leaping up to hurl it at the door where the machine gunner lurked.

"Sergeant!" Collins protested. "That's a bloody church!"

"Bloody, indeed," I said, ducking as the gunner stitched the top of our trough. "When—" My order was interrupted by the explosion, then by a renewed burst of machine-gun fire. I began again: "Take the rest of these and spread out to toss them when I begin firing."

The bird sang. I had come to see it as my good-luck charm, and I stood up to empty my clip through the door. I saw too late that the gunner and his helper squatted on one side on the portico. Fortunately for me, they were distracted by the sudden emergence of my men. I slapped in another clip and shot the gunner just before a well-thrown egg blew both men and their gun out to further defile their civilian victims.

"Now—" Incredibly, the idiot officer was firing at me with an automatic pistol from inside the church, a hopeless shot. Unable to see him, I fired in the hope of keeping him down as I ran forward and waved on my men. Both of them.

Crouching at the door of the church, we kept up a brisk exchange with the officer, who managed to bring Collins down with a shot through the lung before he announced his surrender. "I have no more ammunition," he said, tossing his boxy Mauser out the door and advancing as if to accept a medal. Atkins and I exchanged a look that had become common, the look of Englishmen confronted with the latest outrageous example of Hunnishness.

"I am Hauptmann Walther, Graf von der Hiedlerheim, a great-nephew of Queen Victoria and a graduate of Oxford. I salute your gallantry and determination, my former foes."

In a posh accent that must have recalled fond memories of sculling on the Isis to the sod, I replied: "I never expected to meet so grand a personage, my dear Graf, and can only regret that our acquaintance must be so brief. I am Sergeant Miller, great-grandson of Miller the gallows bird, and I must advise you that you should have surrendered *before* using the last of your ammunition to kill my men."

I then blew his head off.

"Beautifully put, Sergeant," Collins wheezed.

WE carried Collins inside the cathedral, where my hands began to shake so badly as I tried to undo his tunic that I stepped back and told Atkins to tend to him. He would have assumed my tremor was a common reaction to the skirmish, but it was inspired by terror. The blood from the Irishman's sucking chest wound had liquefied the caking of the fabric. The Mud had returned; it stained my hands, it seeped through my own stiff tunic when I urgently wiped them. Striding jerkily, I ventured deeper into the dark cathedral in search of any distraction as I tried hard not to scream.

Our grenades had made a fine mess of the place, blowing out most of the stained-glass windows, but one that was nearly intact gave me pause. It seemed less a depiction of a saint than of an ancient fertility goddess from the Levant, all brown breasts and bum, but wearing a pair of hairy black trousers. The image might have passed muster for decency if one didn't inspect it closely, but I did, and saw that the garment did little to conceal her swollen pudendum; it would have done even less had the labia not been black as the surrounding hair. Then I saw that what I was looking at were not trousers at all, but body hair, foresting her loins and creeping up her extraordinarily swollen belly to the point where a navel might have been. Her nether limbs were concealed by the curls as they spread out to merge with a foreground of black murk shot with brown eddies.

Venus Emerging from the Mud might have been an appropriate name for this nonesuch, but she was identified as Ste. Nigoureth. She held a misshapen flute between her prodigious breasts, but her hollowed cheeks suggested that she was sucking rather than blowing it. I doubted that Collins would be able to identify this saint, probably the goddess of a Gaulish tribe who had been grafted onto the local liturgy without papal sanction; nor could he have done much with the Latin inscription, if Latin it was, for it was remarkably deficient in vowels. I was distracted from my attempts to pronounce it by a sudden recurrence of that birdsong, shockingly loud, as if the bird were inside the cathedral. A fanciful man might have suspected that the music came directly from Ste. Nigoureth's instrument.

"He won't make it," Atkins said at my shoulder, making me jump, but I doubt he noticed as the window seized his attention. "Bloody hell! I knew her sister in Liverpool. You had to clap your hand over your mouth and try to finish fucking before you could start spewing."

I would have thought we had traveled a hundred miles behind the lines, to say nothing of a hundred years, but a map retrieved from the dead officer showed that the front was less than ten miles away. Even carrying Collins, we could leave at dawn and make the railhead at St. Azédarac, our original destination, by mid-morning. Our victory over Huns who had massacred the citizens of a peaceful village would deflect whatever criticism I might have faced for meandering through the countryside.

A prisoner would have been useful, though, to explain what Jerry thought he had been playing at. Why would he infiltrate a crack stormtrooper detachment behind our lines for no apparent purpose other than to murder children and loot a church? After we had supped on Jerry's barkers, along with bread and wine from the sacristy, and lit all the candles and coal-oil cressets we could find in a vain attempt to drive back the gloom of night, we inspected their work.

They had broken into a crypt beneath the main altar and all but unsealed a lead coffin whose lid was sculptured into what could have been a slimmer and more decorous version of Ste. Nigoureth. The resemblance didn't even occur to me until we had torn it open and found that it contained nothing but a replica, or perhaps even the original, of the queer flute pictured in the window.

"I know they ain't half-fond of music, but even for Fritz, this does beat all," Atkins breathed as I lifted the grotesque pipe and turned it over in my hands. "Is *that* what they wanted?"

A dual bulb at the bottom suggested a gourd, although I believed the instrument had been carved from a single piece of very heavy, black wood. Curving upward from this, a thick shaft was perforated with holes that seemed too large and awkwardly spaced for human fingers. These were ringed with gold, and the mouthpiece was of gold, too, but that couldn't account for the value the Huns had put upon it. The hole in the mouthpiece itself seemed too narrow to inject a sufficient volume of air to make music.

I was seized by an irrational urge to try playing it. Yet some of the unpleasantness of the image in the window clung to it, deterring me.

"Give us a tune, then, Sergeant," Atkins urged, noting my fascination. "None of your weepy dirges, either, a nice tootle of 'Pack Up Your Troubles.'"

"Have a go yourself."

He didn't hesitate. His cheeks puffed out and his face reddened as he tried to force air into the mouthpiece, but not one sound came out of the flute. Then he tore it from his mouth with a look of shock and loathing, and he would have dashed it to the floor if I hadn't caught it.

"Why, what—?"

"It *moved!*" He spat. "Bloody thing wriggled like a . . . like a snake."

I didn't believe this, but his horror was clearly unfeigned as I put it to my own mouth and, imitating the saint's technique, sucked on it. This produced such a sudden and unprecedented surge of euphoria that I thought the pipe must contain the still-active residue of an ancient drug. If I had been thinking clearly I would have put it aside instantly, but I could no longer think clearly. I felt exhilarated, as if some cosmic secret were coyly dancing to the dark fringe of my consciousness, about to unveil itself fully in the next instant. The aches drained from my muscles, my limbs shed their weariness, all the unutterable nastiness of the war faded to become merely a rumor of another man's dream.

I fingered the pipe to produce the notes of "La Folia" as best I could, even though I knew that was the wrong tune. Rather eerily, I heard the music, or thought I heard it, not from the pipe itself but from the black vault high over our heads. I suddenly recalled the notes the bird had sung; and when I attempted to reproduce them, I heard them ringing clearly, triumphantly through the cathedral. But once again, the music seemed not to emanate from the pipe I held, but at once from all the shadows of the ancient building.

"Good Lord," I said, reluctantly taking the flute from my mouth. "What was that?"

Atkins answered cryptically: "Rain. You've whistled up a wind, and no mistake, Sergeant."

I strode to the door and was driven back by a wet blast. The darkness outside was total, but it was obvious that the skies had opened. Even in the trenches, rain had always brought a clean smell, however brief, and I anticipated this with pleasure. But the wind that now howled through the vaults and rattled the remnants of the windows carried an odor more foul than any I had ever known.

I recognized it, though. In an undiluted and nearly unbearable concentration, it was the stench of Mud.

ALL night long the rain hammered down, the stench persisted. Our lamps and candles blew out, making the frequent lightning all the more jolting. I soon learned to avoid looking at the window depicting Ste. Nigoureth, her form seemingly twisted to a new and more disquieting posture by each flash, but indelible afterimages of the creature capered on malformed legs in all the shadows. Collins didn't help matters by muttering deliriously throughout the night of a black goat, although most of his ravings were spat and croaked in an unfamiliar tongue that might have been Gaelic. Whatever it was, it recalled most disturbingly the tangled consonants from the saint's window.

I didn't dare touch the pipe again. I didn't have to, for that damnable tune always seemed to hover just beneath the roar of the wind and rain. I felt that something terrible was going on around me, made all the more terrible because I couldn't say exactly what it was, and that I had somehow provoked it by piping the melody. Atkins didn't share my apprehension. He curled into a pew and snored through the night. I'm not sure that he had even heard the music of the flute, but I refrained from questioning him about it for fear of seeming mad. I suspected that I was indeed going mad. Why should a little rain and a foul smell and illusory music—the latter probably brought on by too much exposure to shellfire—so unman me, who had sometimes slept as soundly as Atkins through the very real dangers of a German barrage?

I had no answer, but I fought against sleep. Whenever I began to drop off, the music grew far clearer, it progressed through a series of insane variations to a chaos of tuneless piping, it heralded the sinuous approach of Ste. Nigoureth and her vile embrace. In my dreams I welcomed that embrace, and each time—more times than I had imagined possible, more times than I could bear, until the throbbing of pleasure progressed through increasing degrees of agony—I was woken by the pulsing of a seminal emission. The Mud extended its slimy domain over my loins until I began to fear that I was spending blood to feed it.

THE roar of the storm faded with the dawn, to be replaced by a rattle of gunfire in the distance that grew steadily more intense. I ran to the door. As nearly as I could tell, and I had a good ear for such things, Jerry was dealing a massive punch against a narrow section of the front, having omitted the customary warning of a barrage.

This seemed almost unimportant as I gazed around me in a prickling drizzle and saw that the Mud had followed me, found me, and was now laying siege to the cathedral. The bodies around the wall had sunk into it. The houses across the square seemed to be subsiding into it. The narrow street leading down to the square ran sluggishly with it. Atkins stumbled out to my cry, but his oath of disbelief was lost in a sound like the gods ripping up their blankets. Shells from our own batteries were passing overhead. A steady crump-crump-crump soon rolled toward us from the site of the attack.

Into a brief letup, he said, "I think Fritz is coming this way."

"Where else?"

I was spared making an explanation that would have sounded deranged, I'm sure, as our batteries opened up again. The captain had not returned with the flute, and so a large part of the German Army was coming to get it. The cost didn't matter. My night-terrors had suggested to me that it was a weapon of fearful virulence, a device for summoning the Mud and its guiding demon.

Before I could stop him, Atkins stepped into the square and immediately sank to his knees. His struggles to lift his feet only drove him down deeper. I was somehow able to wrench him free, but only after the Mud had claimed both his boots.

Two men could never have defended the cathedral; a speedy departure was in order. Armed with Jerry's hammers and pry bars, we smashed up the pews and whatever other wood came to hand for makeshift duckboards and stretched them across the Mud in a queasy line. We made a litter for Collins from the intricately carved panel of a confessional screen, overlarge and un-wieldy. The poor chap objected as vehemently to this as if we were trying to lay him on a hot gridiron, but we assumed he was lost in his delirium and tied him down. Once he was secured, I noted that the screen's carving bore a weird motif of goat horns and hoofs in a riot of fantastic foliage, and all of it fit somehow with Collins's ravings: ". . . it's more than a thousand children she has in the wood, you know, and the wood wouldn't be same as the wood that would the greenwood . . . the Wood at the World's End, Gram called it, lying astride this world and the world of the *sidhe*, where the Black Goat pipes . . ."

"This is going to be tricky," I told Atkins, but only knew what a damnable understatement that was when I had taken my first step onto the tilting boards with my arms awkwardly supporting Collins's litter behind me. We had got nearly halfway across when the wounded man redoubled his struggles, thrash-ing and bouncing as if determined to make us lose our slippery grip. He cried hoarsely that *she* was here, that *she* had come to get him, and when I looked over my shoulder I saw that he was craning his neck to stare, bulgy-eyed, at a bubbling eddy in the Mud beside him. "Chub, you bleeding bugger!" Atkins shouted, struggling to keep his balance. "Put a sock in it!"

Thus distracted, I lost my footing and fell to one knee. I threw a hand out to brace myself against the unsteady board, releasing my hold on the litter. Atkins stumbled at the same time, and it was all over for Collins. Litter and all, he slipped over the edge and vanished into the Mud as neatly and quickly as a man buried at sea. In a flash of recovered lucidity, he cursed us bitterly for having tied him down.

"No!" I screamed as Atkins flung himself flat and plunged both arms to the shoulders into the Mud.

"Give us a hand, sergeant! I've got—I think I've got—*good God, it's got me!*" Trembling on the unsteady planks, more like a shipwrecked sailor on a raft than a soldier on duckboards, I watched helplessly as Atkins disappeared. His legs scissored wildly in the air as he was upended and pulled down. I crawled forward on my belly to the point where thick bubbles rose and popped sluggishly. Having witnessed the fate of Atkins, I could no more have put my hand into the Mud than I could have put it in a cauldron of boiling oil, but I told myself that I must, and I was trying to screw up my courage when something broke the surface at a surprising distance from the boards. "Something," I say, because its contours had been so distorted by clinging Mud that I didn't recognize it as a human head until its clogged mouth opened and it gabbled, in a voice very like Collins's, "She's got me, Sergeant, you bastard, she's sucking me into her hairy—" And he was gone. Bubbles no longer broke the surface where Atkins had disappeared, but I at last forced myself to reach in with one arm while keeping a death-grip on the board. The Mud was unexpectedly warm, it slithered around my hand, and I told myself this was evidence that Atkins still struggled down there. Another distorted face rose, this one directly beneath mine, and I swear it was not the face of Atkins. The soldier from Liverpool was bald as an egg beneath his helmet, but this head flowed with long curls, or with Mud that clung to long curls. I recoiled in terror. The arm slung around my neck was bare and soft, but its grip was like iron as it dragged me down.

This wasn't Atkins, it wasn't even human, it could only be Ste. Nigoureth herself, but it felt like human bone and teeth that my fist smashed as I hammered it again and again until it gave up its grip and sank.

Mud

CROUCHING in the thinner Mud beyond the square, I drifted away from the war for a time. I seemed to drowse in a country garden where bees murmured, and I wondered why they should be so active in such wet weather. It took me an unconscionable amount of time to tumble to the fact that someone was shooting at me. Hastily taking cover in the mouth of an alley, I peered out to behold a sight that hadn't been seen at the front since the earliest days—Huns on horseback. They had called up their long-idle cavalry to exploit the breach and retrieve the hellish pipe, and now a cluster of them sat their horses on a low hill beyond the cathedral. Faced with the new lake of Mud before them, they seemed at a loss what to do next, though two or three had hit upon the pleasant diversion of trying to kill me.

But Jerry's murderous intentions seemed almost irrelevant when I looked up and saw the thing that entangled the spires of the cathedral. It was a cloud, I suppose, but it was far darker than the remaining mass of cloud that pressed low on the village. It roiled and folded upon itself, expanded and exfoliated in ways independent of the surrounding atmosphere. Lurid flashes illuminated it from within at odd moments, but I heard no thunder. I thought at first it must be pouring rain on the Mud, but I came to the uneasy conclusion that the Mud was popping and spurting upward from some inner force as it yearned to join the cloud. The more I stared at this anomaly, the more strange details I observed in its depths: eyes, tentacles, horns, random bits of human and bestial anatomy, none of them holding steady long enough to convince me that I wasn't using the cloud as a blank canvas for my fevered imagination. This vision was so alien, so menacing and so damnably real that I conceived an urgent desire to open fire on it. Only then did I discover that I had lost my rifle somewhere along the way. Without intending to, I had retained the pipe, however. I had no doubt that I had called up this thing. But if it could sit on a whole church full of crosses and ikons and holy water, how could I possibly lay it? The Archbishop of Canterbury might have offered helpful suggestions, or possibly Mr. Aleister Crowley, but neither of them was available.

All this while I had been tempted by a strong urge to put the pipe to my lips and play the tune it wanted. I could forget about the cloud, forget about the Huns and recapture the sweet euphoria I had known last night. I feared that this was surely the path to my destruction, and I impulsively tried smashing the pipe against the stone wall beside me, but it seemed indestructible. Worse, my efforts provoked a sudden, angry expansion of the cloud, a more frenzied eruption of the Mud. Jerry was up to something. No longer firing, the horsemen were shouting in unison—at me? No. A shift in the wind brought their peculiar cries to my ears, and it seemed they were chanting a variation of the saint's foul name: "Iä! Iä! Shub-Niggurath!" The flashes in the cloud began pulsing in time to this chant, displaying colors unknown to honest lightning.

I put the pipe to my lips. A hymn—but no hymn that came to mind, I knew, would be a match for the otherworldly power of the theme that even now the German horsemen were bellowing. All other melodies seemed to have been driven clean out of my head. I clutched the pipe until my fingers bled in an effort to keep it still. As cellist in a string quartet before the war, I had known a hundred melodies, a thousand, but none of them . . . and then I remembered the very last thing I had played before the Mud flowed over the world, the final theme of Bach's *Art of Fugue*. All his life he had used his work to praise God, but in that last work he had dropped the mask of Christian humility and taken all the credit with a flourish: I, Bach, a mortal man, did this. If there existed any antithesis to the power of Primal Chaos, it was to be found in the greatest musical mind of all time. I attempted the four simple notes. Once again I had no idea where the music came from, but it filled the air as if the stone walls of the village sang. The Mud cringed back toward the central lake, flowing around my feet so rapidly that I was hard put to keep my footing. Anticipating some spectacularly unpleasant effect, I backpedaled against the tide as hastily as I could, playing one part of the Bach fugue all the while. Oddest of all, I heard the other parts clearly, as if all Nature were joining me in an assault against the Unnatural.

Flashing and boiling all the while, the cloud condensed, darkened and pressed down more heavily on the cathedral. The solid stones of the edifice wavered and began to flow downward, as if it had been nothing but a structure of Mud. Towers lost their clean contours and toppled. Buttresses melted away, the roof collapsed, the great walls folded in upon themselves. Despite this monstrous addition, the lake didn't grow. In fact it shrank more and more rapidly as a vortex developed in the boiling Mud where the cathedral had fallen. Thinned to a pale mist, retaining nothing of its otherworldly imagery, the former cloud fell to the Mud and was absorbed.

I had forgotten the enemy. Understandably chagrined, they had left off posturing and chanting and were devoting their full attention to killing me. They very nearly succeeded.

THE Army believed that I had done something remarkable, since Jerry's attack had recoiled at the very point where I was found barely alive. According to the official version, my small detachment had defended the cathedral so determinedly that the Huns had vindictively shelled it into oblivion. I did nothing to correct this view, maintaining that my severe head wound had produced amnesia. No one mentioned the flute to me, and I suspect that Jerry managed to retrieve it, poor devil. The sudden collapse of his monstrous war machine, the famine and plague and anarchy that seized his homeland, suggested forces even more sinister than human incompetence and confusion. And now this Hitler chap—he does tend to rave on, doesn't he, even more rhapsodically than Kaiser Bill did, about blood and soil? We know what that combination can produce. I fear he may believe that Germany's last attempt to regress the human race to primal slime failed only because not enough blood was added to the mix.

As for the flute of Ste. Nigoureth . . .

Last night Jerry had the effrontery to interrupt a Mozart recital with his damned bombs. We musicians were sheltering in the underground with our audience when our guest artist, Herr Kreisler, said to me, "Did you notice that odd harmonic in the air-raid sirens? It sounded uncannily like "La Folia," didn't it? Except—" And here he raised his violin to demonstrate the melody he believed he had heard.

Much can be forgiven a wounded war hero, I have learned, but assaulting a world-famous violinist and smashing his Stradivarius underfoot may be a bit over the mark. I suspect that my musical career has suffered an irreparable reversal.

Shaped Stones

Nina Kiriki Hoffman

Lexa and Basil clutched the back of Teru's shirt. Teru spread his arms, trying to hide his younger brother and sister from the man who stood before him in the alley.

How could the stranger see through night's darkness to the three children hiding between overflowing ash cans? Teru tried to think himself and his sister and brother into rats. Red-eyed rats, small, squeaking, of no interest to anyone, better left alone. Don't come any closer; we have typhus, smallpox, killer influenza like the one just after the Great War. You're safer staying away from us.

For a moment the man's head turned back toward Broadway. Long, elegant cars purred past, the latest 1932 models; some stopped to let theater-bound patrons climb out of the backseats—women in velvet or silk dresses, jewels, ostrich plumes curling across the fronts of their cloche hats, some wearing fringed scarves around their elbows or short jackets trimmed with black and white monkey fur, men in tuxedos or evening jackets and top hats.

Theatergoers on their way to view dreams and fantasies hadn't proved any more likely to drop pennies into outstretched palms than people in other parts of the city. Those the Depression hadn't touched didn't want to be reminded of what it had done to others. Teru had made Lexa and Basil wash, and had stolen two handfuls of incense smoke from morning Mass to give them a scent other than their own. It hadn't helped.

The children were invisible to rich strangers; but this man could see them.

Rats, thought Teru. Small nothings, hungry bellies, gnawing teeth; we may bite you. Turn away.

"I hear your hunger," the stranger said in a deep voice. Marquee light gilded the short stubble on top of his head, edged his dark jacket in glow.

Squeak, squeak, scree!

"Come with me. I'll buy you supper."

Lexa tugged on Teru's shirt. They had shared moldy heels of bread for breakfast, hours and hours ago. He reached back, trying to squeeze her hand. She had to be quiet. A stranger with a promise: What was more dangerous than that?

The man took another step toward them, and shadows drew him in. He squatted in front of Teru. "How long since you've had a real meal?" He sniffed, grimaced, smiled. "Come. I won't hurt you. I have something to ask, a future to offer."

Basil tugged at Teru's shirt. Teru heard his little brother's stomach grumble. They had been on the street for three months, since Mama died and they were thrown out of their last apartment, the smallest one, one room, and a coffee can for a toilet.

Some nights they hid in doorways or subway stations. Sometimes they sheltered under statues; Teru had touched the stone and bronze faces of angels and war heroes, Balto the hero dog statue in Central Park, busts of famous men who had done things he didn't know, the marble lions crouched above the library steps, but their expressions never changed.

At least they didn't turn away.

When the children's mother was still well, and they walked the streets on Sundays, she had pointed out the stone faces that peered down from above

160

windows, saints and stranger people on churchfronts, the creatures who hid behind waters in fountains. "The city watches," she had said.

Sometimes the children joined others who leaned over steam grates, heating their fronts and freezing their backs. They stood in breadlines, and sheltered in missions some nights when it was very cold. Teru had never found the perfect hiding place, even though he had picturecasting to help.

Some days all they could find to eat were dandelion greens in Central Park. Yesterday one of the apple sellers, a woman with a sad, thin face, had given them a bruised apple. That was a good day.

Teru had no idea what to do next. He used to try to plan out a whole day, but lately his outlook had shrunk to hours, sometimes even minutes. He had trouble thinking, more trouble picturecasting.

Rats weren't working. He tried to cast something simpler. We are just shadows. Just pictures inside your eyelids. We're not really here. Pass on, pass on. Who needs to talk to shadows?

Again the stranger turned his head away. A moment later he looked back. "You are skilled," he murmured. "All the better, little brother. Come." The man reached out and took Teru's hand. His touch sent prickles, needles of warm and cold, skittering from Teru's hand up his arm and all through him, but he couldn't pull away.

"I won't hurt you," the man said. "Not unless you ask me to."

THE waitress gave them a table by the window. Teru, Basil, and Lexa sat on one side of the table, and the stranger sat on the other. The stranger's hair was close-cropped and silver, and his long, thin face had deep crevices around the mouth and across the forehead. His eyes were pale. He wore a big dark jacket that wasn't like any evening wear Teru had seen.

He smiled. His smile was more scary than comforting.

The waitress brought them tall glasses of water. Teru gulped some. So clean, and the glass was clean, too. His hands left smears on it, though, even though he had washed them early that morning.

The stranger ordered them beef stew and bread. Just thinking about such food made Teru's mouth wet. Bread came first, soft, thick, light-crusted slices, and a little bowl with butter in it. He made sure Basil and Lexa got most of it, but he kept a slice of bread for himself. He needed strength to take care of them.

They ate fast. Things got taken away if you didn't.

"You'll make yourself ill," the stranger said.

"We want this kind of sick," said Teru. What if they never got another meal? Better get as much as they could out of this one.

"Work for me and you'll never be hungry again."

"Work? You got a job for me, mister?" Teru sat up straighter. He was almost fourteen, but people with jobs to offer never looked twice at him when there were thousands of men and boys older, stronger, more skilled than he standing in line for every opening that came up. Men with wives and children. Boys who'd finished school before the world crashed.

"Oh, yes," said the man. "I've been looking for a boy like you for a long, long time."

The waitress came and put their stew in front of them. Teru glanced at Lexa and Basil. They watched the man across the table, their eyes dark. They had heard offers from strange men before. In the worst cases, Teru had cast the children's images ten feet away and slipped them out while the men who had offered pursued the shadows. Basil gripped Teru's shirt under the table. *We're ready to run*, he signaled.

Not with stew in front of them, Teru thought, and the man the width of the table away. He picked up his spoon. Lexa and Basil followed suit.

Teru thought of the thin, clear, lukewarm broth of the soup kitchens. Some days they only got a cup of that, little better than warm water.

He took a bite of beef stew. It was the best thing he'd ever tasted. He wolfed it, racing Lexa and Basil to get it all inside.

"Slow down," said the stranger, but it was too late; they had finished. Lexa lifted her bowl and licked it. Teru decided not to tell her to stop. How often did they need manners these days?

Teru's stomach felt uncomfortably full, but he could still taste the wonderful stew. For a minute he just sat, contented to be inside where it was warm, his brother and sister beside him, all of them with full stomachs. He would like it if the rest of his life could be like this.

He stared across the table at the stranger. "What kind of job you got, mister?" he asked. Maybe he should say yes to one of those jobs he always ran from. Wasn't this better than freezing and starving?

"I need an apprentice," the man said.

"What kind of business you in, mister?" If he was in a trade, Teru thought, anything might happen! The stranger could teach Teru, and he'd have to feed him while he taught him. Teru was an expert at making food for one stretch enough for three, so he could take care of the others. Once Teru learned a trade, maybe he'd be able to work.

Basil was eleven; Lexa ten. Maybe they could learn the trade, too. Teru would teach them everything he could. He had tried to teach them picture-casting, but neither of them had the knack.

"This is my business," said the stranger. He held his glass between his hands and stared down at the water. A moment later, he tipped the glass over. Ice spilled from it.

Basil pinched Teru's thigh under the table. *Let's run. Right now.*

Teru thought of his mother lying on a pallet on the floor of their last apartment, shivering, so thin from starving herself for their sakes that her bones poked up almost through the skin of her knuckles. He had cast pictures for her then.

She had talked in her faded voice about the farm in Edmunds, North Dakota, where she grew up, of the rich years during the War, of the barn and the farmhouse, three generations old; the horses, cows, chickens, the dogs, barn cats, and even the mice in the hayloft; the wheat and hay fields, the breakfasts piled high as heaven and the stove blazing hot on winter mornings. How she and her mother had baked! Bread, cakes, cookies, pies with apples right off the tree. How they had eaten! Milk, cream, butter from the cows, eggs from the chickens, potatoes and peas from the garden. The farm was all of the world his mother had known before their father had charmed her into coming away with him.

Teru had listened hard to his mother's memories, pulled up the pictures, and cast them around her so that she died thinking she had gotten home somehow.

Teru reached across the table and closed his hand around some ice. It seared his palm before it melted. If he could cast better, maybe he would have got the heat, too, not just the picture of heat. If Mama had stayed warm, maybe she'd have lasted until spring or even longer.

If Teru could learn to cast heat, Basil and Lexa would never be cold again. Just let him learn to be a stove. If he could share heat with other tramps, they'd share food with his family, surely.

He opened his hand and stared at the damp slick across his palm. Then he glanced up through his eyelashes at the stranger, afraid to show how much he wanted this.

"I'll feed you like this all the time," the man said.

"All three of us?" asked Teru.

The man studied Basil and Lexa. Then he stared into Teru's eyes. His smile started at the corners of his mouth, a faint upward quirk. The corners lifted, pushing up the brackets beside his mouth. He grinned; his pale eyes lost some of their ice. "You have a warm heart, just the kind I need. Yes. I'll see that you and the other two are free from want as long as you remain my apprentice."

"Show us," Teru whispered. "Show us you can pay for this."

The stranger's wallet was fat with paper money, but he seemed to understand that Teru was asking for more evidence. He paid for the food, then led the children out into the street, where he hailed a cab. It was the first time inside a car for the three of them. Lexa stroked the leather seat cushion.

The cab drove a long way, through parts of the city Teru had never seen. As they went farther and farther from the children's usual haunts, Teru's muscles tightened. What if they had to run? They wouldn't know which direction. They would have to learn all over again the architecture of alleys, which ash cans held sustenance and which might offer other treasure, which other wanderers were dangerous and which were not, where was safe to hide and where belonged to someone else who had nothing.

The stranger promised food and a future.

Teru held Lexa in his lap, his arm around her waist. He watched the way their breaths misted the windows, obscuring the cold hard world beyond. The stranger's coat smelled richly of damp wool. Basil leaned against Teru's side and stared around him and Lexa at the stranger.

They were warm and full for the first time in an age.

The cab finally stopped in front of a tall, gloomy mansion with a dome rising from its center and square towers at the edges. Ornate stonework with the inset faces of wild men and women framed the windows and the front door. Smoke wreathed the upper reaches of the towers. Teru felt as though something up there watched him. Lexa and Basil must have felt it, too. They clutched at his hands.

The stranger paid the cabdriver and led the children toward the entrance, up a broad stone staircase to a short portico with twisty stone columns supporting an arched roof, and then to the front door, a huge slab of wood with twelve scenes carved in its panels, fearsome animals and people. The man tapped the door and it opened inward. He smiled at the children. "Please . . . come in."

Basil touched the horns of a goat with a fish tail. Lexa hung back. "Teru?" she whispered. Teru hesitated for a moment, then took her hand and stepped over the threshold into the front hall.

Black-and-white checkerboard marble floored the hall. The ceiling was almost as far above them as the ceiling in Grand Central Terminal. Wide white staircases led up and away; light from a hundred small bulbs fell through the crystal lusters of a waterfall of chandelier to split and shatter in icy brilliance on the hard floor below.

"I can feed you well enough, even if this Depression lasts another twenty years," said the stranger.

Slowly Teru began to believe he and the others would be all right. This man certainly had the money to give them everything they needed. Would he keep a promise, though?

"Follow me." The stranger led them to the left, down the wide hall past dark feather-leaved palm trees in golden pots, past stone and wooden statues of gods and demons in the curlicued dress of other times, other countries, carrying the weapons of other wars, to a door that led into one of the towers.

They climbed stairs, up and up until Teru thought they must be halfway to the sky.

Finally they came to the top of the staircase. A black door led from the small landing. The man waved his hand in front of the door, writing something in the air. In the silence of their standing still, it struck Teru that this house was dead quiet inside, and smelled of nothing; he wondered if anyone else lived here. Who did the housekeeping?

The stranger muttered three words under his breath and the door opened. A strange smell rode the air out of the room beyond, cold and cinnamon and decay, a hint of incense and tobacco smoke. "Come in," said the man.

Bookshelves walled the room on two sides, crowded with old volumes in many sizes. A round table stood in the center, with a black cloth over it, and various odd things on top. Against the far wall, jars with contents suspended in cloudy liquid stood on shelves, and canisters, boxes, jewel-colored glass bottles mingled with them. The fourth wall was covered by a curtain.

"This is my study," said the man. "This is where we will work. Well?"

He looked down at Teru.

Teru stared back.

"You must decide," the man said. "Will you be my apprentice, bind yourself to me and promise to learn what I teach, give what I ask, follow my instructions?"

Teru glanced left to Lexa, right to Basil. Neither looked at him. They both stared up at the stranger.

Teru waited a moment, listening. None of their stomachs growled.

He loved his brother and sister with all his heart. He was so tired of trying to keep them alive all by himself.

"You promise to take care of my brother and sister as long as I work for you so they won't feel hunger or cold or shame? You promise you won't ask me for more than I can manage?"

"I do," said the man.

"Then I'll do it," Teru said.

The man pulled a small, slender knife from a sheath at his belt and touched its point to his palm, leaving a streak of blood in its wake. He held the knife toward Teru.

Teru shivered and tugged his right hand loose from Basil's grip, held it out. The knife was so sharp he felt the cut only as a brief flash of cold. Then the stranger pressed their palms together. "Blood to blood we make this bond," said the stranger, "man and master, to the benefit of both."

.

"MAKE yourselves at home," the man said, gesturing toward the second-floor hallway, and three doors opened at once. The rooms beyond looked strange and sumptuous. Silk covered the walls, never mind the slubs and frayed places where the fibers had bunched up or pulled apart due to age. Ornately decorated furniture crouched on patterned carpets. Each room had its own suite of furniture, carved differently from the sets in the other rooms.

Their last three apartments could have fit into any one of these rooms.

Lexa tugged Teru into the first room, where the walls were bamboo-leaf green and the legs of the bed, desk, chairs, and wardrobe ended in dragon claws clutching colored crystal spheres. She crouched to stare at a green globe in a table leg. Basil walked slowly to the bed, patted its quilted cover. Dust puffed up, fragrant with long-vanished flowers, ghosts of old perfume.

"I didn't have time to prepare," said the stranger. "I didn't know I would find you today."

If there were windows at all, Teru thought, they must be behind the tall, dusty, wine-red velvet drapes that ran from soaring ceiling to floor.

Teru glanced up. The light fixture was close to the ceiling, so high that the room looked dim down where he and his brother and sister were. The air wasn't very warm, but it wasn't wet and freezing. This was much better than a night in a doorway, or in a cardboard shack in a hoovertown.

"Come," said the man.

They followed him through the other rooms, one honey and amber with lion-pawed furniture, and the other lilac and lavender, with spiderwebs embroidered on the bedspread and tatted into the lace curtains.

The stranger showed them where the bathroom was, down the hall. The linen closet was full of old towels and sheets in faded colors, once fine, now dusty but not dirty. The stranger turned on the faucet in the sink. The water ran rusty at first. He laughed. "Strange how the world moves around one when one's not looking," he said, then sobered. "Tonight, I don't want you venturing anywhere but from your rooms to this one. I'll come to fetch you in the morning. Do you understand?"

The children nodded.

"You don't know what you'll meet in my halls if you go where you're not supposed to," he said.

"Please, sir," Basil said.

The stranger smiled. "So you *can* speak. Yes, little man?"

"What are we to call you?"

"How remiss of me. Names! I have no idea what yours are. I am Dominic Cross. You may call me Master Cross. Who are you?"

"Basil. Basil Odessa."

Cross turned to Lexa. "And you, child?"

She stared at the floor. "Lexa," she whispered.

"Apprentice? What is your name?"

"Teru Odessa."

"Curious names," said Cross.

"Our father named us," Basil said. "Mama said he named us to remind him of where he came from."

Cross studied Basil. "Where did he come from?"

"We don't know," said Basil.

Teru said, "He disappeared when we were small."

Cross stared at Teru until Teru felt faint and dizzy. The cut on his hand throbbed.

"Rest," said Cross. "I'll see you all in the morning."

Teru made them wash their hands and faces. They slept curled together under the quilt in the green room, the room with the dragon claws and crystal balls.

"What are we eating?" asked Lexa. She lifted a spoonful of brown glop from her bowl, let it drop back into the main mass.

168

"Put some sugar on it," said Cross, passing her a sugar bowl. He sat at the head of the table and watched the children eat, taking nothing himself. Warm rolls wrapped in a napkin in a basket; plates of crisp bacon, scrambled eggs, buttered toast; a saucer with a stick of butter on it; pots of jam; thick mugs full of hot coffee, with cream and sugar in crockery pots. And the gruel, over which Lexa poured precious brown sugar until it suited her. Unbelievable riches. It all smelled wonderful to Teru. Where had it come from? Who had cooked it? Cross himself?

Basil finished his brown glop. He glanced sideways at Cross, waiting for permission to dive into more food.

"Eat as much as you want," Cross said, smiling at them. There was nothing of kindness or comfort in his smile.

They ate themselves sick.

After breakfast, Cross sent Basil and Lexa out to find a school. "I believe there is a grade school three blocks south of here," he said. "Memorize my address. Register yourselves. Take yourselves away for the day. Teru and I have work to do." He pushed the younger children outside and locked the front door.

"But—" Teru said.

"Now, now. It's a fine day. They won't be cold."

"They'll be hungry and ashamed," Teru said.

Cross's frown was frightening. His eyes filled with cold fire. Teru stiffened his spine and stared at his master. Inside, he shook with sick fear. But it would be better to find out now whether Cross would act with honor.

Muttering, Cross went to the door and slammed it open. "Children!" he called. Lexa and Basil were halfway down the block.

For a moment Teru saw them clearly: ragged, skinny, dirty despite their morning wash in the sink, their hair greasy and brittle, their eyes old. His heart hurt. He had done everything he could for them: not enough.

That had changed. They had all slept dry and had breakfast. Life was better now.

Basil and Lexa stared at Cross, their faces troubled, but after a moment, they returned.

Cross sighed. "You will all bathe," he said. "I'll find you something to wear. Then we will go shopping."

That morning, the children and Cross went to department stores in search of new, serviceable, sturdy clothes. They collected so many packages they had to take a cab back to the mansion. Teru watched carefully and saw that Cross did not care what became of his money. There seemed to be no end to it; he bought whatever Teru asked him for, and more. If Teru asked for one pair of wool socks for each of them, Cross bought three apiece. "It'll save me having to take you shopping again for a good long while," Cross explained.

Teru decided not to tell his master that children, when properly fed, grew out of things. The oath that bound them was tangible now (Teru hugged a packet to his chest: undershirts). Cross would honor it again, wouldn't he?

After they dropped the packages at the mansion and the children changed into their new clothes, Cross walked them to the public school. It was closed. The teachers hadn't been paid in two years. Cross found a private school that was still open and registered Lexa and Basil there himself.

That afternoon, he began to instruct Teru.

TERU had many aptitudes. By suppertime he could make objects the size of teacups float through the air, and he could summon fire from his fingertips.

After they ate supper—the children ate, Cross did not, and there was still no sign of a cook or any other servant—and went up to their bedroom, Teru tried to teach Basil and Lexa what he had learned that day.

Neither could master the simplest thing Cross had taught Teru.

They were happy with their new school, though, and their new shoes that fit without pinching and kept the cold away from their toes, their new jackets, warm and fine. Their underclothes were so soft and clean and fleecy they could scarcely believe it. They showed Teru their schoolbooks, and he sat with them, a pleasant weight of food in his stomach, listening to their delight and feeling warm and comfortable. So what if the children never learned any of Teru's new skills? They were as happy as they'd ever been in their lives.

Days passed. Teru studied and learned; Basil and Lexa studied and learned; good food erased the shadows under their eyes, filled out their cheeks and their spirits.

Sometimes Teru watched the others sleep. He stroked Lexa's hair, felt its new strength, touched Basil's cheek and felt its new clean softness. He listened to their calm, sleeping breaths in the dark room. Though the house was full of strange things seen and unseen, they slept untroubled. No more night terrors. No more empty bellies.

Six months into Teru's apprenticeship, Cross took him behind the curtain in the tower study.

"This is where we do our large work," said Cross.

There was a space here Teru had never even suspected. He had thought the study filled the tower from wall to wall, but here was another room, half again as wide across, its floor black as a cave within a cave, its walls curved and stony. Never a breath of air had escaped this still space to flutter the curtain and hint that it was here. Chills flinched across Teru's back. Something here prickled the nape of his neck and made his face tingle.

"Tonight the dark of the moon comes, and we have large work to do, apprentice," Cross said.

"What kind of work?"

The pale irises of Cross's eyes kindled with bent light. "An opportunity for which I have waited a long time." He stroked a hand across Teru's hair, as one might stroke a dog's head. "I have a few preparations yet to make."

Cross spent that day in a laboratory in the basement, where he had glass-blowing equipment. He did not let Teru watch him work.

Teru drifted through the ground floor of the mansion, entering the library only long enough to finger the gilt-lettered spines of books before his restless feet carried him elsewhere. The kitchen ghost was known to him now, and the big smudge-brown cat who slept most of the day in the front room where diamond windowpanes let in rainbow-stained light. Cross had introduced him to some of the old gods embodied in Oriental sculptures in the front parlor and along the halls, but the sprites and two of the other ghosts who haunted the house remained more elusive. Sometimes they resorted to pranks when displeased. Teru and the others still avoided the third floor, where a bogey lived.

In front of the fireplace in the music room, the auto-chessboard stood on a small table, and as Teru made circuits of the downstairs rooms, he would stop and move a white piece, watch as the board moved a black piece, then wander around before making his next move.

He felt energy pulsing from the workroom below, chill, powerful, seductive, an invitation that spoke to someone or something not himself. Who was Cross talking to? When would he teach Teru the same conversation? What did he give, what receive? In every spell, every rite, every work, there was a transaction, an exchange of some sort. Having tasted some of these exchanges, Teru hungered to learn them all.

The feel of this work prickled Teru's skin with ice. What if what Cross was doing was dangerous? What if he planned to hurt one of the children? Teru went to the kitchen and found a paring knife in a drawer. He made a sheath for it from cardboard and tucked it into his pocket.

Basil and Lexa came home at three o'clock. Usually there was a snack after school, apples or gingerbread or cups of soup set out on the dining-room table. Today they found nothing. The three children went to the kitchen. Teru opened cupboards. Some were empty. Others held dusty dishes, pans, pots. The icebox didn't even have ice in it, let alone food of any sort. Teru checked the pantry shelves. Nothing.

Where did food come from in this household? Who prepared it? In all the lessons Teru had learned so far, there had been nothing about food.

Cross came up from the basement, sweaty and soot-streaked, and found the children in the kitchen. "Oh," he said. "I lost track of time." He moved one hand inside the other, as though he were typing on his palm. "Go into the dining room, children."

There they found thick, heavily frosted slices of rich chocolate cake, and juicy oranges cut into quarters. "Thank you!" Lexa cried, and Basil echoed her before plunging a fork into the cake. Teru lifted a section of orange and touched his tongue to the bright, acid flesh. More than anything he wanted to learn Cross's spell for summoning food. With a talent like that, he could live well the rest of his life. He studied his master, who sat at the head of the table and smiled.

Or, Teru thought, if he never needed to eat, he'd have even less to worry about. But summoning food would be better. Then he could feed Lexa and Basil. Teru bit the orange, and juice spurted into his mouth. Someday he would know everything.

"For supper tonight I want you to dress in the best clothes you have," Cross told Basil and Lexa. "You remember: the last ones we bought. The blue velvet dress for you, Lexa, and the dark blue suit for you, Basil."

"What about Teru?" Basil asked. "Doesn't he have to dress up, too?"

"Certainly," said Cross. He studied Teru. "Wear the black suit, apprentice."

Were they all going out? Where would the master take them, and why? He never made spontaneous gestures. Teru had had to prompt him to let Basil and Lexa use the mansion's library, had had to ask him if they could have after-school snacks and pocket money. Cross always agreed without argument, but he never thought of anything on his own.

"Are we going to the theater?" Lexa asked. She bounced up and down.

"Can we go to the circus?" asked Basil.

"Not tonight." Cross wiped soot off his face. "Tomorrow, if you still want to."

As the children dressed for supper in the dragon room, Cross knocked on the door and came in. He brushed Lexa's hair himself, tied a velvet band around her head so a large bow lay at the top. He brushed Basil's hair as well, confusing them all. "There," he said. "You look fine." He patted the boy's cheek.

Then he gazed at his apprentice.

Teru glanced at his own image in the mirror and thought he looked nothing like all the fancy people who had trooped to the Broadway shows. His face was pale from living indoors all day; his dark hair stuck up in a cowlick at the crown of his head; and the black suit, bought in a hurry and only because Cross had instructed him to buy it, was a size too large.

Teru's eyes met his master's in the mirror. For a moment their gazes locked. Teru's eyes dropped first. He stared at the silver thread of scar in his palm. It itched tonight.

They went down to supper.

After supper, Cross led them to the tower.

"We got all dressed up to walk around in the house?" Lexa asked, disappointed. She picked at a small soup spot on her velvet dress.

Cross smiled at her, one of his wider smiles, self-satisfied and almost friendly. "Don't worry," he said. "I'll show you something new."

They climbed the stairs to the study at the top. Again Cross used ritual to unlock the door; he never left it unlocked, never taught Teru the unlocking words, never left Teru alone inside. Teru watched, every time. He had memorized more than half of it.

Tonight when they entered the room, the curtain was drawn back. Candles blazed in stands all around the room, and the air smelled of burning leaves. Lexa wandered to where the black floor of the secret space began. "Pictures," she said.

Teru closed his hand around the knife, which he had put in his suit pocket when he changed. Ice prickled him again. Why were the children here? Cross never let the children watch them work.

"Don't step there yet." Cross lit a black candle from one of the others and brought it over. Teru and Basil followed him. The floor was scrawled with intersecting white chalk circles, concentric rings, and letters and symbols from arcane alphabets. Teru recognized three of the symbols from his studies, but he had never seen them combined like this before. Gusts and eddies of power flashed through the room, neither warm nor cold: neutral. Waiting.

"What's that?" Basil pointed to something in the center of a small circle. Light glanced off its surface. Something glassy, about the size of a large man's fist.

"That's what I made today, in preparation for tonight. Don't touch anything until I tell you to."

"What's tonight?" asked Lexa.

"Tonight we're doing big things." Cross smiled and smiled. "But they won't take long." He leaned over and picked up Lexa. She looked puzzled. "You stand here," he said, setting her in a small circle. "Don't move outside that circle, all right? Not even your toe. Otherwise it could be dangerous."

"Dangerous?" she asked.

"These circles will protect you. The bogey might come up to see what we're doing, but he can't get into the circles." Cross lifted Basil into a circle beside Lexa's. The glass thing lay in a smaller circle near their feet. "Don't step out."

"Master," Teru said. "What are you doing?" He stared at the symbols, trying to read the ones he didn't know yet, his hand tight around the knife handle, fear flooding him: Cross had already begun the work. Teru did not know how to stop it.

"Strengthening my promise to you," said Cross. "All the lines come together tonight, apprentice, and the omens are good. We will do great work. Tonight I will ensure that your sister and brother are safe, warm, and well-fed for the rest of their lives, even if you should decide not to be my apprentice any longer. In return, I will ask only one thing from you, something in your power to give." Cross came to Teru, lifted him, and set him in a circle across the room from Basil and Lexa before Teru could even pull the knife out of his pocket, let alone unsheathe it. He knew his master was strong, but this effortless lifting shocked him. "Stay here. It won't take long. I have done all the preliminary rituals and summonings."

Teru stood, shivering, knowing that to scuff even the littlest part of the chalk line on the floor might open the door to danger. He ran Cross's words through his mind again. Basil and Lexa, safe, well-fed, warm. Cross hadn't lied to him yet. But he hadn't given him any whole truths yet either.

Cross lit incense in a brazier and set it carefully in a circle between them, then stepped into his own circle halfway round from the others. He knelt to write more symbols on the floor.

Wind whirled around the room, ruffling their hair and clothes. With each symbol Cross chalked, the wind rose higher.

"Teru," Lexa wailed, hugging herself.

"Don't move," he called to her. He had seen Cross conjure creatures before, keeping them captive only with chalk, a fragile cage, but strong enough. Cross had warned him repeatedly about the horrible things that could happen if any of the lines were breached. "Don't even reach across the lines, Lex. Just wait."

"I'm scared," she said.

She was scared, and Teru was terrified. What was his master doing? What did he want? Too late to stop it now. Teru stared at Basil. Wind flapped Basil's pant cuffs. His dark eyes were wide in his pale, frightened face. Teru wanted to hug him. Chalk cut them off from each other. Fear ran like blood through Teru's veins.

Cross spoke, his voice lightless, precise, loud. The words sounded strange. Each grew icier. Then he spoke one loud word like a bell. Lightning crackled across the ceiling, and thunder boomed.

A huge stone-colored face emerged from the ceiling. It looked more human than anything else, but its eyes were pale blanks, its skin was gray and grainy, and it had pointed white teeth. "What is your wish?" it asked in a deep, musical voice.

Lexa opened her mouth. No sound came out. Basil hugged himself and closed his eyes. Teru shivered. His hands clenched into tight fists. What price would this work ask?

"Immortality," Cross said. "Eternal safety for these children, as we have discussed." He pointed to Lexa and Basil. "Eternal thirst for knowledge for my apprentice, as we have discussed." He pointed to Teru.

Eternal safety for the children? Eternal safety: this work wouldn't cost the children anything. It would give them what he hadn't been able to give. Teru sucked in breath, tasted electricity, breathed out terror. The children would be safe. Immortality? Teru didn't care whether Cross lived forever. Eternal thirst for knowledge? Teru already had that, he thought. How big a change could it be?

"What do you offer in return?"

"This child's innocent heart, freely given." Cross pointed to Teru.

What?

The face turned its blind eyes to Teru. "Do you offer that?" it asked.

"What?" Teru gasped.

"It's no more than you can manage," said Cross. "And it will make the children safe forever."

Teru shivered and shivered in the fey wind that swept around the study.

"Child," said the stone face, gently.

Teru looked at his brother and sister. Basil shook his head no, and Lexa was crying. He wanted to comfort them, but the chalk stopped him. He stared at them, saw how fine they looked now that they were fed and clothed and warm. They had nothing of which to be ashamed. Lexa cried now, but if she could be safe forever—heat bloomed in his chest. He could buy that for her.

"Don't do it," Basil called, his words faint in the cold wind.

But it was all Teru wanted. The children, safe forever. After that, what would he need a heart for? He could stop carrying the weight of responsibility his mother had left him months before she died.

"I do," he said to the face. "I offer you my heart." Its blank white eyes warmed to peach for an instant; its mouth smiled. Then it retreated back into the ceiling.

Was that it?

The wind picked up, and lightning danced and flickered from thing to thing in the room, not respecting boundaries or lines at all. Bolts crackled down and touched Basil and Lexa in the same moment; then a bolt struck the glass thing at their feet. The children vanished.

Teru screamed and tried to lunge forward, but invisible walls caged him where he stood. He beat against them. He stood in a tube. The chalk cage: it held him in; it wasn't holding something else out. "Master!" he cried. The children! What had happened to the children? Was death eternal safety? Had his master totally betrayed him? Rage and terror surged through him, hot and choking. He beat on the walls and screamed.

Lightning crackled and sizzled across the ceiling, struck Cross, struck Teru. Teru felt electricity run through him, wash him from skin to bones, sizzle back out again. It shot through the panic in his brain and stirred something up.

Where were the children? He must find out!

Finally a stone arm reached from the ceiling toward Teru. He backed away from it, but the chalk wall stopped him. He had run out of screams. He sagged against the wall and watched as a stone hand thrust into his chest. How could it pass through cloth and flesh without ripping, wounding? Was it the arm of a ghost?

He felt fingers of fire close around his heart. A gentle squeeze. A throb. And then the arm vanished, and the sensations were gone.

The lightning and thunder stopped. The wind died. The room quieted till all the candle flames stood tall and straight on their wicks.

Teru's throat was raw from screaming. He kneaded it with his hand. He felt strange and light. He stared down at his shirtfront and could not see a single thread disarrayed from the stone hand's intrusion.

Cross knelt with his chalk and wrote other symbols on the floor. He drew lines from the circle he stood in, and walked out. He came to Teru's circle and cut it open with chalk lines. Then he stooped and picked up the glass thing.

Teru stepped out of his circle. He stood, studied the chalk drawings on the floor, this time with heightened interest, knowing some of what it could do. He made a mental map of it, complete with all symbols and lines. He would be able to re-create it, but he didn't know what words his master had used, or whom he had summoned. File it, collect more information, he told himself.

Cross rose and came to him, handed him the glass lump. "Here they are, apprentice," he said.

The lump was warm in his hands. Teru studied it. It was shaped like a heart: not a Valentine heart, but a human heart, chambered and valved, twisted and lumpy and somehow beautiful. In one of the large chambers he saw Lexa, curled and sleeping, dressed in velvet. In the other large chamber he saw Basil, elegant and asleep. Both of them smiled.

"How interesting," said Teru.

Shaped Stones

*   *   *

Six months later, Teru and Cross were working together in a cemetery. The rain started when they had dug only halfway down to the coffin. "Blast," said Cross, staring at the wet midnight sky. "That's all we needed. Maybe it will blow over." He leaned his shovel against a headstone and took refuge in the doorway of a mausoleum.

Teru didn't mind the rain. He was interested in getting down to this coffin. Would the body of a murderer really carry a different residue of power from the body of a normal person? But he had dug blisters into his palms, so he decided to take a break too. He ripped the hem off his shirt and, wrapping it around his hands, wandered from the grave.

A marble angel stood above a child's grave nearby, its head bent and its arms spread, beckoning hands aimed at the ground as though to summon the dead. Its widespread wings fanned forward. Teru went to the statue and edged in below its arms and wings, achieving shelter, if only a little.

He wished he had brought something to read. There was enough ambient city light to see by, maybe to read by, even though it was the middle of the night. But he hadn't thought to stick a book in his pocket.

He reached down and took out what he had: the glass heart. He didn't know why he carried it. It made a lump in his pocket, and it was heavy. He couldn't seem to leave it behind, though. One of these days he'd analyze the situation and change it.

He turned it over and over, studying the small, pale, floating faces locked in the intricate craft of the crystal. Cross would teach him more glass techniques soon; Teru knew how to nag and nag until Cross broke down and taught him what he wanted to know.

Leaning against the stone angel, Teru felt something happen in his chest. Something hot, startling and strange. Had he been shot? He hadn't heard a gun go off, but the rain's noise might have masked that. He looked down to see if he was bleeding. No.

Curious heat, prickling like fingers thawing after frost.

He clutched the glass heart and stared down into the face of his sleeping sister. Heat moved into his eyes, his throat. Something hot splashed on his thumb. He raised a hand and touched his face, surprised by tears.

He turned the glass heart over and studied Basil for a while, and still tears trickled from his eyes; heat choked his throat and twisted in his chest. At last he hugged the heart to him, closed his eyes, and wept without sound.

"Let's get on with it," Cross said presently from somewhere nearby.

Startled, Teru lifted his head. The rain had stopped, but his pain was still present.

"Apprentice?"

Teru thrust the glass heart deep into a pocket and stepped away from the angel. The pain vanished. "Huh," Teru said.

They went back to digging. He turned the strange feelings over and over in his mind, but he could make no sense of them.

He needed to know more. What had happened? Why?

Later, when they had spelled the coffin open and as Cross knelt to take what he wanted from the body of a man who had murdered seven children, Teru went back and leaned against the angel.

Feelings flooded him, memories: Lexa showed him a story she had written in school, pointed to the red-ink "Wonderful!" from her teacher, and Teru felt pride, joy, and a helpless, almost hopeless love. Basil brought him a sack of licorice buttons; he'd spent his whole allowance on them, because he remembered that once upon a time, Teru had loved them.

One night before they'd met Cross, Teru had led the others closer and closer to a big fire at the edge of a hoovertown, hoping that if they snuck carefully enough they could share the heat without anyone's knowing, but the man whose fire it was saw them. He called them in and let them sit beside him, and gave them potatoes cooked in the ashes, charred on the outside and flaky-sweet on the inside. Teru burned his tongue and his fingertips, but he didn't care.

"Where've you been? What are you doing? Why didn't you watch me harvest?" Cross stood before him. "I want you to learn those techniques, Apprentice."

Teru straightened and stepped away from the angel, and the feelings and memories faded. "I'm experimenting," he said. "I'll learn the techniques next time."

Teru filled in the grave and they went home. Later, after he had finished his other chores and Cross had retreated to wherever he went when he wasn't teaching Teru, Teru went to a round room in the attic, just beneath the roof-dome. He opened a tiny window he had only looked out before, and climbed onto the roof, then crept to the south tower. A narrow staircase led up its side, unrailed and crumbling, fogged in at the top. For the first time, Teru climbed up into that eternal fog to see who was hiding so far above the street.

He found a black marble sphinx sitting there, her wings half-spread as she leaned forward to look between wisps of mist at the world below. Her lion's back was broad enough to sit on. He crawled up onto it and leaned his back against hers. With the glass heart in his hands, he felt the same rush of feelings he had felt leaning against the cemetery angel.

He sat and let it wash through him, anxieties and regrets, horror, sadness, guilt, Lexa's starving face, Lexa's healthy face, Basil's skeletal hands holding a slice of apple, Basil's wonder as he touched the new clothes Cross gave them, and Mama, tickling Teru and laughing with him when he was just a baby, putting her own coat around him when he was small and crying with cold, hugging him up out of a nightmare.

Presently Teru sat up. He stroked the black marble back, touched the tip of the lion tail that curled up over the sphinx's haunch. Then he slid to the roof and stepped away from the statue, losing contact with the black shaped stone. Instantly the memories and feelings shut off, but he had memories of the memories now, and cool distance and intellectual rigor with which to study them.

A pleasant puzzle, one he could poke at.

But not tonight. Tonight he set the glass heart with his brother and sister inside it on the table beside his bed, and turned the lamp up high so he could read the next chapter of *Gray's Anatomy*, "The Organs of Special Sense." Cross had told him some special senses couldn't be found with an autopsy, but anatomy was still a good thing to know.

"The Membranous Labyrinth," Teru read. The broken blisters on his hands stung. His eyes kept falling shut and blinking open; his head drooped forward. Every night was like this, his mind racing faster than his body could keep up with until he fell asleep with the page printing itself on his cheek. Somewhere beneath the surface of his thoughts, a question whispered: Why did stone creatures give him visions? He knew he had surrendered his heart, and he didn't think he cared; life was simpler, less painful, without it. And yet.

He still didn't know to whom he had given his heart. A god of stone creatures? One who didn't mind sharing?

If he hadn't given his heart away forever, was there a chance that the children weren't eternally safe, that somehow he could get them out of the crystal?

What if Teru didn't want his heart or the children back?

The book thumped to the floor beside the bed, rousing him enough to turn down the lamp. He collapsed sideways on the covers, his hands cupped around something intangible.

No color touched his dreams.

Wanderlust

M. Christian

The moan of radials on asphalt; a high-octane, four-stroke, eight-cylinder growl under the hood.

The white line vanishing under, then appearing behind. The near landscape moving fast, far landscape slow. Then it was day pines and jagged peaks, blurs of snow, and stoplights swinging in a biting wild. The clouds above were thick and dark, heavily laden with imminent hard rain.

Dancing on his dash, spring-loose hips knocking back and forth with each shimmy and engine knock, she smiled up at him: a beatific image of absolute love in cheap, sun-faded plastic. Every once in a while he found himself looking at her, entranced for a moment by her smile—but most of the time he tried to ignore her, pretend the Mustang's dash was void of cheap hula girls.

The road lifted and dropped under him till the sun set, cutting itself on a distant mountaintop—bleeding a bright red sunset. Reaching down, he hooked two fingers around a peeling, chrome knob and pulled. High beams stabbed out, revealing a picket line of trees beneath a dark canopy of thick branches and strong needles.

The needle tapped E. Around one bend, a gas station—antique sign lovingly preserved: GAS & FOOD. Then a restaurant, flashing by his right-hand window—a hospitable glow from within dusky log cabin walls, through thick gingham curtains.

A quick turn, tires only beginning a scream of protest. With his foot on the brake, the exultation of being on the road, of traveling, fell away from him. Stopping felt like putting on a heavy cloak. Before he opened the door he took a deep breath of mental preparation.

Out and into the station. Dark deco pumps, like drained Coke bottles, under buzzing lamps circled by flights of huge moths. The air was crystal—hard and jagged with cold. Plunging hands deep into leather jacket pockets, he moved across the concrete toward the buzzing neon OFFICE sign.

Inside, the place was as familiar as . . . well, as his home had been, so long ago. It had the usual touches, as regular as the gas in the pumps: jerky and maps, cigarettes and potato chips, lighters and a GIVE can; a guy behind the counter in overalls, backward gimmie cap, face craggy with exhaust and exhaustion—and with that special grease and spark plug viewpoint they all seemed to have, that special kind of bitterness.

"Howdy," the gas station man said, "anything I can do you for—?" Then he stopped. Frozen, arrested, his eyes staring wide. He'd been drawn in, completely taken.

"Yeah, I need gas," he said. As the door closed behind him, he took another deep breath, feeling the soft leather press against his chest.

"Take what you want, please," the gas man said, his voice soft, cooing like a pigeon. "Anything you want, it's yours." It was a tone he had probably never used before, and would never use again. Not a two-stroke sound, not a fuel-additive sound; it was so sweet it was almost comical.

"Thanks," he said, turning and walking back out to his car, the pumps. He didn't laugh.

Dipping the nozzle in and squeezing the handle, he sensed the gas man standing behind him, lingering close by. With another breath, tired this time, he turned to look at him.

Turning his gimmie cap in his dark, wrinkled hands, mouth hanging open just enough to show his yellowed, picket-fence teeth, eyes glimmering, flashing with fascination, the gas man said, "Uh, mister, I, ah—"

He turned completely, to look at him directly. Sometimes he just walked away, or drove off—feeling bitter guilt for a few miles. Tonight, though, he felt a pitiful affection for the man. "For the gas," he said, kissing him on his chapped lips, listening to his little sigh, his pathetic moan of ecstatic release.

Then, toward the restaurant. Suddenly, the wind surrounded him, nipping at his exposed skin, howling with feral glee—carrying away most, but not all, of the gas man's sobbing, beatific joy.

He hoped the restaurant wasn't crowded. He prayed it wasn't crowded. The door was heavy (halved logs again) but pushed open easily. Inside it was warm, comfortable, like burrowing under many layers of blankets. Maybe a dozen tables, a dark jukebox, red-and-white checkered tablecloths, little electric lamps at each table, stuffed moose on one wall, antlers on the others. From the back, the clatter and bang of a busy kitchen.

Maybe four people—not many: an older couple dressed simply, warmly— obviously locals; a pair of women wearing simple but pretty dresses—on their way to, or home from, something formal.

"Hello—," the waitress said, and he turned to look at her. Maybe forty, bright red hair, skin the color of new cream. She was a big girl, but strong— she moved with a comfort in herself, not without a certain grace, a certain sensuality.

Her eyes were bright green, like the stoplight that he'd seen swinging, and very, very wide—drinking him in as completely as they could. Looking at her, he watched them dilate till they were nothing but jade-ringed deep pools.

"I'd like to have something to eat. A steak, some potatoes. Oh, and a beer," he said, turning away from their rapture.

She nodded, unable to speak. She licked her lips—once, twice, three times. Finally: "Yeah, sure—right. How . . . how do you want it cooked?"

"Medium," he said, trying not to smile, trying to keep his face cool and immobile. "I'll sit over there," he said, indicating a table near the window.

He sat in silence, everyone's eyes on him, their conversation dead. Their attention was like a growing heat, making his skin and face feel almost burned. Even the kitchen was quiet, the cymbal clashes of pots and pans gone.

He turned, looking over his shoulder at the kitchen door. The waitress stared at him, immobile in her bliss in the doorway. Next to her, partially eclipsed by her shoulder, was the cook: an old man with a bad toupee, his eyes the size of skillets.

"I'm in kind of a hurry," he said, and the cook disappeared, hastened by the simple request. The waitress looked startled, as if surprised by the time limit—and vanished back into the kitchen as well.

Someone was stroking his jacket. Looking over his shoulder he saw that it was one of the fancy-dressed women sitting behind him, her face frozen in joy, her eyes wet with ecstasy, her hand moving with cautious delight up and down his back.

"Please don't do that," he said with kindness. Shocked, she jumped back, looking like a fawn trapped in headlights: frozen in place, caught between adoration and the fear of losing the source of it. "It's okay," he said softly, "just don't touch me."

Delighted, she squealed, curling her legs under her—staring with fascination as he took a napkin from the stainless dispenser and neatly arranged it on the table.

"Your . . . your beer," the waitress said, putting the chilled bottle on the table in front of him, her hand grazing his. With the contact, her eyes rolled back into her head and she quivered, ever so slightly.

The others watched as well—eyes wide, mouths slightly agape. He wondered, again, what they saw. The answer was simple, but somehow unfulfilling: They saw what they wanted to.

The steak came—quicker, he knew, and prepared better than the cook had ever prepared a steak before—with a steaming baked potato. With the food in front of him, his stomach complained loudly.

He ate quickly, cutting the steak with a few deft strokes of the cheap knife, following every other bite with a swig of beer. They all watched, staring at each movement, adoring him totally, completely. Every gesture, every breath, every blink was perfect, ideal, beatific.

Halfway through the steak, blade scraping against white bone, a frown creased the waitress's forehead—a quick spasm of facial muscles.

He didn't need to, especially with time slipping away, but sometimes he wanted to release the guilt, to explain—if just a little. His years on the road, the salesman of all salesmen—mile after mile, selling this and that: his car, his home, his bible, an AAA map, his family, the grim faces that pumped his gas.

A swig of beer, a big bite of tender steak, hot potato. He'd driven those roads day after day, night after night—miles and months blurring. At first the cheap little figure on his dashboard had been just that: an image of cartoonish happiness in red plastic, found in a junk shop attached to a service station somewhere. At first it was a kitschy trinket to keep his spirits light, give him company on his journeys. But all those miles he'd put in, all those roads, his life as the salesman of salesmen—it had attracted the attention of . . . something. Something that had come to inhabit that hula girl. Something that had come to possess her—and in so doing, possess him.

Wanderlust, you'd have to call her: a priestess of the interstate, a goddess of the roads. The endless white lines were her altar. His endless traveling, it seemed, had gotten him noticed, and then loved by her. And she had a powerful, divine affection.

She loved him so much, in fact, that she'd given him a gift, a little something to remember her by whenever he left her immediate domain: a little something that made him glow with splendor at every new stop, made him beautiful to every new face he saw. His face had become the mirror of her adoration.

And now his dashboard lover reflected the pleasure she drew from him: a tiny smile on the face of that cheap plastic hula girl. A smile on the face of Wanderlust.

The waitress's frown creased further, deepening. He ate faster, cutting with even greater speed, almost choking down the meat, the hot potato. Then the older man sneered, his lip quivering; and the waitress's frown dropped into a scowl . . . her eyes narrowing at him.

A sudden clattering explosion of metal from the kitchen startled him, and his beer almost slipped from his hand. Glancing up, he caught the cook standing in the doorway, disgust on his face.

The waitress got up and left, quickly retreating toward the back of the cafe. The women followed, shading their eyes behind shaking hands. The older man looked pale, as if the life had been quickly drained from him.

He ate quickly—soon very little of his steak remained, but there was still a good portion of potato. Not finishing meant getting hungry—so he tried to force the food down.

The waitress retreated into the kitchen, moaning pitifully as she glanced over her shoulder at him. The older man turned a light shade of green and started to painfully retch in a distant corner. The three women held each other—faces turned away, trying to avoid even the slightest glimpse of his grotesqueness.

The last piece. The last swallow. He rose, his chair skidding across the floor. The older woman looked up at the sound, deep reflexes betraying her fear. Seeing him, she screamed. It was a sound of terror and revulsion that came up from down deep—even deeper than that betraying instinct. Seeing his primal ugliness, her body convulsed, snapping her head back against the hard wall with a heavy, hollow sound and rocketing her arms and legs out stiffly.

He ran toward the door—a piercing chorus of agonized repulsion tearing through the air from behind as he moved. It was a sound of ultimate abhorrence, absolute disgust. He knew what they saw, now, as he slammed into the heavy door, bolting out into the bitter night—it was what they never, ever wanted to see: an image of ugliness that was lurking in them all, painted on his face.

As he ran toward his car, he felt a bolt of sadness tear through him. He used to apologize—first with words and then, later, just in thought. But it had been too many miles, too many roads. So he just ran — trying to get into his car as fast as possible.

The gas man was standing by the door to his office, absently wiping his hands with a red cloth — his movements stiff and awkward, still recovering from his dose of pure joy.

The man looked up, his face instantly frozen in a mask of exaggerated horror: mouth and eyes too wide, hands clawing outward as his legs tried to push him as far away as possible. His scream, when it came, was a shattering noise, a sound of witnessing his own personal terror.

As quick as he could, with the sound of the gas man's screams still tearing at his ears, he climbed in, started the engine, and pressed the accelerator to the floor. The sound of squealing tires on wet asphalt was an angels' choir, a concerto of escape.

MILES later — time not having any meaning, anymore — his heart slowed a bit, was no longer hammering in his chest. As he relaxed — sinking down into the seat, resting his hands on the wheel — distance slipped by faster.

So many highways, so many roads, so many white lines vanishing in front, reappearing behind. Yes, she loved him — his goddess of the roads. Loved him enough to give him that special gift: He wore her love as a mask of beauty.

But she also wanted him with her, always. So, toward the end it turned, he turned . . . ugly: His face invariably changed into a reason to return to the road — to return to her.

Mile after mile, the road sometimes weaving, sometimes straight, always ahead. Foot down, hands on the wheel, he drove — following the road wherever it took him, stopping only when he absolutely needed to.

While on the dashboard, the hula dancer smiled up at him — her cheap plastic face a stern image of eternal possession.

Giotto's Window

CHELSEA QUINN YARBRO

They found him locked in the bathroom of the sixteenth-century B and B, smearing the walls with what he found in the catbox. The images were hideous, disturbing; the smell was nauseating. His robe was in tatters and his nails were broken and bleeding; he kept muttering profanities in English and Italian, his face set with a rigidity born of fury.

The police came, very polite and voluble as Italians are apt to be, and two psychiatrists; they conferred while the landlady wrung her hands and said to anyone who would listen that nothing like this had ever happened in her house before, appealing to the saints and all her previous guests to verify this for her. No one paid much attention to her; the psychiatrists made a few routine inquiries when the police had collected Thomas's passport, making sure they understood how the incident came about; they drugged Thomas enough to keep him from hurting anyone; and then they drove him off to a small hospital in the hills on the south side of the Arno, to a room that overlooked the glowing beauty of Florence, where they left him while they contacted the American Embassy and began the slow process of deciding

190

what to do with the young man. When Thomas woke, he began howling, making sounds that hardly seemed to come from a human throat. He ran himself against the walls, the sound of impact shuddering through them. He cursed. He screamed. He slammed his head into the bars over the window, which was when the four attendants came and injected him with a powerful sedative. Thomas kicked and muttered while the drug took hold, then he lapsed into an enforced sleep.

"Such a pity," said the oldest nurse, a middle-aged man from Pisa with a nose like a potato and big, fleshy ears. "He looks like an angel."

Asleep, Thomas Ashen did. He had the kind of regular, well-proportioned features that would not have been out of place in a Renaissance portrait; his hair was a sunny light-brown and curled just enough to make a nice frame for his face. With his eyes closed, the wrath that smoldered within was hidden. Lying on his utilitarian bed he seemed serene, but that was the result of his stupor.

The other three men agreed, one of them reluctantly; the man from Modena said, "One of the Fallen Angels." There was a long silence while they made sure he could not lower the sides of his bed, and then they left him alone.

It took nearly a week for Thomas to be calm enough to talk. When he did, he struggled visibly to control his anger and to hide his dread; he was drugged to help him maintain command of his emotions and to keep his apprehension at bay. He slumped in his chair, his head and shoulders rounded forward as if he was about to fall forward into an abyss; his slippered feet dangled as if he could not see the floor, or did not trust it to support him. He listened to the gentle promptings of the psychiatrist with increasing loathing on his countenance.

"*E impossibile, Dottore,*" he said, slurring his words a little as the drugs did their work.

"What is impossible?" Doctor Giacomo Chiodo asked in perfect Americanized English, the legacy of two years at Stanford Medical.

"Everything. *Tutti quanti*. It's all for nothing." He held his arms crossed tightly over his chest and he glared down at the soft slippers on his feet. "You don't know what's out there. You are blinded by reason, by rationality. You think what you see is what is there." He had to stop himself from saying more, to keep to himself the tentacles he saw writhing out of the psychiatrist's shoulders, or the huge bird talons that served him as feet.

"If I don't know, will you tell me?" Doctor Chiodo appeared calm, even mildly disinterested, but beneath that facade he was paying close attention.

"That's a psychiatrist's trick, isn't it? Turning the matter back on me so you don't have to risk anything." He scowled at the floor; it was too difficult to look at the man and ignore the tentacles. "You don't want to admit it."

"Admit what?" Doctor Chiodo sounded politely interested, as if they were discussing film at a cocktail party. He waited, seeming to be in no hurry, his ferociously beaked face as benign as something that nightmarish could be.

"That you know what I see, that you know it's real." He glared at the Italian. "You aren't as much a fool as the rest of them. You listen to so much—I can't be the only one who has seen . . . You must know more, the reality."

"What do I know is real?" Doctor Chiodo asked with the same determined courtesy.

"Well, *look!*" he burst out. "Do you mean to tell me you don't know? Don't you look in the mirror? Can't you see what's out there?" He used his chin to indicate the window. "Do you have to think I am crazy in order to be sane yourself? Can't you see?"

"I see hillsides and the western half of Firenze," said Doctor Chiodo quietly, doing hardly more than glancing toward the north-facing windows. "With the Arno cutting through the city. What do you see?"

His jaw angled defiantly. "I don't pretend. I see what's really there; I see the monsters and freaks and grotesques. You've gotten used to them, haven't you? You think you see a man's face when you shave, that the people you pass in the streets are not macabre creatures in a macabre landscape. You pretend you haven't got a beak, that no one has one." He lowered his eyes. "You're as bad as the rest of them. You don't let yourself recognize what is there," Thomas said, then added in a soft, desperate tone, "No one believes me. No one wants to believe me."

"Why do you say that?" It was a standard therapist's ploy, and it worked well enough.

"You sound as if you don't believe me, either, but I know you aren't really convinced that what you think is there is real, not doing what you do." His eyes went sly. "You want it to be like Giotto's window, where you can show the order of what you think is there. But you sense that the order is false, a trick of geometry, or you should, a man in your line of work. If you don't, then—" He made a sound of contemptuous scorn. "You're as bad as the rest of them. Admit it. You don't want to see what I see. You'd rather look for reason and beauty than for the madness that is here. You have been seduced by all those lines Giotto drew out his window, forgetting it was all just a trick." He kicked at the chair leg with his soft slippers. "This isn't Giotto's window—that's the illusion you have accepted. The world is Bosch's, with bird-headed men and flowers in walking cages. That's what surrounds us. All the rest is sleight of hand."

"If that is so, what are you?" Doctor Chiodo kept his tone level and his gaze indirect.

"Oh, I am as much a monster as any of you, but at least I know it. I have seen my beak and my leathery wings, and my talons. I know that mirrors can lie if you are afraid to look at the truth. I am not afraid to see what I am." He snatched at the air as if to gather his thoughts. "You would see, too, if you permitted yourself to see them—I do. Oh, not the same monstrousness as mine, but some things all your own. I know you for what you are." He sounded almost proud, but he would not face Doctor Chiodo as he went on. "I can see what you are. You're one of the false men, with pink skin over the scales of a lizard, and fangs like a wild beast. The streets are full of beasts like you, chimeras and gargoyles and monsters; you all go on as if you were men. You have an armored raptor's head, your arms are not arms at all, and your feet are clawed."

"Is that what you see?" the doctor asked quietly as if they were talking about the pleasant Tuscan weather. "Is everyone so hideous?"

"Yes. And you would see it if you would let yourself," Thomas insisted again. "You will not let yourself look because you know I'm right."

"If you insist," Doctor Chiodo said, maintaining his calm and prepared for more repetition. "How does it happen that you can see these things and the rest of us cannot?"

Thomas laughed. "Because I am not afraid of seeing the world as it is." He leaned farther forward in his chair. "I know that if I fall from here, I will sink into the earth for miles. Don't pretend you don't know that, too. I can see it in your face."

"Which face is that? The pink one or the lizard one with fangs?" He wished the words unspoken as soon as they were uttered. He strove to regain the removal he sought. Finally he coughed gently. "You should be able to inform me."

"You won't believe me," said Thomas, so quietly that Doctor Chiodo had to strain to hear him. "No one believes me."

"So you keep telling me," said Doctor Chiodo. "I wish you'd tell me more."

"Why? So you can say I am hopelessly delusional, spending my time hallucinating? So you can embrace the dream of rationality and tell yourself you are sane? So you can proclaim the triumph of rationality?" His sarcasm sounded exhausted; his defiance was fading, giving way to increasing dejection. "Look in the mirror, Dottore. *Guard' al viso.*" He swallowed hard. "If you used your real hands, you could touch your real face. You are not as lost as most are—you still have the capacity to know yourself." The doctor's tentacles waved at him, and the large, beakish horn that went up his nose and over his eyebrows dipped as the psychiatrist nodded.

"No doubt," said Doctor Chiodo. He wanted to pursue the matter later, when Thomas had rested, for the young American was slumping in his chair, his head nodded down onto his chest. "When you are more alert we will continue this."

"You think I won't know you for what you are? Do you think anything you do to me will change that?" Thomas challenged in a whisper. "The world

194

isn't rational, Dottore. It never was." There was nothing Doctor Chiodo could think to say; he rang for the orderlies to escort Thomas back to his room.

"I am Jane Wallace," she said as she presented her passport and her letters of authorization; Director Bianchi glanced at them and took them carefully. "You were told to expect me? I'm here to . . . to escort Thomas Ashen home." She waited while the director of the sanitarium examined her credentials. "How is he?"

The director sighed with Italian eloquence as he gave her back her passport and letters of authorization. "He is still delusional, as Doctor Chiodo says in his report. This does not seem to have changed, although it is difficult to know. He is not saying much to us, but he flinches when he is with others, and he refuses to look out the window, so we have assumed he is continuing to see something other than what the rest of us do." This was as soothing as he could make it, and he watched Jane's response; then he waved to the chair across his desk. "Sit down, sit down. We must discuss this, you and I, if you are planning to travel anywhere with him." His face was slightly pinched, as if he had smelled something not quite wholesome.

"I wonder if it will be safe to travel with him at all, given what your reports say," she said to him as she sat down. "I read them quite thoroughly on the flight over. His family wants him back as soon as possible, but I don't know if it would be wise." She tapped the folder that held the evaluations. "I appreciate your faxing them to me before I left. It was all done in such a hurry—" She broke off. "Has he been violent?"

"Only to himself. This morning he hit his head on the door two times before we stopped him; he said he was trying to leave an impression of his beak, to prove he has one. He still attempts to eat feces if we leave him alone in the toilet. He has scratched his arms, saying that the scrapes prove he has talons instead of hands." The director sighed. "I cannot emphasize this strongly enough: He has not improved in any creditable way since we undertook his care." He folded his hands. "He is filled with despair, insisting he is surrounded by monsters." He shook his head again. "Doctor Chiodo has kept him moderately sedated, and that has made him easier to handle, but it does nothing to alleviate his condition."

"No," Jane said quietly. "I can see how it is advisable, however." She was just tentative enough to encourage Director Biancchi to continue.

"You would be well-advised to keep him under heavier sedation while you are traveling; I know you are not required to, but I do think it would be prudent," he told her, a slight edge in his voice. "He has not been violent, as I have told you, but if he is closely surrounded by those he sees as monsters, I cannot promise he will not lash out. If he is in a stupor, he might endure his surroundings well enough for you to get him home."

"That's not very encouraging," said Jane.

"No, it isn't," Director Biancchi agreed. "You are a psychiatric nurse and you know how easily some patients can be overcome by their delusions. I'm afraid Thomas Ashen is wholly given over to his beliefs and regards all attempts to change his mind as confirmation of his worst suspicions." He tapped the shiny top of his wide desk.

"So I gather," said Jane, her manner a bit more assertive. "That makes him doubly troublesome; we must assume he will be responding to his hallucinations at all times. It will make traveling with him more difficult." She stifled a sudden yawn. "I'm sorry. Jet lag."

The director nodded, his manner politely concerned. "*Capisco.* You have come a long way, and you must travel again in another day or two; it is very demanding." He indicated the tall windows. "There is a guest cottage on the grounds, if you would like to rest until evening. Your bags have already been taken there. We can discuss this case further when you have restored yourself." His smile was genuine and practiced at once, the smile of a man who has spent his life putting frightened people at ease. "I will have the most recent reports prepared for your review."

"Thank you," she said, rising. "I am very tired." She started for the door. "I'd appreciate as much information as you can give me on the nature of his delusions. That way I can deal with him more effectively."

"Of course, of course; I will have all the information you need made ready," said the director. "I'll arrange for you to talk with Dottore Chiodo

196

this evening." He rose and remained standing until she left his office; then he went to the window and looked out on the vine-covered Tuscan hill, taking solace in the beauty he saw.

DOCTOR Chiodo and Director Biancchi had a glass of pale sherry and a small plate of cheese pastries waiting for Jane when she came into the study at the Institute; it was glowing dusk beyond the windows as the day drained away to darkness. The building itself was alive with sounds, for most of the residents were being given their dinners just now, and some were expressing themselves vociferously. Director Biancchi shut the door, muffling the loudest of the noises.

"Does Thomas eat on his own?" Jane asked when their introductions were complete. She was in no mood to dawdle over social pleasantries, and sensed that the two men would be glad to lose themselves in small talk if they had the opportunity.

"Yes, he can feed himself," said Doctor Chiodo. "He is messy—he claims his beak gets in the way, that he can't hold on to utensils with his talons— but he is capable of eating food." He sighed.

"That's something," Jane said, trying to make herself more alert, for in spite of her nap she still felt swathed in cotton wool.

"You would think that the hallucinations are the product of a fixation in childhood, but if that is the case, he has not revealed it to me directly or indirectly. He is not very forthcoming about when he began to experience these perceptual episodes." He sipped his sherry. "I have rarely encountered such consistency in a delusion as he appears to have."

"You've had him here for three weeks; given the severity of his condition, that doesn't seem a long time, if, as you suppose, the hallucinations have been building for some time. Your report suggests as much." Jane did not want to be the first to sit down, but she found standing about awkward. "I spoke to his mother at length before I left St. Louis; she told me he has drawn monsters all his life, most of them similar to monsters in comic books. She supposed he would grow out of it in time. She was under the impression he had given it up before his father became ill."

"And he may have done," said Doctor Chiodo. "But if that was the case, something triggered a resurgence of those perceptions. Perhaps his father's illness contributed to the son's deterioration, assuming such predilections existed before his father became ill, as I suppose must be the case, given the comprehensive nature of his delusions." He popped one of the little pastries into his mouth, chewed it vigorously, then finished off his sherry before going on. "And given the possible connection to a family tragedy, I want to have one more hour with him before I inform him he is to be taken home."

This startled Jane a bit. "Why delay telling him?"

"I am concerned about his understanding of the reason for his return home; it would be better for him if he did not perceive it as a punishment." He poured more sherry into his glass and held out the crystal decanter to Jane and then to Director Biancchi; only the director accepted his offer. "I would like to try to discover more about his home life before I send him back into it, no matter how briefly, in order to minimize the possible distress he might suffer because of it. Surely his family would prefer he not respond negatively to this transfer? He will need proper care, of course, and the sooner he is hospitalized, the better for everyone."

Jane nodded, frowning as she spoke. "I think his mother wants to have him at home, in familiar surroundings, for a few days before she arranges . . . anything. She's hired me to stay with them until—" She stopped, not knowing how to explain Catherine Ashen's hopes to the two men.

"If you will pardon me for saying so, Nurse Wallace," Director Biancchi said in the silence, "Missus Ashen is not being very wise. I know this must be very painful for her, but if her son had suffered a medical injury, she would want to speed him to the best hospital she could find as soon as he arrived. This emergency is as genuine as broken bones are, and needs as expert care as soon as possible if he is to have any hope of a good recovery." He glanced at Doctor Chiodo. "Wouldn't you agree, Giacomo?"

"Most certainly. It cannot be sufficiently elucidated." He gave Jane a long, thoughtful look. "You have experience with delusional patients. Surely you must know that what you and I see as normal and reassuring—familiar—can be terrifying to a patient in Thomas's condition?"

Jane resented his patronizing tone but kept that to herself. "I've worked in the field for seventeen years, Doctor Chiodo. I have a grasp of the problem."

Doctor Chiodo metaphorically retreated. "An excellent one, I am sure." He coughed gently. "I will be sure you have enough medication to keep him quiet for as long as necessary. I only wanted to impress upon you the volatility of his current state."

"I believe you made the problem clear in your notes, Doctor," said Jane, a bit stiffly. "Rest assured, I will not underestimate the severity of his condition." She looked from the doctor to the director and back again, hoping the intensity of her gaze would be sufficient emphasis to convince them of her conviction. "He is my responsibility now, not yours." As she said this she saw the two men exchange a glance that was clearly an indication of shared relief.

"As you say, Nurse Wallace: Thomas Ashen is your responsibility now," Director Biancchi concurred.

THOMAS's head lolled as he was buckled into his first-class seat; an attractive stewardess hovered nearby, her features distorted by worry. "You're sure he won't cause any trouble?" she asked Jane uneasily; her Midwestern accent revealed her origins as much as her fresh-faced good looks.

"He'll sleep for five hours; I have a second dose to administer later," Jane replied, more efficient than cordial. "There is no reason for concern while he is dozing, and I will give him my full attention once he awakes." She had shepherded him through Rome's Leonardo da Vinci airport, maneuvering his wheelchair with the ease of long experience, making sure he was undisturbed by the press of travelers around them. Now that he was aboard the plane and in his seat, Jane knew she could relax.

"Well, at least first-class is half empty," said the stewardess, sighing as she readied herself to tend to the other passengers.

Jane made a careful check of Thomas's seat belt, then wiped his lip of the shine of drool. She hesitated in this simple act, noticing that his flesh felt unexpectedly hard.

Thomas half-opened one eye and tried to make sense of her face. "Oh," he mumbled. "You're one of the sad ones." The eye closed and his head rolled onto his shoulder. "Long beak," he added, then fell deeply asleep.

A short while later the plane lunged into the air, heading northwest for Montreal, St. Louis, and Houston. The sound of the engines penetrated Thomas's drugged slumber for a brief instant; he saw the stewardess in the crew seat beside the door, and he gave a little shriek of dismay. "Teeth, long teeth," he whispered, then looked away toward the window, and went pale as he slipped back into his stupor.

If that's the worst I have to deal with, Jane told herself, this is going to be an easy flight, and let the acceleration and climb push her back against the padded seat until the pilot announced that they had reached cruising altitude. Relaxing, Jane let herself be lulled by the loud purr of the engines as the plane continued onward.

"Something to drink, ma'am?" the stewardess asked a short time later; she studied Thomas's slack visage and adjusted her own smile. "He's really out of it, isn't he?"

"As required, for his safety and that of the rest of your passengers," said Jane, more sharply than she had intended. "Hot coffee, black, and something light to eat—a croissant, or scone."

The stewardess stared at her. "Ma'am?"

"That's what I'd like for now—coffee and breakfast pastry. I don't care what the hour is." Jane sat straighter, squinting as she saw the stewardess move back. There was the oddest look about her, thought Jane, a shininess that seemed out of place on so perfectly made-up a face. She dismissed this as the oddity of the moment, a nervousness left over from getting Thomas to the plane. When the coffee was brought, Jane noticed the shine again, but out of the corner of her eye; again she dismissed it, reminding herself that she was a jittery flier. She leaned back, sipping on her coffee, and stared past Thomas out into the cerulean expanse. When the stewardess returned with two croissants and a sticky bun to accompany her coffee, Jane saw the suggestion of a chitinous mass on the stewardess's face; she ignored it.

There were two movies to choose from for the personal screens, and Jane selected the costume drama about skullduggery at the court of Elizabeth I;

it held her attention even though she found it heavy-handed and anachronistic. Only twice did she find her attention wavering: once when the stewardess brought around an elegant tray of cheeses, and once when the man in the seat across the aisle rose to go to the bathroom and revealed a long trunk dangling from the front of his face. Jane blinked and the proboscis disappeared; she reimmersed herself in the sixteenth-century drama as quickly as possible.

Over Nova Scotia Thomas became restless and struggled against his seat belt, murmuring bits of protestations that caught Jane's attention. She reached over to quiet him and found herself staring into his open eyes. "You know. You know," he said, his voice made distant by his drugs. "Don't pretend."

"Of course not," said Jane, reaching for the kit that contained the tranquilizers he would need for the rest of the journey. "Don't upset yourself." As she administered the injection, she thought she saw a gleeful grimace on the beaked face of the stewardess, but in an instant it was gone, and the young woman's smile had nothing sinister about it.

"Is he going to be okay?" the stewardess asked as Thomas nodded off into sleep once again.

"Oh, yes; I think so," said Jane, doing her best to sound optimistic.

The stewardess patted Thomas's shoulder. "Good."

Thomas shuddered and huddled back into his seat as if he were aware of the presence of the stewardess and found her frightening.

As Jane settled herself again, she noticed the long, distorted arms of the other stewardess in first-class, and she suppressed a shudder, reminding herself that delusional people could be very persuasive; no doubt Thomas had gotten to her. She closed her eyes, and kept them closed until the plane landed at Montreal. Watching some of the passengers leave the plane, she reminded herself that none of them really had such heads, or such limbs. Frightening as they were, they could not be as hideous as what she saw. It was impossible.

THOMAS'S mother, her carefully maintained appearance less than perfect for once, sat in the living room, her hand to her eyes. "We hoped the year in

Florence would do the trick," she said wearily, turning the last word to a tasteless joke. She collected herself enough to look up at her brother as he came in from seeing Thomas off in the ambulance. "What did they say?" Her spindly arms ended in narrow paws, more like a cat's than a human hand.

"They'll call you tonight, when they have completed their evaluation." He sat down heavily in the recliner that had been Alec's special chair. He stared at his hands as he spoke to the third person in the room. He seemed wholly unaware that his vest enclosed not ribs but a birdcage in which sat a monstrous crow with a lizard's tail. "I don't know what to say. We thought he was doing so well." The last words were lost in the wail of the ambulance siren as it pulled away from the house.

Jane Wallace could think of nothing to say to either Thomas's mother or uncle. She decided to try the oblique approach. "You said he wasn't doing anything out of the ordinary until this morning?"

"No." Catherine Ashen sighed, glancing uneasily at her brother. "Well, not for Thomas. He kept to himself when he got home. He spent most of yesterday looking out his window, making sketches. He said he was showing the lie." Her voice grew unsteady but she kept on. "They weren't of anything specific. Just the street. You know, perspective drawings, sketches of the houses along the block. They're very good," she finished desperately.

"Thomas is a talented young man," Jordon Pace announced as if saying it importantly enough would create a validity through ponderousness.

"No one who has seen his work doubts that." She tried to think of something more she could say that would help Thomas's family to deal with his obsessions, but nothing came to mind.

"He says the monsters are self-portraits," his mother whispered. "He drew a number of them yesterday, every one worse than the last. How can he think that? He's such a handsome young man. Everyone thinks so." Her cheeks colored, as if she expected to be contradicted.

Jane sighed. "That has been part of his pattern. That's what Doctor Chiodo's evaluation says."

"And it's absurd," Jordon Pace announced firmly. "It's foolishness."

"No it isn't," said Jane firmly. "It isn't foolishness." She studied the man for a long moment, trying to decide how to approach him. "If he believes his work is self-portraiture, then we have to assume that, in some sense, he is telling the truth." It was as much as she dared to say, and she kept her voice low, not wanting to give herself away to such a creature as his uncle.

Catherine put her hand to her mouth; her fingers were trembling. "I can't bear to think that," she confessed, her head lowering and her eyes averted.

"For now, you will help him the most if you do not argue with him, especially about his art." Jane gave Uncle Jordon a steady look. "This isn't something he can be coaxed or cajoled out of."

Jordon Pace pursed his lips. "I should have taken him in hand as soon as Alec became ill," he said, inclining his head toward his sister. "I should have, Caty. I'm sorry I didn't."

As gently as she could Jane said, "I don't think it would have made much difference. Thomas's drawings have been . . . unnerving for some time."

"It was Alec's illness," Jordon insisted, needing to fix blame somewhere. "To have to watch his father go through such—" He shoved his hands into his pockets and looked away. "It would give anyone nightmares, let alone a boy like Thomas."

"Don't speak against him," said Catherine faintly. "His drawings were strange long before Alec got sick."

"Of course not; of course not," Jordon soothed. "But I can't help but think that those two years took a toll on the boy." He swung around to Jane, silently challenging her.

"Oh, don't talk about it," Catherine pleaded. "Today is bad enough without bringing all that up."

"They took a toll on everyone," said Jordon. "We all know how hard it was for you."

Unlike Jane, Catherine seemed to find his condescending manner comforting. She reached out and patted her brother's hand. "You were so helpful. I couldn't have managed without you." Then she blinked and turned her attention to Jane, chagrin in her expression. "You must think very poorly of us, talking about something that happened so long ago."

"Not at all," Jane responded in an even tone. "I'm sure there were many factors leading to your son's crisis, and no doubt his father's illness was a contributing factor."

"Just what I've been telling her," Jordon declared. "It's not the kind of thing a man puts behind him easily, and a boy . . . well." He shrugged.

Knowing it was a very difficult task, Jane did what she could to turn the subject back to the present. "Has Thomas talked about his father's death?"

"Not really," said Catherine, her eyes evading Jane's gaze. "It was . . . so unpleasant."

Jane wondered if Catherine had encouraged the silence; that was for another time. "Did Thomas see most of the course of the illness?"

"Well, of course he did," said Jordon, blustering afresh. "Alec was at home for most of its duration." He indicated the recliner. "He practically lived in that chair—if you call that living."

"Jordon; please." Catherine put her hand to her eyes.

There was much more to be found out, Jane told herself, but later. Today she had to follow Thomas to the hospital and try to be sure he was properly admitted. She wanted to see what kind of beings would be caring for Thomas. "I know this has been a very trying time. I won't distress you any longer," she said to Catherine. "But in a day or two we must talk. For your son's sake."

Catherine nodded numbly, her eyes fixed on a distant place; her brother took it upon himself to escort Jane to the door.

"She is not very strong," he said in a low voice. "I'm sure you'll take that into account in your dealing with her. She has had to bear so much already." He opened his hands to show he had done all that he could.

"I understand," said Jane numbly, because she did. She turned away and walked down the steps to her car; for an instant she caught a glimpse of her reflection in the window-glass. The sight of her long beak no longer distressed her, and she got into the driver's seat with little more than a flinch; she sat there and kept her full attention on the traffic, watching the cars instead of the drivers as she signaled in preparation for leaving, her mind deliberately focused on the ordinary sights. She refused to acknowledge the monsters around her, for that way was the end of reason, the loss of perspective that she had done so much to maintain. There was nothing to be gained in seeing the hideous apparitions that filled the streets; she glared at the two young men riding skateboards; they had the heads of ibises and the wings of vultures.

"I'm glad Thomas has someone like you to help him," Jordon said as he stood back, allowing Jane to depart.

"So am I," said Jane, driving away from the house into a world of monsters.

Masks

JACK KETCHUM AND EDWARD LEE

"The bedroom's down this hall," he said. "You'll find a box at the foot of the bed. I'd like you to wear what's inside. *Only* what's inside." He smiled and poured them each a second glass of whiskey, handed one to her. The crystal sang against her fingernail. She drank and touched the delicate silver chain around his neck, felt its warmth between her thumb and forefinger—*his* warmth—and let it fall.

She turned to do as he said. On the wall in front of her was a mounted stone image of the triadic *Shiva Maheshvara*. The face on the left was female, on the right, male. In the center was the mask of Eternity. An ancient masterpiece. *Where in God's name did he plunder this?* she thought. Below, on a pedestal, stood a terra-cotta figurine from Tlatilco over seven hundred years old—the dual-faced "pretty lady" that the Toltecs buried with their dead. And on the opposite wall, a relief carving, in black granite: Kali.

His apartment was filled with treasures. Scythian goldwork. Bassari and pre-Christian Polynesian sculpture. The restored fragments of twelfth-century

Norman mosaics—*two* of them—occupying an entire wall in the living room. A "Harrowing of Hell" from a fifteenth-century psalter.

The dealer/collector in her was reeling.

So was the woman.

It wasn't the cognac. It was the man.

She'd waited a lifetime for one who just might be her equal.

"Christine," he said.

She turned and saw him backlit by the glow of the fireplace. He raised his glass to his lips. "When you get in there, be sure to light the candles."

His bedroom was modest and spare, though every piece spoke quietly of his taste. A simple walnut mirror hung over a Hepplewhite chest of drawers. An old, primitive oak wardrobe that had probably once belonged to the servant class. A Saladino bookcase, a Louis XVI drop table and a Louis XV bergère. A William and Mary four-poster bed.

Old wood plushly scented the room. Two candles stood on the Louis XVI, two more on an inlaid cherry nightstand by the bed. Wooden matches lay in a Georg Jensen silver pit plate. She lit the candles and turned off an oil lamp.

From the wall beside the bed sprang a wooden Magdalenian *atlatl* carved in the shape of a horse. Yet another masterpiece.

Christ . . .

A plain white hatbox sat on the bed. She opened it, parted the taupe tissue within.

She stared into the face of an African lioness.

Magnificent.

She touched it. The fur was real, smooth and soft in the direction of its growth, and coarser as she moved her fingers against the grain. A linen lining had been sewn in. Rich, creamy leather fashioned the wide nose and thin, dark lips, and carbon-black lashes seemed to flutter above each eyeslit. She could not imagine what time and care it had taken to do this. Perfect, genuine whiskers lanced from the snout.

She picked it up. Her fingers teased around the edges; some sort of plate obviously had been slipped inside, to give the mask some rigidity, plastic or thin wood. The mask felt surprisingly light, and delicate as Tibetan silk. *Beautiful*, she mused.

The ears lay back flat against the head. They and the open mouth gave the lioness an appearance of waiting. She could almost see her in the tall, waving grass of some veldt. Crouched, scenting the wind.

She stepped out of her kidskin heels, unzipped the back of her dress and allowed it to flow down her shoulders, heard its silky hiss to the floor. She gingerly draped it over the back of the bergère. Then the stockings and the black slip and finally the sheer lace bodysuit. She stood naked before the mirror, aware that already she was participating in some sort of arcane ceremony with him. That this was not just sex but ritual. The thought excited her in the way that sex itself hadn't for a very long time.

Her body was the object of that ceremony.

Her body . . . and the mask.

She'd never had a child. She had never allowed the tight smooth flesh of youth to disappear. At forty her body still deserved to wear the mask.

She took it to the mirror.

There was no strap. It was designed to extend across the back of the skull almost to the neck. Her own coiffured hair was nearly the same color as the lioness's fur. She could simply tuck it in.

She slipped it on.

The fit was perfect.

She leaned in close to the mirror and turned her head from right profile to left. Then stepped back and gazed at herself.

The mask hugged her like a second skin.

She was aware that she was trembling. It was warm in the room but her nipples stuck out rigid, dark.

A cat, she thought.

A predator.

You've never been so beautiful . . .

Trace sweat gathered between her breasts. Droplets, like diminutive jewels, glittered at the very ends of her nipples. In the mirror she saw the door open slowly behind her. He stepped silently into the room. He'd changed into a sheer, plum-colored kimono. She saw him smile at her image. She turned.

"You like it?"

"Stephen, it's . . . spellbinding."

"I'm glad," he said.

He moved across the room to the bed, reached beneath it and withdrew a second box. He smiled again.

"It's Tutsi, isn't it?"

His smile widened as though impressed. Or—

"You knew this was coming, didn't you?"

She nodded, smiling too beneath the mask.

He opened the box, extricating its contents from the tissue. He looked up at her and opened the kimono and let it fall off his shoulders. He was naked. She saw that, like her, the years had barely breathed on him.

In his hand he held up the massive head, its mane trailing eighteen inches at least. Its dark wide mouth hung open in a howl.

She sensed the sudden pull of him as he held his arms out to her and she saw the muscles of his arms twitch and the muscles of his shoulders. She crossed the distance between them and the supple grace of her walk seemed like something unknown to her.

She knew what sex with him would be like. Something crimson. A crimson gash in time.

She wanted his hands on her, the long, polished nails tearing.

She gazed into the eyes behind the mask, saw them flick across her body like the tongue of a whip. Were his eyes different? No, just keenly hungry. His hands were electric as he reached for her—power flowing from fingertips, bared wire-ends. Power that had nothing to do with wealth or position or even intellect, but something deeper and much older.

She could feel it clawing out of her too.

A power of her own.

＊　　＊　　＊

IN the morning the masks lay beside them on the bed.

She watched him sleep.

He was Stephen and she was Christine and they lay in bed in a Manhattan loft in Soho. Outside, below the windows, were shops and galleries. One of them was her own—she, Christine, with a master's in history and a doctorate in art, who had never wanted for anything nor failed at anything, born of New York privilege, who had been engaged not once but twice only to find each man bereft and even empty in both the moral courage to stand up to her and the wisdom not to try. Who had neither regretted these men nor missed them. Who had been quite content alone to this very moment.

And beside her lay Stephen Gannet, of whom she knew so very little. She knew only that he was exorbitantly wealthy from old family money rolled over in investments. He said he'd been in the military once but he didn't seem the type. Before and after, he'd prowled the world while his fortunes amassed. He'd been on digs but spoke of them as though bored. He supported the arts and was notorious for ignoring all other forms of charity. They'd met at the Vivian Beaumont Theater, at a benefit for the Lincoln Center Library for the Performing Arts. They'd talked about sculpture, architecture, Expressionism and Post-Impressionism, and Post Neo-Expressionism. She found him more than knowledgeable. And amazingly attractive. They went to bed. And now . . .

Her body ached, stung.

Yet she'd given as good as she'd received. She had only to look at his shoulders.

Cats, she thought. A mating of lions.

God knows what we did.

She could remember only in knifelike flashes of flesh on flesh, torso to torso, torso to back. At some point they'd discarded the masks to use their mouths, their tongues, their teeth, but that seemed to change none of the scarlet animal fury of their lovemaking. Something had worked its way inside of them. Some primal kiss of fantasy, some gossamer *thing* that lit her nerves and dropped her into an ecstatic, spiriferous bliss.

"Morning," he said.

"Good morning."

"Any regrets?"

"No."

"Good. That's good."

Her eyes focused on him, with her thoughts. He was an arcana. "You're so unique. Who *are* you?"

"A collector, nothing more. Rich by design like yourself." One finger idly traced a scratch at his neck. "My travels in the military showed me how rife the world was with whispers of the past. I collect little pieces of cultures, anything that's left. There's truth in those pieces, and it can be said that there's power in truth. All too often, those little pieces provide the only remnants of entire civilizations."

Little pieces? Her eyes accessed the room. His nonchalance astonished her; so much of what he so errantly referred to as "little pieces" were actually priceless relics. Each room here could be a museum worth millions.

"You must've been everywhere," she said, still in awe.

"Nearly. From Troy to Knossos to Nineveh. From Hastings to Golgotha to the Seven Hills of Rome. Yes." His voice turned sonorous. "From cenotes to ziggurats."

Fascinating. But his previous words resurfaced, like shadows standing just behind her. Little pieces. Power. Truth.

The wounds of his passion radiated on her skin.

She shook her head. "But I wish I knew . . ."

"What happened? Last night?"

"Yes. Not that it really matters. It was . . . wonderful."

His face grew stolid. Like a mask. "Of course it matters. Do you want to know what happened? I mean what *really* happened?"

Her thoughts dripped. She nodded.

"It was the masks. *The masks* happened."

She nodded.

"The *masks* . . ."

"Yes, but . . ."

He leaned up on one elbow. "The military showed me that we're living in an age that's been so thoroughly demythologized, there's nothing left. You know that, Christine—you know that as well as anybody in our field because you see it every day in your gallery. Art today has no mythology. Which is why so much of it is empty, drained of its real vitality, exsanguinated, and why we prefer the works of former eras, other cultures, things . . . so . . . old."

She stared at his words more than his face.

"People think that masks are about nothing more than children at Halloween. But take a *good look* at Mardi Gras and you see what masks can do. Even today. People get monumentally, fabulously drunk. They trash the streets. They do drugs they wouldn't ordinarily touch. And they fornicate with anything that moves, regardless of gender. The masks release them, Christine. The masks separate the chaff from the real seeds of the soul. But what they forget, and what *we know*, is that all they're doing is tapping into a kind of vestigial power based on a much, much earlier magic. When the powers that the masks invoke weren't just psychological. They were ever-reaching. They were cosmic, limitless, without parameter."

Her mouth fell open.

"There *are* no parameters," he said.

"You're saying *we* did that? Tapped into—"

"Something we don't understand. And why? Because of what I just said. The parameters don't belong to us. So many cultures, so many different imprecations . . . There's so much to dissimulate, you know?" His bare shoulders shrugged. "What do *you* think?"

He lifted a finger, traced the fine clawmarks on her bosom, then down her belly, then down her white thighs.

She shuddered—then laughed.

"I think it bears . . . further investigation," she said.

"So do I."

THEY arrived in a Rolls-Royce White Shadow. Date of manufacture: 1916. Original owner: Nicholas Romanov.

Masks

The crowd at the door parted for them immediately.

The Rolls matched her own plumage. The white owl was Athena's bird. *Athena. Wisdom. War.*

The feathers of her mask were real, luxuriantly arranged over a light wire frame with a soft satin lining, which was then affixed to the lined insert. The beak was a carven horn.

Stephen's was a faceplate of pressed gold, the image, perhaps, of the sun god Apollo. Athena's brother.

They wore white-satin, floor-length cloaks, and when they handed them to the woman at the club entry they were naked but for the masks, and wholly anonymous. He attached three silver chains to the pressure rings on her nipples. The sensation hummed through her.

They moved down the hall, and the crowd parted for them a second time.

Heavy chains and black leather manacles hung from walls and ceiling. A corpulent man tied by ropes to the steps of a wooden ladder was being whipped with a riding crop by his mistress. A couple made love in an iron cage as a crowd stood watching. But Christine felt all those eyes shift to her as they passed. Then she realized that most of them had begun to follow.

He led her to a dais inside another cage. She raised her arms to the manacles above her head and spread her legs wide to those who fixedly stared. *Captive bird.* He turned and spoke to the crowd.

"My sister," he said. "I give her to you. To touch, to know. To love as you see fit."

Nods from the crowd, eagerly submitting to his will.

Music blasting. Slayer. Danzig. Killing Joke.

The hunger in their eyes, and the smell of leather.

He stepped aside. The sun god offering up his bounty.

She felt serene. Soaring.

Stroked by a dozen hot winds.

*   *   *

IN the dream she stared. Beyond the dusk she saw cities, or things like cities: cities so old they were black, odd architectures which extended along a vanishing line of horrid lightlessness. A raging terra incognita. Horizons crammed with stars sparkled close against the cubist chasms. She saw buildings and roads, or things like roads, tunnels and pyramids, and strange flattened edifices whose chimneys gushed oily smoke. It was a necropolis, systematized and endless, endless as eons. Squat, stygian churches sang praise to mindless gods. Ataxia the only order. Darkness the only light.

She lay paralyzed in the black, nattering dream. Small, soft nubs prodded her. Hands, or things like hands, reached out to touch her lambent white flesh.

She saw it all. She saw time tick backward, death bloom into life, whole futures swallowed deep into the belly of history.

But later she awoke to the sound of him crying.

He no longer lay in bed with her. He sat naked in the dark at an Edgewood secretary, its mahogany writing lid opened.

A hand-dipped candle flickered.

"What? What's the matter?" she said.

Sleep had refreshed her. Even the dream, so oddly terrifying, seemed to rekindle her. His crying thrust into her consciousness.

"Stephen?"

"I'll lose you," he said.

"No you won't."

"Of course I will."

"Come to bed. You're not going to lose me."

A pause in the fluttering light. "You'll be the first, then."

"Yes. I'll be the first. Now come to bed."

The Windsor chair creaked when he rose. The candlelight licked his skin. But she stopped him as he crossed the room.

"And bring the masks," she finished.

*   *   *

Masks

LAMB and wolf.

He was the wolf.

Nanticoke, she guessed. Or Wicomico or Conoye. Tribes which had thrived along the East Coast from 10000 B.C. until the 1600s, when England had christened the New World with metallurgy, gunpowder and smallpox. These masks were all that remained of them.

She was the lamb, in rut, squirming beneath the cunning predator. The masks clicked when their faces touched; they were wood, hand-carved a thousand years ago by shark-tooth awls gingerly tapped with hammers of flat slate. Both, again, had been laced to the linen-covered insert plates, whose eyeholes matched those of the masks. The inserts felt soft as baby's skin.

The wolf's eyes hovered over her. They seemed strangely murky-blue, not like his eyes at all, nor a wolf's. Her crude passion paused. She looked at the eyes behind the mask as if studying something acrostic. Sumerian cuneiform. Druidic glyphs. The Runes of the ancient Norse.

Mindless now. Something as dead as all those languages.

She sensed sapor and heat. She felt the flavor of his sweat, and tasted the sound of his panting breath. She lay impaled, pinned to the bed. Her own eyes rolled upward, her teeth crimped her lower lip.

Then the lamb was felled.

Later, the wolf rolled off her, slaked. The veneer of sweat cooled her skin as it dried. She even continued to climax briefly, little pelvic hiccups, long after he'd withdrawn. The tracery of scratches on her body felt luminous, sensorial glitter running along her nerves.

Jesus, she thought, her breath husky beneath the mask.

She fell asleep—

—AND dreamed again. The strange, milky-blue eyes peered querulously at her. She lay naked, procumbent now. The lamb stretched out before the butchers?

No, this wasn't like that. Beyond the scape of sheer black, she heard a nattering. It seemed echoic, sullen. Small soft things touched her all over, between her fingers, between her lacquered toes. Hands, or things like hands, smoothed over her sleek back, down her thighs, the backs of her calves, the bottoms of her feet.

One climax after the next, subtle yet strangely powerful and so different. Her mind felt like a labyrinth now, an eighth-century Chinese puzzle box only now beginning to open.

What had he said?

You'll be the first, then.

And the black nattering drew on and on.

LATER she wakened again, her face hot behind the mask. She didn't want to take it off. He slept silently beside her; the candle had burned to a stub, its light diminished. She slid out of bed, then padded barefoot past countless relics and out of the room. She was still wearing the mask.

Down the carpeted hall.

In the paneled den stood a Federal Period highboy, circa 1760. Over it hung a British "Brown Bess" musket, and below that a blunderbuss whose hand-forged barrel must've been made a century before that.

She noted a Stradivarius in a frame, complete with rosined bow. On the facing wall hung a crude iron mask of Xipe, the Aztec god of good fortune. And beside it, Quetzalcoatl. Would these be the masks they wore next?

Or would there even be a next?

She parted the French doors, stepped out into the evening's sultry heat. A flavescent moon blundered above a reef of lit clouds. She stretched on the balcony, offering her nakedness to the night. The street below remained half-alive, but up here?

No one could see her but the gods.

Her dark nipples stood erect. She rubbed her navel with her finger and flinched. An electric sensation. Then she touched herself lower and sighed.

In the phosphoric moonlight, she let her hands open over the tight contours of her body. More electricity. Through the double-layered eyeholes of the mask, she gazed upward.

The moon shifted to a blur.

The sky turned black-pink.

A *hundred dead cultures*, she thought. A *thousand. They've all looked at this same moon. A century ago, or fifty centuries.*

Her mind flowed; something gripped her. She knew she loved him more than she had ever loved anyone in her life. Perhaps the loves of her past hadn't been real lovers at all but just a long line of spoor leading to the point of time in which she now stood. Naked. Satiated. Exuberant.

Her vision shifted, gazing high. Not a dream this time, but a waking scape of abstraction. The black nattering kissed at her ears. She rose on her tiptoes, slim and sleek, when she half-sensed the tiny proddings. She felt so different now, brimming with an alchemy of desires, and she knew it was because of him, because of Stephen.

The man of her dreams? Nothing quite so trite. A man forged of the world, a man with sensations so far removed from the fodder of flesh that was her past.

A man to love, to be a part of.

She let the night's caress release her, then traipsed back in. The mask—of thick carved wood plus the insert—should have felt heavy by now, but instead it felt like a cutting of rice paper. Her gaze roved the room.

From Troy to Knossos to Nineveh, she thought as her eyes strayed over countless relics. *He's been everywhere. Everywhere on earth.*

She stopped before a Shogun mirror with fabric inlays. Her image—her *masked* image—looked back.

She was beautiful, but . . .

The eyes.

Blue as the ocean, with a skein of milk.

Not her eyes at all.

Unsettled, she whisked the mask off. Tricks of candlelight and the denouement of passion. Her senses, now, had grown obvolute, folded over a hundred times by a hundred plush new consummations.

The Asian carpet felt warm under her bare feet. She wandered back to the highboy, opened the center drawer, set with mother-of-pearl and flower petals of white pine.

A folder in there, atop a mound of clutter. She picked up a piece of the clutter and found it rigid, yet thin as newsprint. A curved beam the color of balsa wood didn't even flex when she tried to bend it. What was this stuff? And what was in the folder?

Only one way to find out.

She set the wooden lamb mask on top of the highboy's veneered mantel. Yellowed sheets of paper filled the folder, along with grainy black-and-white photographs.

Here was a picture of Stephen, in a military uniform, bending over a long piece of something in the sand. The thing looked similar to the cryptic balsa beam. Another photo showed the beam close, with markings, much like glyphs, embossed along its center.

She picked up a sheet of paper out of the folder, and read:

TOP SECRET, SPECIAL ACCESS REQUIRED.
TEKNA, BYMAN, DINAR
21 April 1979

Dear Mr. President:

Enclosed you will find our official analysis of the aforementioned incident concerning the vehicle tracked by NORAD on 18 April 1979. Crash perimeter verified, 198NE, 2017S, near the Nellis Military Reservation. All Army CIC and recovery personnel have been properly debriefed. Recovered material now in transit via INSCOM Technical Escort Unit, 61st Ordnance, to W-P AFB. Please advise in compliance with AFR 200-1.

Signed,
Stephen D. Gannet, Major General O-7
Commander, Air Force Aerial Intelligence Group
Fort Belvior, Virginia, MJ-12/Dept. 4

She stared at the sheet as though it were a skiver of human skin in her hands. Behind her, the door clicked open.

"Indeed, from Troy to Knossos to Nineveh," came his flowing voice. "From Galilee to Agincourt to the blood-fields of Zama where Hannibal lost his dream."

The room hushed in her stare.

He was still wearing the mask, but his eyes seemed so blue, with a lacteal tinge. He stepped forward once, then twice, then a third time. His hands opened out like those of a preceptor on an ancient mount, before smoking crevices and plinths of obsidian and granite dolmens encrusted with the blood of the innocent.

"And from Kingman to San Angelo to Roswell," he said. Now his voice resembled a sound akin to crumbling rocks. "There is such truth in little things, be they from here or from places we cannot conceive. The little things, in a sense, are ghosts that haven't quite given up all their flesh."

She snatched up her mask from the highboy top. Her fingers pressed against it. The wooden lamb mask stared up inert. But beneath it . . .

The insert. The satin-covered lining.

She untied the insert from the mask's carved holes. The mask clunked to the floor — just dead wood.

The covered insert lay in her hands now, like something stillborn. She unlaced its velvet strings, slipped the insert from its delicate lining.

And withdrew . . . *another* mask.

It shone silver, like metal, in the candlelight. It had no weight at all.

"So much power in truth, and so much truth in culture, Christine." His milky-blue eyes stared through the face of the carven wolf. "*All* cultures, *all* relics. It's a symbology of life, isn't it? Mythology needn't belong exclusively to us. We'd be inept to believe that."

Only then did she fix her eyes on the insert, the mask within the mask. What looked up at her was this:

A curved plate in the shape of an inverted pear. The tiniest slit for a mouth. Only a bump for a nose.

And two spacious holes for eyes.

Her own eyes rose, then, back to him.

The wolf leapt.

And as the lamb was finally taken, the black nattering rose again from the deep, deep well of her soul.

At Eventide

KATHE KOJA

What he carried to her he carried in a red string bag. Through its mesh could be seen the gleam and tangle of new wire, a package of wood screws, a green plastic soda bottle, a braided brown coil of human hair; a wig? It could have been a wig.

To get to her he had come a long way: from a very large city through smaller cities to Eventide, not a city at all or even a town, just the nearest outpost of video store and supermarket, gas and ice and cigarettes. The man at the Stop-N-Go had directions to her place, a map he had sketched himself; he spoke as if he had been there many times: "It's just a little place really, just a couple rooms, living room and a workshop, there used to be a garage out back but she had it knocked down."

The man pointed at the handmade map; there was something wrong with his voice, cancer maybe, a sound like bones in the throat; he did not look healthy. "It's just this feeder road, all the way down?"

"That's right. Takes about an hour, hour and ten, you can be there before dark if you—"

"Do you have a phone?"

"Oh, I don't have her number. And anyway you don't call first, you just drive on down there and—"

"A phone," the man said; he had not changed his tone, he had not raised his voice but the woman sorting stock at the back of the store half-rose, gripping like a brick a cigarette carton; the man behind the counter lost his smile and "Right over there," he said, pointing past the magazine rack bright with tabloids, with *Playboy* and *Nasty Girls* and *Juggs*; he lit a cigarette while the man made his phone call, checked with a wavering glance the old Remington 870 beneath the counter.

But the man finished his call, paid for his bottled water and sunglasses and left in a late-model pickup, sober blue, a rental probably and "I thought," said the woman with the cigarette cartons, "that he was going to try something."

"So did I," said the man behind the counter. The glass doors opened to let in heat and light, a little boy and his tired mother, a tropical punch Slush Puppy and a loaf of Wonder bread.

ALISON, the man said into the phone. It's me.

A pause: no sound at all, no breath, no sigh; he might have been talking to the desert itself. Then: Where are you? she said. What do you want?

I want one of those boxes, he said. The ones you make. I'll bring you everything you need.

Don't come out here, she said, but without rancor; he could imagine her face, its Goya coloring, the place where her eye had been. Don't bring me anything, I can't do anything for you.

See you in an hour, the man said. An hour and ten.

HE drove the feeder road to the sounds of Mozart, '40s show tunes, flashy Tex-Mex pop; he drank bottled water; his throat hurt from the air-conditioning, a flayed unchanging ache. Beside him sat the string bag, bulging loose and uneven, like a body with a tumor, many tumors; like strange fruit; like a bag of gold from a fairy tale. The hair in the bag was beautiful, a thick and living bronze like the pelt of an animal, a thoroughbred, a beast prized for its fur. He had braided it carefully, with skill and a certain love, and secured it at the bottom with a small blue plastic bow. The other items in the bag he had purchased at a hardware store, just like he used to; the soda bottle he had gotten at the airport, and emptied in the men's room sink.

There was not much scenery, unless you like the desert, its lunar space, its brutal endlessness; the man did not. He was a creature of cities, of pocket parks and dull anonymous bars; of waiting rooms and holding cells; of emergency clinics; of pain. In the beige plastic box beneath the truck's front seat there were no fewer than eight different pain medications, some in liquid form, some in pills, some in patches; on his right bicep, now, was the vague itch of a Fentanyl patch. The doctor had warned him about driving while wearing it: *There might be some confusion*, the doctor said, *along with the sedative effect. Maybe a headache, too.*

A headache, the man had repeated; he thought it was funny. *Don't worry, doctor. I'm not going anywhere.* Two hours later he was on a plane to New Mexico. Right now the Fentanyl was working, but only just; he had an assortment of patches in various amounts—25, 50, 100 mgs—so he could mix and match them as needed, until he wouldn't need them anymore.

Now Glenn Gould played Bach, which was much better than Fentanyl. He turned down the air-conditioning and turned the music up loud, dropping his hand to the bag on the seat, fingers worming slowly through the mesh to touch the hair.

THEY brought her what she needed, there in the workshop: they brought her her life. Plastic flowers, fraying T-shirts, rosaries made of shells and shiny gold; school pictures, wedding pictures, wedding rings, books; surprising how often there were books. Address books, diaries, romance novels, murder mysteries, Bibles; one man even brought a book he had written himself, a ruffled stack of printer paper tucked into a folding file.

Everything to do with the boxes she did herself: she bought the lumber, she had a lathe, a workbench, many kinds and colors of stain and varnish; it was important to her to do everything herself. The people did their part, by bringing the objects—the baby clothes and car keys, the whiskey bottles and Barbie dolls; the rest was up to her.

Afterward they cried, some of them, deep tears strange and bright in the desert, like water from the rock; some of them thanked her, some cursed her, some said nothing at all but took their boxes away: to burn them, pray to them, set them on a shelf for everyone to see, set them in a closet where no one could see. One woman had sold hers to an art gallery, which had started no end of problems for her, *out there in the workshop, the problems imported by those who wanted to visit her, interview her, question her about the boxes and her methods, and motives, for making them. Totems, they called them, or Rorschach boxes, called her a shaman of art, a priestess, a doctor with a hammer and an "uncanny eye." They excavated her background, old pains exposed like bones; they trampled her silence, disrupted her work and worst of all they sicced the world on her, a world of the sad and the needy, the desperate, the furious and lost. In a very short time it became more than she could handle, more than anyone could handle and she thought about leaving the country, about places past the border that no one could find but in the end settled for a period of hibernation, then moved to Eventide and points south, the older, smaller work-shop, the bleached and decayed garage that a man with a bulldozer had kindly destroyed for her; she had made him a box about his granddaughter, a box he had cradled as if it were the child herself. He was a generous man, he wanted to do something to repay her although "No one," he said, petting the box, "could pay for this. There ain't no money in the world to pay for* this."

She took no money for the boxes, for her work; she never had. Hardly anyone could understand that: the woman who had sold hers to the gallery had gotten a surprising price but money was so far beside the point there was no point in even discussing it, if you had to ask, and so on she had money enough to live on, the damages had bought the house. And besides she was paid already, wasn't she? paid by the doing, in the doing, paid by peace and silence and the certain knowledge of help. The boxes helped them, always: sometimes the help of comfort, sometimes the turning knife but sometimes the knife was what they needed; she never judged, she only did the work.

Right now she was working on a new box, a clean steel frame to enclose the life inside: her life: she was making a box for herself. Why? and why now? but she didn't ask that, why was the one question she never asked, not of the ones who came to her, not now of herself. It was enough to do it, to gather the items, let her hand choose between this one and that: a hair clip shaped like a feather, a tube of desert dirt, a grimy nail saved from the wrecked garage; a photo of her mother, her own name in newsprint, a hospital bracelet snipped neatly in two. A life was a mosaic, a picture made from scraps: her boxes were only pictures of that picture and whatever else they might be or become— totems, altars, fetish objets*—they were lives first, a human arc in miniature, a précis of pain and wonder made of homely odds and ends.*

Her head ached from the smell of varnish, from squinting in the sawdust flume, from the heat; she didn't notice. From the fragments on the table before her, the box was coming into life.

HE thought about her as he drove. The Fentanyl seemed to relax him, stretch his memories like taffy, warm and ropy, pull at his brain without tearing it, as the pain so often did. Sometimes the pain made him do strange things: once he had tried to drink boiling water, once he had flung himself out of a moving cab. Once he woke blinking on a restaurant floor, something hard jammed in his mouth, an EMS tech above him: *'Bout swallowed his tongue,* the tech said to the restaurant manager, who stood watching with sweat on his face. *People think that's just a figure of speech, you know, but they wrong.*

He had been wrong himself, a time or two: about his own stamina, the state of his health; about *her,* certainly. He had thought she would die easily; she had not died at all. He had thought she could not see him, but even with one eye she picked him out of a lineup, identified him in the courtroom, that long finger pointing, accusing, dismissing all in one gesture, wrist arched like a bullfighter's before he places the killing blade, like a dancer's *en pointe,* poised to force truth out of air and bone: with that finger she said who he was and everything he was not, *mene, mene, tekel, upharsin*. It was possible to admire such certainty.

And she spared herself nothing; he admired her for that, too. Every day in the courtroom, before the pictures the prosecutor displayed: terrible Polaroids, all gristle and ooze, police tape and matted hair but she looked, she listened carefully to everything that was said and when the foreman said *guilty* she listened to that, too; by then her hair had come in, just dark brown down at first but it grew back as lush as before. Beautiful hair . . . it was what he had noticed first about her, in the bar, the Blue Monkey filled with art school students and smoke, the smell of cheap lager, he had tried to buy her a drink but *No thanks*, she had said, and turned away. Not one of the students, one of his usual prey, she was there and not-there at the same time, just as she was in his workshop later, there to the wire and the scalping knife, not-there to the need in his eyes.

In the end he had gotten nothing from her; and he admired her for that, too.

When he saw the article in the magazine—pure chance, really, just a half hour's numb distraction, *Bright Horizons* in the doctor's office, one of the doctors, he could no longer tell them apart—he felt in his heart an unaccustomed emotion: gratitude. Cleaved from him as the others had been, relegated to the jail of memory but there she was, alive and working in the desert, in a workshop filled with tools that—did she realize?—he himself might have used, working in silence and diligence on that which brought peace to herself and pure release to others; they were practically colleagues, though he knew she would have resisted the comparison, she was a good one for resisting. The one who got away.

He took the magazine home with him; the next day he bought a map of New Mexico and a new recording of Glenn Gould.

SHE would have been afraid if it were possible, but fear was not something she carried; it had been stripped from her, scalped from her, in that room with

*the stuttering overheads, the loud piano music and the wire. Once the worst
has happened, you lose the place where the fear begins; what's left is only scar
tissue, like old surgery, like the dead pink socket of her eye. She did not wait
for him, check the roads anxiously for him, call the police on him; the police
had done her precious little good last time, they were only good for cleaning
up and she could clean up on her own, now, here in the workshop, here where
the light fell empty, hard and perfect, where she cut with her X-Acto knife a
tiny scrolling segment from a brand-new Gideon Bible:* blessed are the merciful, for they shall obtain mercy.

*Her hand did not shake as she used the knife; the light made her brown
hair glow.*

THE man at the Stop-N-Go gave good directions: already he could see the
workshop building, the place where the garage had been. He wondered how
many people had driven up this road as he did, heart high, carrying what
they needed, what they wanted her to use; he wondered how many had been
in pain as he was in pain; he wondered what she said to them, what she
might say to him now. Again he felt that wash of gratitude, that odd embodied
glee; then the pain stirred in him like a serpent, and he had to clench his
teeth to hold the road.

When he had pulled up beside her workshop, he paused in the dust his
car had raised to peel off the used patch and apply a fresh one; a small one,
one of the 25 mgs. He did not want to be drowsy, or distracted; he did not
want sedation to dilute what they would do.

*HE looked like her memories, the old bad dreams, yet he did not; in the end
he could have been anyone, any aging tourist with false new sunglasses and a
sick man's careful gait, come in hope and sorrow to her door; in his hand he
held a red string bag, she could see some of what was inside. She stood in the
doorway waiting, the X-Acto knife in her palm; she did not wish he would go
away, or that he had not come, wishing was a vice she had abandoned long*

ago and anyway the light here could burn any wish to powder, it was one of the desert's greatest gifts. The other one was solitude; and now they were alone.

"ALISON," he said. "You're looking good."

She said nothing. A dry breeze took the dust his car had conjured; the air was clear again. She said nothing.

"I brought some things," he said, raising the bag so she could see: the wires, the bottle, the hair: her hair. "For the box, I mean . . . I read about it in a magazine, about you, I mean."

Those magazines: like a breadcrumb trail, would he have found her without one? wanted to find her, made the effort on his own? Like the past to the present, one step leading always to another and the past rose in her now, another kind of cloud: she did not fight it but let it rise, knew it would settle again as the dust had settled; and it did. He was still watching her. He still had both his eyes, but other things were wrong with him, his voice for one, and the way he walked, as if stepping directly onto broken glass and "You don't ask me," he said, "how I got out."

"I don't care," she said. "You can't do anything to me."

"I don't want to. What I want," gesturing with the bag, his shadow reaching for her as he moved, "is for you to make a box for me. Like you do for other people. Make a box of my life, Alison."

No answer; she stood watching him as she had watched him in the courtroom. The breeze lifted her hair, as if in reassurance; he came closer; she did not move.

"I'm dying," he said. "I should have been dead already. I have to wear this," touching the patch on his arm, "to even stand here talking, you can't imagine the pain I'm in."

Yes I can, she thought.

"Make me a box," as he raised the bag to eye level: fruit, tumor, sack of gold, she saw its weight in the way he held it, saw him start as she took the bag from him, red string damp with sweat from his grip.

"I told you on the phone," she said. "I can't do anything for you." She set the bag on the ground; her voice was tired. "You'd better go away now. Go home, or wherever you live. Just go away."

"Remember my workshop?" he said; now there was glass in his voice, glass and the sound of the pain, whatever was in that patch wasn't working anymore: grotesque, that sound, like a gargoyle's voice, like the voice of whatever was eating him up. "Remember what I told you there? Because of me you can do this, Alison, because of what I did, what I *gave* you. . . . Now it's your turn to give to me."

"I can't give you anything," she said. Behind her her workshop stood solid, door frame like a box frame, holding, enclosing her life: the life she had made, piece by piece, scrap by scrap, pain and love and wonder, the boxes, the desert and he before her now was just the bad-dream man, less real than a dream, than the shadow he made on the ground: he was nothing to her, nothing and "I can't make something from nothing," she said, "don't you get it? All you have is what you took from other people, you don't have anything I can *use*."

His mouth moved, jaw up and down like a ventriloquist dummy's: because he wanted to speak, but couldn't? because of the pain? which pain? and "Here," she said: not because she was merciful, not because she wanted to do good for him but because she was making a box, because it was her box she reached out with her long strong fingers, reached with the X-Acto knife and cut some threads from the bag, red string, thin and sinuous as veins and "I'll keep these," she said, and closed her hand around them, said nothing as he looked at her, kept looking through the sunglasses, he took the sunglasses off and

"I'm *dying*," he said finally, his voice all glass now, a glass organ pressed to a shuddering chord but she was already turning, red threads in her palm, closing the door between them so he was left in the sun, the dying sun; night comes quickly in the desert; she wondered if he knew that.

He banged on the door, not long or fiercely; a little later she heard the truck start up again, saw its headlights, heard it leave but by then she had already called the state police: a sober courtesy, a good citizen's compunction because her mind was busy elsewhere, was on the table with the bracelet and the varnish, the Gideon Bible and the red strings from the bag. She worked until a trooper came out to question her, then worked again when he had gone: her fingers calm on the knife and the glue gun, on the strong steel frame of the box. When she slept that night she dreamed of the desert, of long roads and empty skies, her workshop in its center lit up like a burning jewel; as she dreamed her good eye roved beneath its lid, like a moon behind the clouds.

In the morning paper it explained how, and where, they had found him, and what had happened to him when they did, but she didn't see it, she was too far even from Eventide to get the paper anymore. The trooper stopped by that afternoon, to check on how she was doing; she told him she was doing fine.

"That man's dead," he said, "stone dead. You don't have to worry about him."

"Thank you," she said. "Thank you for coming." In the box the red strings stretched and curled from top to bottom, from the bent garage nail to the hospital bracelet, the Bible verse to the Polaroid: like a Jacob's ladder, a voudou vévé, like roads marked on a map to show the way.

That Glisters Is

TANITH LEE

When he was a child, he understood as a child ... through a glass, darkly. ...

The child remembers, when he was seven years old, how his uncle Talva drowned at the top of the stairs.

But the Face had been seen before that. Their maid, Ersenne, had seen it, and because of seeing it, had fallen down the whole flight, hurting her foot so badly that for half a year she had walked with a limp.

When the child is ten, they move from the house on the hill. The child has no more rights in this matter than the family dog.

(The dog, incidentally, has seen the Face countless times, never showing dismay or much surprise.)

✻　　✻　　✻

DURING adolescence the child, now a boy, has various dreams, but all his dreaming seems infected by a general lunacy, and more and more often by sex. Also he rarely recalls very much, once awakened. He is dimly aware that certain elements recur. But then, so do other certain elements of other dreams (figures which undress but disappear at the last moment, savage wolves— which creature he was made afraid of when small, and which he has to fight and kill). Of the particular dreams, he does keep a memory of fire which glimmers in water, and of a shadow, enclosing a burning core.

THE family is constantly moving, all over the city, though never quite out of it. His father's irksome job necessitates this.

By now the boy knows his own name (rather than merely answering to it, like the dog). He is called Conraj.

Conraj enjoys the constant moves. Conversely, his mother hates them, cries and grows red in the face with anxiety, faints, and has to be put to bed. Ersenne left them some years before. The new maid is pert, dirty, and virtually useless. One day she contrives to let Conraj, now thirteen, see her partly naked. He is quite uninterested.

NOT long after this the dog, grown old, dies peacefully.

Conraj is distressed, but as helpless, naturally, as anyone in a confrontation with death.

He soon experiences, however, a series of wonderful dreams, which he will retain.

Conraj dreams he and the dog are racing, side by side, on feet swift as if winged (as are the god Mercury's) along a wide white highway unlike anything seen in the concreted city. In the dream it is either near sunset or just after dawn, the sky golden, and there are glimpses of mountains and high, terraced rocks. The dog is young and full of strength. Conraj too feels a strength he has never felt, even at full pitch in the waking world. There is a sensation—not of joy—but of some powerful elation, slightly tinged by a bright fear—which is *not* fear.

That Glisters Is

*   *   *

WHEN Conraj is seventeen, his father decrees that he must forget any ideas of college and instead start at once to work in his uncle Lutyer's firm. (The family finances are not good.)

Conraj is resignedly horrified. But also, at seventeen, feels the boundless miles of time yet before him. Surely things will change? So he goes meekly to Uncle Lutyer's establishment, stiffly dressed in a cheap dark suit and strangulating tie. He supposes Uncle Lutyer will be considerate, seeing they are related, but Uncle Lutyer is not. He puts Conraj into the low-paid post of an overseer on the factory floor. Here Conraj is automatically loathed and despised by all the workers, insulted strategically by grander employees, and ignored by his uncle, except for once every month. Then Uncle Lutyer invites Conraj to take lunch with him in the management canteen.

This canteen is quite spectacular. It has velvet banquettes and bronze light-fitments. The favored feed on such things as cold rare roast beef, squab, oysters, chocolate soup, pineapple — food to which Conraj is unused, and after which he tends to feel queasy. Wine, though, is never served him, only to Uncle Lutyer, who takes half a bottle of Caesar's Blood regularly at each meal. (Including, rumor has it, breakfast.)

They do not converse. Between courses, Uncle Lutyer pontificates. Work is always his theme. Fine work, or shoddy work. How one must apply oneself. He has many anecdotes of great men who have worked hard, and lost creatures who have not.

One day, after a particularly difficult entrée, Conraj speaks to his uncle. That is, he waits until his uncle begins on the soufflé, and then Conraj says, "I was thinking of Uncle Talva last night. I've never understood how he came to die."

Uncle Lutyer raises his boiled eyes from the cindery moustache — his face by now seems only to comprise these two features.

"What?"

The word does not mean *What?* It means: *Be silent.*

Conraj fails to heed.

"They said that he drowned. On the stairs. What could that be?"

"Pneumonia," states Uncle Lutyer. He sits up, dabs his lips with the napkin, pushes back his chair. Rising, he leaves the canteen.

Conraj waits a moment, then also gets up.

As he too is leaving the canteen, a well-dressed man of Uncle Lutyer's age approaches him.

"I was the friend of Talva," says this man. "Do you know the Thirteenth Hour on West Boulevard?"

Conraj says that he does know of it.

"We will meet there at nine tonight."

THE Thirteenth Hour is the haunt of prostitutes, but Conraj is unaware of this. He decides the women there are very glamorous, and free, even though they have no sexual interest for him. Later he notices a young man with golden hair and mascaraed eyes, but before Conraj can even blink, the old man appears, Lippenkitz, his dead uncle's friend.

"TALVA," says Lippenkitz, "was obsessed by your house. I mean, of course, your father's earlier house, on September Hill.

"He would often," Lippenkitz continues, "go to visit your father, really only wanting to be in your house."

"Why?" asks Conraj.

Lippenkitz inquires what Conraj remembers of his uncle Talva, and looks sad when Conraj cannot remember much at all, apart from the fact that Talva drowned at the top of the stairs.

"What then," says Lippenkitz, "did that involve?"

Conraj is clear that it is he who has asked this question but, without answering, Lippenkitz is now asking it himself.

However, in order to have made plain something which, for some reason, has increasingly begun to nag at him, Conraj racks his brains. He describes an evening dinner, when his family was more prosperous, and Uncle Talva rose from the dinner table about ten o'clock, as it seemed only to seek the lavatory on the floor above.

"Suddenly," says Conraj, recollecting how sudden it had been, "we heard a thrashing noise, and a strange sound, which was, presumably, my uncle—drowning. My mother ran out and so did our maid, who, at the time, was still Ersenne. There were then screams. Then my father ran out. After a while, Ersenne came back in—she still limped then—very white, and hurried me away to bed, saying I shouldn't have been allowed to stay up so long. But later I heard the doctor on the landing, shouting that Uncle Talva had drowned. He accused my father of drowning Uncle Talva in the bathtub on the upper floor."

"So you have never questioned your father about any of this?"

"It would be impossible."

"Yes," says Lippenkitz, even more sadly. He sips his brandy and says, "Let me tell you about Talva. He was, in his youth, a very handsome man, and something of a dandy. He started a whole fashion based on black and white. As he grew older and his looks waned, as unfortunately they normally do, he began to brood. One night, he said to me, 'I believe there is something in my brother's house.' "

Conraj says, "You mean in my father's house?"

"On the hill, yes. I was accordingly invited to a dinner there, but saw nothing."

"What did you expect to see?"

"I had no idea. Talva was excited but vague. And although I saw nothing, Talva would keep on going back there. He said to me, 'It shines. I know it does.' "

"What shone?"

"I have no idea."

Lippenkitz says, mournfully now, "He told me he was determined to find it."

"What?"

"I have no idea. But he was determined. I said, 'Talva, let me go with you.' He said, 'No, you can't see it. It isn't for you.' I was hurt. We quarreled. I let him go. That very night—he drowned."

"But *how?*"

Conraj waits for Lippenkitz to answer that he had or has no idea.

Lippenkitz says, "There was another Place there, by the bathroom, on the landing. Did you ever notice? I heard one of the maids saw something. . . . Whatever it was, Talva saw it too. My poor Talva, he saw it and stumbled."

"He *drowned.*"

"Yes, stumbled into some water. He must have been startled to do so — he was generally neat on his feet."

"You mean the bath —"

"No, no." For a moment Lippenkitz is not sad, but impatient. "No, not *bath*water. Some pool. Or lake — it was freshwater in his lungs, you know. Nothing clean or sanitized from a tap."

Conraj frowns, also out of his depth.

Lippenkitz says, "Your father was cleared of all blame. But there has been a stigma on him ever since. Oh, if only Talva had watched his step."

After this conversation, which leaves Conraj more perplexed than ever, Lippenkitz sneaks slyly away.

Presently realizing the old man will not return, Conraj gets up. He then sees again the exquisite mascaraed young man beckoning to him from a curtained doorway. As if in a trance, Conraj follows him, and in the subsequent acute delights of the evening, forgets, temporarily, what he has gone to the Thirteenth Hour to learn.

In the morning, though, at Uncle Lutyer's firm, Conraj discovers he has been dismissed. No reason is ever given.

OVER the succeeding months, aggravated and frustrated by his father's ceaseless tirades — Conraj looks for, but has not yet found, another job — Conraj stays out of the house as much as he is able. "Go, you parasite!" screams his father. "Spend my money on booze and women!" In fact Conraj walks the city. If he drinks, it is a cup of coffee. As for women, he likes them, but not in any way that makes it necessary to pay them or buy them presents.

That Glisters Is

After an interrogation for a job in a printing works (which Conraj fails to secure), he finds himself near the old house on September Hill. The house, with some others, is being demolished, and Conraj stands watching, shocked. It is as if someone is rubbing out the early chapters of his life. A month later, Conraj returns, and walks about the empty lot. And now it is as if the chapters *are* rubbed out.

Curiously, part of the stairway of the house — the fatal stairway — remains. As dusk falls, Conraj climbs the stair and sits at the top, near where, perhaps, the bathroom had been.

Above, stars come out, and below lights pierce the city. Conraj feels the pressure of a possible event — but nothing happens. Then a night watchman appears with a torch, and orders him to get down, as the stair is dangerous.

THAT evening, in a café, Conraj overhears a small item. A young male prostitute from the Thirteenth Hour, a popular blond, has vanished without trace after entering a tobacconist's. The tobacconist has sworn hysterically he never saw the young man, or anyone, walk into the shop. The young man's friends have never seen him emerge. Foul play is suspected, reviewed, debated, and dismissed. Someone in the café cites the instance of a grandfather who disappeared at a station, in similar bizarre circumstances. Neither case will ever be solved.

YEARS pass. Conraj obtains work as a journalist. That is, he types or pastes up the work of others, fetches them tea and beer, and sometimes attends them at funerals, weddings or murder inquiries.

The family by now exist (maidlessly) in a large damp flat. Although they have little money, Conraj's mother has acquired a dog, a stray that she began by feeding, but which now lives with them. Conraj is fond of the dog, but conscious it is not *his*: it is his mother's. One day Conraj's mother runs away with the dog, leaving a brief insulting note. They are never seen again by Conraj or his father.

Conraj's father sits drinking cheap vodka. "What will become of you, you parasite?" he asks Conraj. Then he throws a bottle at Conraj, which almost misses him. Conraj goes to the hospital for stitching up, and then moves to a small room near the dye works.

THAT spring, Conraj has to attend another important reporter at the interview of a woman who, alone, has won the annual, and significant, city lottery. The woman who has won is none other than Ersenne.

Conraj is prepared for vast differences, but recognizes her at once, despite the time which has passed. Ersenne is heavier, but radiant, healthy, and smart in wonderful clothes, hairstyle, and jewelry.

Conraj does not say who he is during the interview, but Ersenne begins to glance at him oddly. When he returns, rather cautiously, to her apartment later, she opens the door and at once throws her arms round him. They drink strawberry juice—neither much likes alcohol—on Ersenne's balcony. She tells him about the new house she is buying at the Carousel Gardens. For ten years before her lottery win, she had nursed a tyrannical sick aunt in this apartment. "The day after her funeral, I bought the lottery ticket," says Ersenne, proudly.

When Conraj rises to leave, Ersenne too gets up, and stays him with one plump hand on which a sapphire now burns blue.

"Let me help you, Conraj. I know things can't have been easy for you at all."

Conraj is appalled, having feared all along she will think he is here with her to beg. "That isn't what I'd like. What I *would* like is to see you from time to time. To see your new house. And, Ersenne—"

"Yes, dear?"

"Will you tell me about the thing you saw on the upper landing of the house on the hill?"

"The thing I saw—"

"The Face."

Ersenne has become very still. She sits down again, then lights a cigarette with a platinum lighter.

"I asked my uncle Lutyer—he promptly sacked me. Or, that may have been for another reason, I've never been sure. An old friend—I think a lover—of my uncle Talva's insisted Talva drowned there. Which, anyway, I knew. I also know there was something—I dream about it. Particularly since I began to live by myself. But—I can never properly remember my dreams. Except about my dog. We were running fast with wings on our heels, in golden light."

"The golden light, yes," says Ersenne gently. She puts away the cigarette, allowing it to consume itself. "I dream of that. And the Face is of gold. The Face—showed me the lottery numbers, reflecting in the grotto pools, Conraj, dear."

"At the house on the hill—all those years ago?"

"No, dear. Last month only."

"So you've seen it here, in your aunt's flat?"

"Everywhere. In dreams. Since she died."

"But it was on the stairs in our house—"

"For a moment. That was why I fell, you see. It made me jump. And those stairs were always awkward."

"You hallucinated?"

"I thought so. But no. It *was* there. Your uncle Talva saw it endlessly. He used to sit up there on the landing, and wait for it. Oh, he never said so, but it was obvious to me. He was very nice, your uncle Talva. He used to slip me money—not because I did anything for him—oh, he wasn't inclined that way."

"Neither am I."

"No, dear, of course you're not."

"Ersenne, how did he die?"

Ersenne folds her hands, and the flicker of the sapphire catches her eyes. She raises it smiling, and kisses it. The gesture is utterly charming—loving, not acquisitive.

"Poor Talva. He made some mistake. I can't explain it. But somehow he mixed them up—that Place, and this place. And fell between the two."

Conraj does not understand. But that is all he expects now, on this subject. Not to understand.

"Others, of course, see it as well," abruptly adds Ersenne. "Let me take you to the bank."

Conraj protests. Ersenne insists. A taxi manifests and they are whisked to the huge new city bank on South Boulevard. Once in the foyer, Conraj realizes Ersenne has not brought him here to embarrass him with proffered money, but to show him that, inside, high, high up on a wall like rippled green onyx, is a Face of Gold, beautiful, remote, savage and wild.

The moment he sees it, Conraj remembers it from his dreams. *There* it is contained inside vast cliffs, high on a wall curtained by green water—which the faux-onyx approximates quite well.

Two weeks later, at a lavish party in Ersenne's mansion, Conraj meets the artist who made the Face of Gold for the bank. His name is Maturinn, and at forty he is thirteen years older than Conraj. Nevertheless, the momentum between them begins immediately. They become lovers, and presently Conraj is living with Maturinn in eight strange eight-sided rooms by the river.

LIVING with Maturinn and his silvery dog Auroris, Conraj now begins to dream regularly of the high cliffs, the wide road, the grotto where the golden Thing stands from its wall of water, perfect as an egg. Even so, Conraj never really remembers what each dream is about. He is aware now, however, that some not only occur at night, but are set during night, in darkness, when torchlit processions, like burning snakes, move up the cliff.

A cat comes to live with them, too. It has one eye, three legs, and a coat like silk. Conraj definitively calls the cat "the Cat." While Conraj is never sure if Auroris sees in their rooms the Face—or other elements he himself sees only when asleep—the Cat undeniably does. At first, the Cat stares, the one eye locked, or moving, on some image which, to Conraj and Maturinn (if not the dog), is invisible. After a while, however, the Cat tends three-leggedly to spring to higher furniture, as if wishing to be nearer whatever it is it sees.

That Glisters Is

Maturinn tells Conraj that he often dreams of the Cat inside the caverns of the cliff. The Cat, in the dreams, has both eyes and all four legs. It is also winged, skimming easily over pools of water on the grotto's floor, reflecting in them like the torchlight, and the Face.

CONRAJ and Maturinn do not much discuss the oddity of their similar dreams, nor the oddity that Ersenne also seems to experience them. Maturinn eventually mentions he has, elsewhere in his life, met two men and a woman, none known to the others, who have seen the Face of Gold.

"I designed the facsimile for the bank, so it would be recognized," he tells Conraj, after they have been together a year. "In case there are more who know it, here. Almost certainly there are. I recall once reading of a hermit who saw visions of a saint, in that form, like a golden mask. That, though, was in the Middle Ages."

The following year, Maturinn suffers a minor heart attack. A Warning, as the scowling doctor disapprovingly and ominously tells him.

"It seems," says Maturinn, "I work too hard, drink too much, and make love too often."

Conraj, shaking, says that Maturinn must therefore work less, drink less, make less love.

"In other words," says Maturinn sternly, "*live* less. What's the point in that? I might as well live properly, until I die."

There is then a passionate and distressing row between them, which Conraj ends in terror, seeing Maturinn begin to look gray.

Later, Maturinn tells Conraj that he has no fears of death, not even any fears of leaving Conraj, since he will not, in fact, be dead, but *there*, where Conraj will eventually be himself, and where Conraj, if Conraj so wishes, will always be able to meet with Maturinn, in the meanwhile.

"What are you talking about?"

"*There*," says Maturinn. "Do you still not know?"

*   *   *

SEVEN years later, Conraj has a short affair, while Maturinn is away in another country. Returning in the early hours of the morning, devoured by unease, Conraj walks into the eight-sided rooms, and goes out on the wooden deck to watch the night river.

The Cat is already there.

Conraj starts to talk to the Cat, which sometimes purrs, like a polite acquaintance whose mind is on other things.

For some reason, Conraj has become obsessed by an old argument from his typing and pasting-up days, years ago. One of the important reporters had extravagantly used the phrase (from Shakespeare's *Merchant of Venice*) "All that glitters is not gold," which Conraj had seen as quoted wrongly. Having altered the word *glitters* to the correct *glisters*, he was later shaken and punched by the drunk reporter, who accused Conraj firstly of bad typing, and when Conraj detailed the error, of idiocy. The piece duly appeared in the journal with *glitters*.

"*Glisters*," Conraj now insists to the Cat.

Then he breaks down and tells the Cat everything about the affair. The Cat stares all the while at the dim benighted barges on the river (perhaps scenting rats).

Weeks later, when Maturinn returns, Conraj struggles to put the affair from his mind. He nearly faints when Maturinn says, "Oh Conraj, don't worry about those two or three nights in summer. These things happen. Forget it."

Conraj blusters.

Maturinn says, "I'm perfectly well. You haven't harmed me, or yourself. Remember. All that glisters is not gold. But some that glisters is."

Then Conraj is silent. He can only conclude the Cat has told Maturinn the story (putting Conraj's side very tactfully) among the cliffs of their composite dream.

CONRAJ is now so used to those dreams, that Place, the Face of Gold, to the *idea* of it, that he only questions Maturinn properly ten years after all that, when Maturinn is dying, not from heart failure, but a street accident involving someone else's car.

This is because, instantly following Conraj's reception of the telephone call from the hospital, something happens in one of the eight-sided rooms.

Conraj, having thrown down the phone, is rushing to get his coat and wallet and dash to the ward where Maturinn is lying, dying, and Conraj is weeping, and he passes a mirror and sees himself as now he is, and does not know himself. All he can identify, in fact, is the pale scar left over from the night his father threw a bottle at him.

And then, the room is filled by somewhere else.

Although to Conraj it is almost as familiar as the city, and more so than anywhere else he has ever been, he staggers to a halt.

Gilded rock towers up, and cascades down. A high-ceilinged sky is the color of amontillado, and great birds wheel slowly. There is a cave-mouth, the entry to the grottoes, dripping crystal fringes of water, patched by pyrite, and through the shadow of these caves, a glow of gold, shining like a lamp.

Conraj notices vaguely that he is dressed in white clothing, and holds a burning torch. He feels a buoyancy which drinkers have described to him, and which he has never himself experienced. All his agony over Maturinn's accident is gone.

But then, something makes Conraj glance down, and through the miles of rock on which he is standing, a black shape is cutting its way like a shark through smooth water.

Conraj watches aghast as this creature, gigantic and blackly gleaming, moves smoothly through and through the rock, as a needle would puncture through layers of thick velvet. But then the beast emerges clear of the cliff, into the sky. And Conraj sees it is an airplane, a metal machine of his own world, with lights and cabin windows.

Then he screams and falls, and as he does so, for a second the torch scorches and water laps over his face, and he almost swallows some and chokes—but he is not Talva, and this does not quite happen. Instead he finds himself sprawled on the polished floor of the eight-sided room. Springing up howling, Conraj rushes out into the winter street, coatless, where only the compassion of a taxi driver takes him to the hospital without any money.

"No, I'm in no pain," says Maturinn, "and do you know, they say my heart is excellent, would have lasted me another thirty years.

"Don't cry," says Maturinn. "I've nothing to fear. Nor you, darling."

Then Conraj blurts the story about the Place he has seen, in their rooms, and the airliner which carved through it.

"Really?" says Maturinn. "How fascinating—oh, but of course. Physically we are still here. Things of this world do pass in and out of *there*—how else can we do so in our physical sleep?" Dreamily he says, "But once we're really there, that won't matter."

"Where is it? Where?" cries Conraj, clutching at Maturinn's sheet, and at straws. "Everything—every country, region, area—is *known*! In space then? Out there—in some other galaxy—?"

"Certainly *in*," says Maturinn. The morphine has made him distant and beautiful as a saint. "In *here*." He touches his own chest.

Conraj shakes his head.

"Inside us, each of us—that's where it is. The thing we call the heart, which isn't the physical heart at all. The true heart and core of us. *Inside.* Do you recall that little statue I carved, with an empty part where the upper stomach was—*there*. You joked and called it Hunger. But it is hunger of a sort."

"How can we go *inside*?" barks Conraj, furious with fear.

"As you've said, the rest is taken, built over. Where else could heaven be? Where else is there room? Where else could we go?"

"But—"

Maturinn says, "Have you ever heard of persons who vanish, suddenly and inexplicably? Perhaps everyone has these worlds within. I've always thought so. And groups of us have the *same* world. That's the thing, Conraj. You and I, for example. And those few people I've met. And Ersenne. And animals—the dogs, our cat. When we're alone, or better, if we're with companions that have the same world in them that we do, the effect is heightened. But others have other inner worlds. Not ours. Theirs.

That Glisters Is

"Think of it this way," says Maturinn. "We are standing back to back, you and I, pressed close. Flesh, the lovely illusion, melts. We sink inward to this inner land common to us both. Now imagine it isn't only you and I, but all the countless ones who also have our world inside them. Imagine it, Conraj, as if we are all standing in a ring, yet facing outward. Outside, in front of our seeing eyes, *this* world. Within the ring, unseen, the inner world. We sink down into it. That's where at last we go. Who can doubt it? Where I shall go presently. And you, one day. Nothing lost. All to come. That Face we see, is it a god? Or the mask of a god . . . Visions pass into the here and now, also water, lottery numbers. . . . Just as the airplane passed the other way, through the golden cliff. I wonder what they saw, and if the pilot will report it. My God, Conraj, the plane — it could only be — it must have been full of the ones that share that Place with us — how else — did they get there?"

Skin pure and almost metallic from the hospital lamp, Maturinn stares with shining eyes. His face is the Face. Conraj gazes at it and does not, until a doctor comes hurrying, know that Maturinn is gone.

As Conraj will write, grief is a flower best left to rot.

(He does not, at that time, notice the reference in a newspaper to an airplane mysteriously lost over the Atlantic.)

Conraj is a celebrated writer, now seventy years of age. He lives alone, but for a housekeeper, above the river, with an old dog, which will be, he says, the last. The dog does not apparently have the same inner world, but another, of its own. (Perhaps the same one as the housekeeper's? They are close and sometimes seem to be telepathic.) But Conraj and the dog get on very well. They may be seen sitting together in the sun on the deck, or walking stiffly in the Carousel Gardens.

Sometimes Conraj dreams of Maturinn, but these dreams are never set in any particular place, though always in this world. And he and Maturinn are often old in the dreams, have grown old in each other's society. (Conraj cannot, anymore, see as a child does, darkly. . . .)

The golden face at the bank on South Boulevard was taken down last year. Now they have a bust of the bank's president, an impressive man with fat eyes.

Ersenne's not especially opulent grave is in the city cemetery. Uncle Lutyer also lies nearby, in the large mausoleum, which houses additionally the remains of Talva. If not, it would seem, Conraj's father.

Conraj has never visited any of these graves. The graves are, he suggests, only stone bookmarks left in pages of earth. (Maturinn was cremated. There is a plaque to mark his life and passing, somewhere or other. Conraj has never looked.)

Life does pass so swiftly. Only the dream takes its timeless time, and, never changing, is always constant. Conraj senses these dreams, even when he fails to remember them.

Conraj writes: "And now there abide these three, Faith, Hope, and Kindness; but the greatest of these is Kindness. And why is Kindness the greatest? Because Kindness demands of us some extra muscle. Faith and Hope are actually native."

He smiles, writing this, and touches the sapphire ring Ersenne left to him.

Conraj does not "believe," has no faith at all, nor any hope. Is more comfortable without them. (Anyone might hallucinate, particularly under stress.) He has amicably decided, and written, that after death there is nothing, simply a well-earned rest.

But sometimes it occurs to him how absolute and momentous his dreams, whatever they are, seem to him in the first instants of waking, although then he forgets them, often utterly, as reality returns. If it were a fact, that inner world which Maturinn so entirely credited, no doubt life too would quickly fade, on waking there.

Then the last old dog, alert, pleased, lifts his head, moves his eyes, seeing something, some image that Conraj cannot. No doubt a gnat, or tiny fly.

Graven Images

M. Christian's work can be found in such books as *Sons of Darkness, The Mammoth Book of Short Erotic Novels*, and John Skipp's *Mondo Zombie*, as well as other anthologies and magazines. He is also the editor of the anthologies *Eros Ex Machina, Midsummer Night's Dreams, Guilty Pleasures*, and *The Burning Pen*. His collection of short stories, *Dirty Words*, is due out from Alyson books in 2001.

Storm Constantine is the author of the *Wraeththu* trilogy, and has written fourteen novels as well as numerous short stories. Her new trilogy, *The Magravandias Chronicles*, will be published by Tor this year, starting with *Sea Dragon Heir*.

Esther M. Friesner has had twenty-nine novels and over a hundred short stories published, besides editing five anthologies, including the popular *Chicks in Chainmail* series. She won the Nebula Award twice and was a Hugo Award finalist once. She lives in Connecticut with her family, mad cats, and obligatory hamster.

Nina Kiriki Hoffman has been writing for seventeen years and has sold lots of short stories and a number of books of various lengths. Her latest novel is

A *Red Heart of Memories,* which came out from Ace in 1999. She lives with many cats and imaginary friends.

Jack Ketchum is the author of the novels *Off Season, Hide and Seek, Cover, She Wakes, The Girl Next Door, Offspring, Joyride, Stranglehold, Red,* and *Ladies' Night,* the novella *Right to Life,* and the story collections *The Exit at Toledo Blade Boulevard* and *Broken on the Wheel of Sex.* "Masks" is his third short story collaboration with Edward Lee. Ketchum has four cats via the ASPCA and lives in New York City.

Kathe Koja is the author of five novels and a short story collection. She lives in the Detroit area with her husband, artist Rick Lieder, and her son.

Edward Lee is the author of a dozen novels and many short stories, novellas, and comics scripts. He is also a contributing editor for *Barnes & Noble Online.* "Masks" marks his third short story collaboration with veteran novelist Jack Ketchum. The two plan to coauthor more projects in the future.

Tanith Lee was born in England in 1947, and became a full-time writer in 1975. Lee has published sixty-six books and two hundred short stories, written for TV and radio, and won three major awards. She lives in England with her husband, the writer John Kaiine.

Brian McNaughton was born in Red Bank, New Jersey, in 1935 and attended Harvard. He has written too many paperback novels (all out of print) and more than two hundred short stories. A book of his tales, *The Throne of Bones,* won the 1998 World Fantasy and International Horror Guild awards for Best Collection.

Yvonne Navarro has had eleven novels and sixty-plus short stories published and recently resigned from her job of fourteen years to make a dubious living as a full-time writer. Those brave enough to accompany her on this terrifying journey can find updates at http://www.para-net.com/~ynavarro.

Contributors' Notes

Kathryn Ptacek has had twenty-one books published, as well as numerous articles, stories, essays, and reviews. She is also the editor of *The Gila Queen's Guide to Markets*, a newsletter that goes to writers and artists around the world. She lives in New Jersey.

Robert Silverberg's many novels include the best-selling Lord Valentine trilogy and the classics *Dying Inside* and *A Time of Changes*. He has been nominated for the Nebula and Hugo awards more times than any other writer; he is a five-time winner of the Nebula and a four-time winner of the Hugo.

Lois Tilton's novels are about vampires in strange times and places. Her short stories have appeared in many magazines and anthologies of fantastic fiction.

Lawrence Watt-Evans recently celebrated the twentieth anniversary of selling his first fantasy novel. Watt-Evans is the author of about thirty novels — most recently *Dragon Weather* — and over a hundred short stories in various genres; one of those short stories received the Hugo Award in 1988. He served two terms as president of the Horror Writers Association. He lives in the Maryland suburbs of Washington with his wife, two kids, a cat, and an albino corn snake.

Gene Wolfe is the author of many books, including the classic and critically acclaimed *Book of the New Sun*. His most recent books are the collection *Strange Travelers* and the novels *On Blue's Water* and *In Green's Jungles*, all from Tor Books.

A professional writer since 1968, **Chelsea Quinn Yarbro** has worked in a wide variety of genres, from science fiction to westerns, from young adult adventure to historical horror. Her Saint-Germain books are widely considered classics of the vampire genre. Aside from writing, Yarbro has worked as a cartographer, has read tarot cards and palms, and has composed music, all of which she continues to do.

About the Editors:

Nancy Kilpatrick has published thirteen novels, two collections, a hundred twenty-five short stories, and has, with *Graven Images*, edited seven anthologies. She specializes in mythological themes, from vampires to gargoyles, to Día de los Muertos. Currently, she lives in beautiful Montreal with her black cat Bella, and spends her spare time traveling and visiting unusual and compelling sites with her companion, photographer Hugues Leblanc. You can visit her website at: http://www.sff.net/people/nancyk.

Thomas S. Roche is a music journalist and a writer and editor of horror, fantasy, and crime fiction. His hundred-plus short stories and articles have appeared in a wide variety of magazines and anthologies. He is currently at work on his first novel. Visit www.thomasroche.com or send e-mail to thomasroche-announce-subscribe@onelist.com to subscribe to his monthly newsletter, Razorblade Valentines.